THE TURNING

THE PATRICIAN PROPHECY SERIES

BOOK TWO

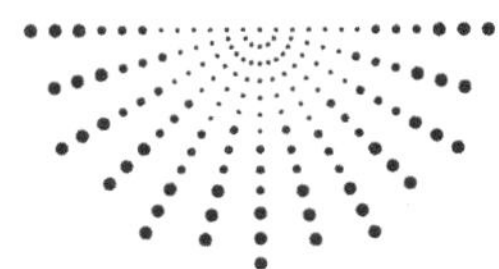

MICHAEL PENOSKY

THE PATRICIAN PROPHECY BOOK TWO: THE TURNING BY MICHAEL PENOSKY
Published by Brimstone Fiction
1440 W. Taylor St. Ste #449
Chicago, IL 60607

ISBN: 978-1-946758-62-0

Cover design by Elaina Lee www.Forthemusedesigns.com
Interior design by Meaghan Burnett, MeaghanBurnett.com

Available in print from your local bookstore, online, or from the publisher at: www.brimstonefiction.com

Brought to you by the creative team at Brimstone Fiction:
Casey Carpenter, Rowena Kuo, and Meaghan Burnett.

Library of Congress Cataloging-in-Publication Data
Penosky, Michael.
The Patrician Prophecy Book Two: The Turning / Michael Penosky 1st ed.

Printed in the United States of America

To the Only Wise God who turns the darkness to light and works all things after the counsel of His will.

"To and fro we leap
And chase the frothy bubbles,
While the world is full of troubles
And is anxious in its sleep"
— W. B. Yeats, *The Stolen Child*

"Arise, shine; for your light is come . . ."
Isaiah 60:1

CHAPTER ONE

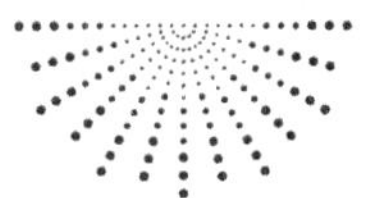

Professor Saorla O'Rourke woke to the noise of metal clanging. She bolted upright in the small twin bed attached to the cinderblock wall. She'd slept sound, quite a feat given she'd spent the night on a rock-hard mattress in the Dublin jail.

"Take care of yourself, O'Rourke," her cellmate Tara said. Tara was a superwoman with a half-shaved head. She towered over the male guard that led her away. Whoever Tara's foe happened to be in her next UFC fight deserved all the pity in the world.

"Good luck in your match," Saorla called out after her.

"I've never needed luck, O'Rourke," the woman yelled without turning back, as she trudged away in lockstep with the guard.

Saorla sprung from her bed and brushed her teeth at the small sink in her cell with the toothbrush and paste the jail guard had issued her last night. The peace that had overtaken her before she fell asleep was still clinging to her.

A couple minutes later the same guard returned. "You want to make that phone call now?"

"Why not?"

"Better take this," the guard said, handing her the mobile phone they'd taken from her person when they'd booked her. "All conversations on the jail phone are recorded. Mobiles are forbidden. But I don't always follow the rules. I'll be back in fifteen minutes to collect your phone."

"When do I get out of here?"

The guard chuckled. "I wouldn't count on getting out if I were you. You've got a court appearance at eleven. Your judge is known as the hanging judge. Right now, you're charged with obstruction of justice, punishable by up to five years in prison, and maybe they will add further charges." The guard laughed harder.

Some of her peace fluttered away.

"Who knows when you'll get out?" he continued. "A guard will walk you over to the courtroom shortly. And don't bother calling a barrister. One has already been appointed for you."

"Do you know who?"

"Ian Shaw."

Saorla smiled at the news of the appointment. Soon, she'd see Ian again, tell him all about the decisions she'd made last night. Decisions that had set in motion the unexplainable joy that had been about to burst out of her last night.

It made no sense that any calm still lingered, facing a charge as serious as the one she was facing. There was also the trauma of almost being blown to pieces by a car bomb yesterday. Her grad assistant, Myrna, was injured in the blast and wound up in the emergency room. No further word on Myrna's condition had yet made it Saorla's way.

The guard tossed a copy of the *Irish Times* in her direction and left. She dialed the hospital, asked to speak with Myrna Cahdan, but was placed on hold. Seated on her jail bunk, she glanced down now at the newspaper that lay at her feet and read the lead headline: "Book of Kells Vanishes."

No surprise there.

But just below it her eyes settled on an article that normally would have been the top story. David Braden, the billionaire high king who everyone was claiming had descended from the blood-line of the high kings of old, had just been voted by the Oireachtas, the Irish parliament, to succeed as the new taoiseach, or prime minister of Ireland. Braden's ascension to the chief governing role, the article explained, followed closely on the heels of the resignation of the former prime minister for unspecified health concerns. The national general elections were just five months away and Mr. Braden would take the former prime minister's place on the ballot, it was announced.

The car bombing hadn't made the front page.

She didn't want to spoil her peace by looking to see if a story about it appeared anywhere else in the paper, but was just about to turn to the second page when the phone crackled to life and a nurse from the hospital patched through. The information pelted her in rapid fire. Myrna was in surgery, unable to talk, and no further information was available. Saorla's first question was interrupted with the refrain, "No further information was available nor could be it be divulged if it was."

It would be futile to press it further, she knew. She ended the call and sighed.

God, I hope she's all right.

The peace dissipated a wee bit more. A measure of angst slipped in to fill the vacuum. How was she was going to get out of this place so she could see Myrna, to tell her how sorry she was for getting her involved in this whole mess?

With the guard gone now from her immediate wing of the jail facility, Saorla rang her father, but then remembered he was probably out hunting or fishing at this time of the morning in the rolling glens near the old family home in County Donegal. The call went unanswered; her father didn't even have voice mail.

Oh well, there was always her friend Meegan, a fellow faculty member at the college, a good listener and she could be trusted to keep secrets. The perfect person to tell about all that had been transpiring with this strange life she now found herself living. Finally, for once, she might just outdo her friend with this yarn, even given the limits of what she could tell her in earshot of possible jailhouse snitches. Besides that, she needed to ask her to take over her class today.

Saorla tapped on her colleague's contact and made the call.

"Saorla, dear God, where are you? The most fantastic rumors are flying around on campus. Some say you've taken up with an American movie star. Others say you've joined a religious cult. There's even a claim that you were found at the scene of the murder of that retired professor down in Wexford. But the one I like the best is that *you're the one* responsible for stealing the Book of Kells!"

Meegan laughed, and Saorla aped along, hiding her nervousness, like it was all a big joke.

Only one problem. A wee bit of truth formed the basis for all those rumors, especially the last one about the Book of Kells theft. But there was no way she could tell Meegan about that now. And anyway, she hadn't actually meant to *steal* the Book of Kells.

It was more like borrow it for a mite.

Just long enough to see the code that led to the next clue. But then things had gone horribly wrong and ... well, here she was in jail.

"You have a minute?" Saorla asked.

"I'm all ears. You know I can't resist a good story."

"Well, this one might even top all the adventures you've regaled us with over the years."

Meegan chuckled. "That's a high bar, you know?"

"Yeah ... listen, I found God."

Meegan let out a long sigh. "So, they're right ... you joined a cult."

"It's not like that."

"Oh, really." A tone of sarcasm tainted her words. Saorla hoped Meegan hadn't been talking with Claire, her other colleague at Trinity College who'd already expressed her concern about Saorla's spiritual search.

"You remember when I told you about the American who came into my office with photos of supposedly ancient artifacts, and I threw him out because I thought it was a hoax?"

"Yeah. We all had a good laugh about that. I still think you were on to something when you suggested going along with the hoax to drum up excitement, and thereby enrollment for the college, so that the cuts to our department could be avoided."

"That's what I've got to tell you—it's no hoax."

"You're kidding, right?"

"No."

"Dean Grady's going to love this fantasy of yours when he finds out about it."

"Except it's not fantasy. You remember the night of my thirtieth birthday party when the American gave me that gift, the leather satchel everyone thought was a keen imitation knockoff of an ancient relic?"

"Yeah. Mac and I both said later that it was uncanny in its ability to fool."

"You have to promise me you won't tell *anyone anything* about what I'm about to tell you."

"Cross my heart, swearing on me grandma's grave."

"Ok, well, it was *no knockoff*. Dated to 469 AD—"

Meegan gasped. "You can't be ser—"

"And there's more. A week before this, I took some sleeping pills with mega glasses of wine and—"

"I was afraid something like that was going to happen to you. Sorry I wasn't there for you as much as I should have been after your husband ..."

"It's not your fault. I kept you ... everyone on the outside for so long after Stuart passed. Anyway, my housekeeper Sophie found me unconscious out in the yard, revived me, then prayed for me. She gave me an obscure verse from the Bible. Made no sense, or so I thought. It said, *It's the glory of God to conceal a matter, and the glory of kings to search it out*. I had no clue what that meant. Then came the birthday party when the American, Ian Shaw, gave me that satchel. On it, *that very verse* that Sophie gave was inscribed in Old Latin."

A silence settled, and Saorla waited for Meegan to take it in.

"So, you quit giving him the cold shoulder after that?" Meegan finally said.

"I'd never heard that verse before, not until my housekeeper came that day I was strung out on the lawn. Then, a week later, it's in front of my face again on an artifact that had been in the ground for sixteen hundred years. So yeah, you got it. I started to pay attention to Ian. And it turns out the verse seems to be some sort of encouragement to take this quest I've been on now for the last few weeks."

"Oh dear, you're letting a coincidence dictate your course. Are you sure it's not because the American is so handsome that you 'found God?'"

"Believe me, I know he's handsome, but that had nothing to do with my agreeing to help him get to the bottom of the mystery posed by artifacts."

"Mystery?"

"Well, Ian's grandfather found a number of artifacts on his farm. The old man was led by a dream to dig in a certain part of his bogland. There, he found a chalice. He took it to a shop in Belfast and got no help there. On the return trip, he had an accident and a heart attack. It's more than a wee bit unclear whether it was really an accident. He says he was run off the road by an SUV and someone stole the chalice from him. After that, the old man's wife, Ian's grandmother, called Ian over from his home in San Francisco to help get to the bottom of it. He's a smart attorney and quite capable of handling himself. Anyway, other artifacts we found are so incredible you would *not* believe me if I told you everything. The long and short of it is that Saint Patrick himself is leading us from one clue to the next."

A wordless void ensued on the other end of the line.

"Meegan?"

"You're losing me now. You think a saint is talking to you from the grave?"

"No, not talking. He's left clues, before he died that is, for us to follow." Saorla let out a nervous chuckle. She had to be well beyond the danger zone of sounding like an insane person.

"To what end?"

"This is the part where I might really lose you."

"If it's truth to you, I want to hear it."

"That's what I love about you. Okay, first, the old man says he thinks there's a literal treasure to discover. But, honestly, the things we've already uncovered are priceless."

"Well, there's the satchel and the chalice. Did you find anything else?"

Saorla wanted to tell her friend they'd found the original of the famous *Breastplate* poem, and that it was penned by the hand of St. Patrick himself. All scholars thought it was crafted a century after Patrick's death. But she'd have to wait to tell Meegan all about that. First, she and Ian would have to at least try to find out the meaning of the code they'd uncovered from the Book of Kells. See where that led. Only in the end would she be able to tell Meegan the whole story. But at least her friend wouldn't feel like she'd been kept utterly in the dark.

"I can't tell you exactly what I think we've found yet. We're still pursuing leads, which brings me to the second thing the American's grandfather thinks." Saorla hesitated about whether to go any further, but then decided to let her friend in on the ultimate theory they were working under. She couldn't see the harm in that as long as she didn't get into anything about how the code they'd found in the Book of Kells might relate to all this. "He thinks the mysterious artifacts and clues we are finding will ultimately lead to a prophecy from Saint Patrick addressed to this generation, and it has the power to profoundly change the country for the good."

Saorla waited for Meegan to say something but there was only silence on the other end.

"I know, I know, you think I've gone off the edge into some crazy cult," Saorla said finally. "But something happened to me last night, quite apart from my work. I actually *believed,* chose to believe really, in the God of historic Christianity. Not any cult. And something happened to me. I know it. I—"

"O'Rourke, it's time for me to take back the phone," the guard said.

"Do you want the professor to get out on bail or do you want to keep her in the slammer longer?" Kirby asked. He sat across the chessboard from Lorcan Duihbur in Lorcan's government office.

Lorcan remained stone-faced with his fingers on a chess piece, not taking his eye off it.

"It could go either way," Kirby continued, "We have people at the courts that can make this come out however you want."

Lorcan nodded. "Have our men search the room of the American and also a thorough look through the home of the professor. If we find the book, we'll get what we need, see what they saw. Then we can keep her in jail for a long time, even forever. If we don't find the book, then arrange her release so she can lead us to it." He moved his queen across the board, took his hand off the piece, then leaned back in his chair. "Checkmate, my friend."

Kirby could only curse.

By 10:45 a.m., Ian Shaw had made his way to the Criminal Courthouse on Parkgate Street. He set himself up at the defense counsel's table in an empty courtroom drinking a cup of coffee he'd purchased at the corner cafe and waited for Saorla's case to be called. The paucity of onlookers was a good sign. It meant that so far the media hadn't been tipped off that an arrest had been made in the Book of Kells heist. But, as the minutes passed and the room began to fill, he grew increasingly anxious that the newsrooms had been given a hot lead.

A minute before the scheduled start of the hearing, a side courtroom door opened with a bailiff leading Saorla, handcuffed and shackled at the feet. Ian rose and was about to make a vociferous complaint but stopped himself when he saw the bailiff free her. Saorla's eyes met his and she smiled. Despite the night spent in jail and the shackles, she didn't look the worse for it. In fact, a glow emanated from her.

She headed straight for him, then flung her arms around him and squeezed him tight. It was the first time a client had ever hugged him *before* a hearing.

"Hey there," Ian said. "I'm so sorry. I tried to—"

Her eyes were steady, looking into his, when she cut in and said, "I know you can get me out of this."

"I wish I was as confident as you."

Silence sliced between them for a moment.

"I wanted to see you last night," Ian said. "You know that don't you?"

"It's okay. God met me in jail." She smiled momentarily, then her brow suddenly wrinkled, and her shoulders stiffened. "Do you have any news of Myrna?"

"Oh yeah. She's going to be okay."

Her shoulders dropped. "I couldn't keep from thinking it could have been ... should have been me."

The courtroom bailiff interrupted their conversation. "All rise, the Honorable Kathleen Shea presiding."

In walked a petite, middle-aged woman in a long black robe. She took her seat on the bench which rose several feet above the rest of the courtroom. Ian hoped she was inclined toward leniency. He'd gathered some general advice from his supervisor at the legal aid clinic on how to navigate the labyrinth of the Irish legal system, but he wished he'd asked if there were any special tips on how to proceed with Judge Shea.

She nodded in Ian's direction. "Counsel, you may address the court."

He suppressed the urge to yawn; lack of sleep was probably the prime culprit, but tense situations had always made him yawn unless they were off-the-charts-crazy tense, like a day at Mavs back home when it was firing and sending surfers to the hospital, or worse to the morgue. He took a sip of his coffee and stood erect at the podium facing the bench.

"Your Honor, there is no probable cause to connect my client to any crime. The elements of obstruction of justice, as the Director of Prosecutions has charged it here, requires an endeavor to render false testimony to investigating officials. The Director has no evidence that will show that standard has been violated. Now, Your Honor, what we do have is a situation where my client, a distinguished professor at

Trinity College, has never had any trouble with the law in her entire life. Her dear friend and research assistant was terribly injured in the bomb blast, the origins of which are unknown and under investigation at this hour. Now, I want to—"

"Excuse me, your honor," the Director of Public Prosecutions, Joseph Egan, was on his feet, cutting in, addressing the judge, fire flashing from his eyes. Ian's supervisor at the legal aid clinic had been dead-on in his assessment of Egan as a tough-as-nails guy who looked like a bird of prey with his neatly shaped beard and dark hair slicked back from his forehead ending in a ducktail. "In the interests of justice, I would like to present an oral motion to disqualify Mr. Shaw from acting as counsel in this case. Your Honor, if I may explain?"

"Of course, you may. Go right ahead." The judge nodded vigorously.

"Thank you, Your Honor," Egan said, with a quick flash of a smile. "It is my contention that Mr. Shaw is disqualified on the basis that he is part of this whole sordid incident. He was at the bombing. He's a close, personal friend of the defendant. He was interviewed at the scene of the bombing as an eyewitness. We would therefore call Mr. Shaw at any trial in this case. Now, I don't have to tell you, Judge, that the law prohibits a solicitor from being a witness in a case in which he also represents one of the parties."

"Your Honor, this is absurd," Ian protested. "This is a preliminary hearing on the matter of probable cause and bail. There are no witnesses that the defense would need to call at this point, and it's the Director's burden to establish probable cause, which I maintain he cannot do."

Egan took a step toward the judge, glanced at Ian, and then addressed the judge. "I ask that the defense motion to dismiss for lack of probable cause be denied and the case transferred to circuit court for trial."

Judge Shea removed her eyeglasses and leaned back in her chair. "I am prepared to rule only on the matter of bail today after I hear arguments on that issue. I will have to further consider the nature of Mr. Shaw's conflict. I won't be making a ruling on the probable cause issue raised by the defense. I'm going to take that matter of probable cause under advisement. I will, however, allow Mr. Shaw to proceed with his argument as to bail."

Judge Shea put her glasses back on, shuffled some papers, and pulled one out. Her eyes grew wide. "The director in his pleading before this court requests that bail be set at five-hundred-thousand euros."

Ian quickly did the math. Under Irish law, a defendant would be required to pay one-third of the amount set to obtain his release. In this case, it would require a payment of over €166,000 to procure Saorla's freedom. The money would be returned to Saorla when she appeared in court on the charges, but neither of them had that kind of cash in the first place. The amount Egan was attempting to set was impossibly high.

Judge Shea peered over the top of her eyeglasses in Ian's direction.

He took a deep breathe, then said, "Judge, Ms. O'Rourke requests that she be released on her own recognizance and that any bail amount be waived in this case."

The Director shot up from his seat as if stung by a wasp.

"Your honor, we strongly oppose that request. In fact, we would ask to orally amend our recommendation. We now request that bail be denied altogether, and that defendant be remanded to the custody of the Gardai station until such time as she is brought to court for trial on the obstruction charge. As we will show in our argument, Ms. O'Rourke poses a significant danger to society."

Ian jabbed a hand in the air. "Judge, there is no question this is a bailable offense. My client is not charged with murder, war crimes, treason or genocide or anything of that nature, which would warrant a finding that she is *per se* ineligible for bail. Now, looking at the statutory factors that you must consider in making your decision, my client isn't a flight risk. She isn't going anywhere. Hasn't even been out of the country in the last two years. Basically, you're looking at a lifetime resident of Ireland other than the time she spent living abroad for her education. She hails from the hills of Donegal, growing up speaking the native Irish language. She has strong ties, gainful employment as a distinguished professor of linguistics and Irish history at one of Ireland's finest institutes of higher learning, an honored member of the community. She owns her own home, has a Mercedes and a Land Rover SUV. And I say all this to point out that she has property and ties in the community. She isn't going to leave her life and possessions in Dublin to flee from … with all due respect, Your Honor … what I would call a relatively minor charge that will never be proven by the prosecution."

Ian took another sip of coffee.

"Anything else from the defense?" the judge asked.

"Not at this time," Ian said. "But I would like to reserve comments for rebuttal." Ian gathered his coffee and papers and left the podium for his seat.

Saorla reached over and placed her hand on top of his. "Thank you," she mouthed, smiling at him.

He felt the warmth from that touch spread over his body. Time to return his focus to the courtroom. The director was already standing at the podium.

"Please proceed when ready, Mr. Egan," Judge Shae said. Her words were comfortable, familiar. The two were probably long-time pals.

"What Mr. Shaw is not telling you is that there is a cloud of suspicion swirling around this woman. In this month alone, she was found present at the scene of the murder of a retired professor at his seafront home in Wexford."

Judge Shea's eyes were growing wider by the second. Ian had to do something and quick.

"Judge, I object to that line of argument."

"On what bas—"

Ian cut Egan off mid-sentence and sprung to his feet. "For one thing, the premise is false. Defendant reported the crime, and she was there to visit the professor at his request. But more importantly, the whole line of argument is prejudicial—"

Egan turned his eyes from the judge to glare at Ian. "Judge, this will all become clear," Egan said, "if Mr. Shaw will let me finish my argument."

"I quite agree," the judge said. "Mr. Shaw, please refrain from interrupting. You'll have your chance in rebuttal to speak your piece. But during Mr. Egan's argument, I'm going to warn you most adamantly to hold *your peace*. Understood?"

"Yes," Ian said, as he sat down in his chair.

Egan cleared his throat. "As I was saying, she was at the scene of a violent murder. An elderly man was stabbed numerous times in his home. She was there. Then, and this is where it gets profoundly interesting. The Book of Kells goes missing, and this defendant's ring is found at the scene of the crime the next morning."

There were audible gasps from the spectators in the back of the courtroom. Was it just Ian's imagination or did there seem to be several people busily scribbling notes in the back? If this got out to the media, it would certainly complicate matters.

CHAPTER TWO

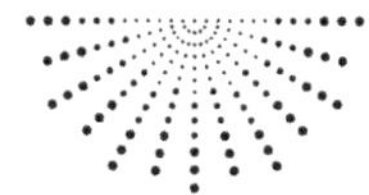

"It's *her* ring," Prosecutor Egan told the court. "What was it doing there? We don't know yet. She hasn't been forthcoming in that investigation."

Ian suppressed the urge to scream out another objection. Heaven knew his client had given a reasonable explanation for the ring's discovery on the floor of the Treasury. She'd been showing the book to him; that was the sanitized version anyway. But an objection would be futile. He'd probably be held in contempt of court if he decided to speak out of turn again. And, on second thought, it probably wouldn't be a good idea to remind the court that he had deep ties with this witness. At least it wouldn't be a good idea if he wanted to avoid being disqualified from representing Saorla in this case for future proceedings.

"We have a book of incalculable value—missing," Egan said. "What is that book worth on the black market? A billion dollars? Nobody knows for sure. But what we might guess is that the person that has it would be a flight risk, happy to leave Ireland forever if they could disappear somewhere in the islands of the South Pacific, let's say, with a new identity. Staying in Ireland would suddenly not seem so important for many placed in that position."

"But there is more, Judge. We have the bombing incident last night where somehow this defendant escapes harm, but someone else is gravely injured. There are a lot of coincidences here if you buy the notion they are merely coincidences. I don't. I think there's more than enough here to give the court pause in allowing bail at all. And I am asking that defendant be remanded to the custody of the Gardai station without bail. Thank you, Your Honor."

"Thank you, Mr. Egan. Mr. Shaw, do you have a rebuttal?"

"Yes, thanks, Your Honor. First of all, Ms. O'Rourke's presence at Doctor Greenwald's home is easily explained. She has emails to show his invitation to visit on the day in question. They were to work on some historical research together. She rang the doorbell even though the door was ajar, waited a long time for him to answer. It was only out of fear for the old man's health that she entered his home and discovered the body. She immediately called police and reported what had happened."

"The ring incident is also easily explained." Ian winced at the half-truth he was about to tell, as he remembered the night Myrna disabled the security and he and Saorla had taken the book from its glass case to look for the secret code that was supposed to be there and was there. And then security rebooted prematurely and there was no time to get the book back to where it belonged in its exhibit at the college. "The professor had been to see the Book of Kells exhibition that day and was showing a visitor around. Lastly, the explosion last night had nothing to do with my client other than she appears to have been a target too. She was on her way to get into the same vehicle. I don't see how any of this supports an obstruction charge."

"Let's keep focused on the issue at hand—which is bail," the Judge interrupted. "Is defendant a flight risk? That's what I want to know."

"I apologize, Judge, my mistake," Ian said. "The Book of Kells's disappearance is, admittedly, a matter that has the whole country on edge, but there is nothing to suggest that my client has it or would attempt to flee the country with it. And I am sure that if the Gardai really believe it to be a possibility, they will watch my client closely to prevent her from taking flight. I would ask that Your Honor not punish an innocent woman for the angst that is permeating our community over that beloved book, and I would ask the court to set bail at a reasonable amount, say €5,000. Thank you, Your Honor and Mr. Egan."

Ian nodded in the judge's direction and took a seat. All that remained now was to hope, hope that the judge would take his recommendation, show some leniency. Under Irish law, the attorney for the accused was not allowed to post the bail from the attorney's own resources. So, he'd called Sophie that morning and asked if she knew anyone at church that could help post bail. Saorla, he explained, would pay the loan back as soon as she had a chance to get situated at home.

To his amazement, Sophie herself said she'd cover it, explaining that she'd saved more than $5,000 in her bank account since arriving from Poland and would bring it to court in cash. Ian knew she was an incredibly hard worker who put in long hours every day. Still, his admiration for her kept growing.

Ian turned to look over his shoulder. Sophie sat in the back row of the courtroom. A young blonde-headed immigrant from Warsaw was now acting as surety for Ireland's treasure book and bailing out its robber.

Whoa boy, would the press love that story.

Ian told himself that everything would be sorted out soon enough; the book could get back to its rightful resting place. He tried to comfort himself with the thought that it had not been the first time the beloved book had disappeared.

He remembered from Saorla's lecture that it had been stolen for a two-month period in 1006-07 AD, its golden cover removed and never recovered. Even then, it was described in the literature of the time as the chief treasure of the western world. Ian longed for the day when it was back where it belonged with nothing missing or destroyed.

But more than that, he hoped that Saorla was not remanded to the custody of the jail. He desperately needed her to help with the clues that would chase down the mystery. Without her, he wouldn't be able to advance the ball down the field.

And there was something else too.

He tried to fight the thought away, but he had to admit it—he'd come to profoundly enjoy her friendship.

The judge was busy with pen in hand, jotting down some notes. When she finished, she flipped her glasses off.

"I am ready to make my ruling at this time. Bail is set at ten thousand euros, which means the accused must post one-third payment of that amount to secure her immediate release. I will not require a surety to guarantee her appearance, but she must not leave the island until this matter is concluded. The motion to disqualify counsel and any defense motions will be continued to a hearing date three weeks from today. Thank you, Mr. Egan and Mr. Shaw."

Ian turned to Saorla; she was flashing a grin at him.

"Good news?" she asked.

"Good news and bad news. You are out of jail for the time being. But they want to put you there eventually. If they can convict you, that is."

Saorla hugged Ian, then drew back. "It's him," she said, looking over Ian's shoulder. Her face was losing its color.

"Who?"

"Callahan, the SDU detective that had me put behind bars."

"Relax, this is going to be okay."

Saorla looked a little unsteady, so Ian took her hand and walked her out of the courtroom. Callahan was waiting in the hallway.

"This isn't the end," he said, glaring at them. "People wind up dead and injured around you. I'm going to find out why."

"Give that dutiful cop stuff a rest," Ian said.

Callahan pointed a finger in Ian's face. "You're going to make a mistake, and I'll be there when you do."

Eager to see Myrna at St. James Hospital, Ian and Saorla quickly left the courthouse after Saorla signed the bail bond, paid, and thanked Sophie profusely, promising to have the money she'd lent back in her account as soon as possible. Sophie assured them she was glad to help, then parted ways, saying she was in a hurry to catch up on some cleaning jobs she'd missed in the morning.

After arriving at the hospital, Ian and Saorla were informed that Myrna had been moved from the intensive care unit to a private room on the third floor. They found her lying in bed, sipping water from a straw. Bruises covered her face, and scratches were visible on every exposed part of her body.

Saorla wiped a tear from the corner of her eye. "Oh dear, you look pretty good for having been blown up by a bomb."

Ian laughed but Myrna managed only a mischievous smile. "Do either of you want something to eat? If you're smart, you'll say no"

"Hospital food is bad in the States, too," Ian said.

"It's gotta be worse in Ireland," Myrna shot back.

Saorla came to the side of the bed and put a hand on Myrna's cheek. "How are you feeling?" Saorla asked.

"I lost a mighty amount of blood even though the injuries were sort of superficial. I nicked my eyebrow and that bled like crazy. I had four stitches there. The biggest problem, though, was the cut to the artery in my arm. Thankfully, they got the bleeding stopped in time. The ambulance came quite fast, didn't it?"

"I kept thinking not fast enough," Ian said.

"My ribs hurt like heck. They say none are broke, just badly bruised. I'll have to take their word for it. All in all, I feel like I just got done with a UFC sanctioned fight and got knocked out in the fifteenth round."

The odd reference to UFC fighting caused her thoughts to drift to Tara, Saorla's cellmate from the jail. "Actually, you both look like you went fifteen rounds of MMA," Saorla said as she glanced at Ian's nose. It was still quite swollen, and his right eye had continued to blacken up.

"I didn't know you were a fan," Ian said.

"Actually, I wasn't until last night."

Ian's head tilted. "Huh?"

Saorla shrugged her shoulders and flicked her hair over her ears. "Never mind; it's a long story, which we don't have time for now."

Myrna flashed a wry smile. "Ian and I can walk down the street now as a couple and say we are Connor McGregor and Aisling Daley." Saorla knew from her conversation in the morning with Tara that McGregor and Daley had been internationally famous male and female UFC competitors from Ireland.

Ian laughed. "You bet. We'll have to do it soon before we heal up unless some of this is permanent. In that case, it will give your face some character."

Saorla winced at the attempted bit of humor about scarring.

"Oh no, wait, the doctors didn't say there would be permanent disfigurement or scarring, did they?" she asked.

"No, they assured me I should be healed up quite well in a couple of months. But the good news is I get out soon and then—."

A garda officer, a young and handsome one, suddenly entered the room. "My shift's up," he said to Myrna. A second garda came into the room and joined the first. The first one said to the second, "Take good care of her. She's special." He then turned to Ian and Saorla. "Someone will be here around the clock, and then, when she gets out in a few days, a garda will be posted outside her residence until further notice from the higher ups."

Saorla let out a sigh of relief about the added protection for her home but then began to ponder the ways it might cramp her secretive mission of pursuing this strange quest her life had become. What if the Gardai were using the need for added security as a pretext to keep a closer eye on her activities?

CHAPTER THREE

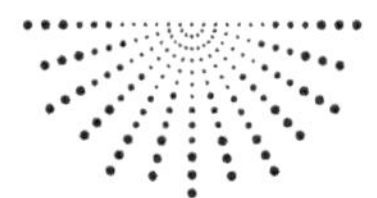

Saorla was concluding her last lecture for the week when Ian sat down in the back of her classroom. Word had spread on campus that she'd been questioned in connection with the car bombing and the Book of Kells heist. She chose to focus on Ian's eyes rather than the eyes of the students boring in on her soul. His face calmed and comforted her as if she was kicking off her shoes to meander barefoot in the summer grass.

When she finished and the last student left, Ian met her at the front of the classroom. "Hey there, you look like you could use a little R&R. What do you like to do to unwind?"

"Shopping on Grafton Street," she said without hesitation. More than a couple dozen months had passed since the last time she'd really shopped. She couldn't count it as shopping the time she recently thought about throwing herself through a store window and instead ended up buying a bottle of wine that ended in her attempting to drink herself to death to avoid the memory of her anniversary. The second one now without Stuart, without the love they'd shared. But the worst of that was behind her now; she'd found a new love in God she knew would even outlast death.

"Let's do it," Ian said.

His enthusiasm was contagious, but she wasn't willing to let him know that. "You're kidding, right? I just spent a small fortune on bail."

"You're forgetting to add that you owe me legal fees," he said, a teasing glint in his eyes.

She punched him in the arm. "You're forgetting there's no way you can afford my consulting fees. So, checkmate!"

Two hours later, they strolled down Grafton with their hands full of shopping bags. Ian suddenly stopped and pointed to an outfitter store across the street. "Our next target."

"You think you can satisfy your adventure itch by looking at outdoor gear?"

"Who said anything about *just looking*?"

Ian stepped toward the store, but then turned back to face her. "I know we're supposed to be unwinding, but work awaits. We're going to need the gear. This part will be fun; I guarantee it or your money back."

"What money?"

"Are we still talking about money? We sound like a couple with marital problems."

What did he mean by that? She felt her face smiling. It had to be one of his jokes, but it also registered that she hadn't thought about Stuart much in the last week. There had never been any fights about money, of course. But with the unusual reference to marriage, a warm pensiveness poured through her.

The store was called Outdoor Happening. They entered under a sign that displayed the figure of a man carved in white on the top of a rock summit. Obviously, Ian's kind of place. He commandeered a pushcart and began filling it as if he'd won a free two-minute shopping spree: coils of heavy rope, a fistful of carabineers, a climbing harness, headlamps, water bottles, a couple of backpacks, a multitool with a knife.

"You planning on a long holiday?" Saorla asked.

Ian grabbed a power bar, threw it in the cart and looked up at her. "Huh? Uh . . . no. But we're going to the cliffs on the sea tomorrow and maybe kayaking out to an island."

"Won't it look suspicious if I leave town, Mr. Attorney?"

"Live a little," he said. "Besides, there's a mystery to solve. Are you forgetting about that?"

How could she possibly forget about the quest? She gave a quick shake of her head. "We're like a couple of Agatha Christie wannabes, eh?"

Ian grinned. "A couple of sleuths for God and country."

Saorla looked over Ian's shoulder and saw a man peering at them from around the corner of the merchandise set up at the end of the aisle. "I feel like we're being watched from all sides, and not just God. And some of those sides aren't playing nice."

The smile left Ian's face. He leaned in close to her. "I should have seen the danger coming, should never have led you into it."

"Don't go there."

"Letting you stay in jail a couple of extra days for your own safety is what I should have done . . ." He looked down at the rope in his cart, ". . . while I do this. But I think you'd be safer with me at this point. I wish I could turn back the clock."

"Don't do that to yourself. It was my choice. I wouldn't miss this for the world, even if it means I die trying. I mean that."

Ian's mouth fell ajar. He nodded his head slowly. "You're special."

"On some level I can't explain, I don't think we're going to die." Saorla's voice was a whisper now. "I feel God's protection."

"You're so strong now," he said. "I'm not as certain as you."

She could feel his breath as he spoke centimeters away from her face now. He smelled musty and woodsy. She smothered the urge to bridge the space between them.

"I just wish there weren't so many grey lines ethically with the book," he said. "We need to get this over as quickly as possible so we can return it."

Yeah, get it over quickly so I don't have another urge like I'd just had. She pulled back from him, put some distance between his lips and hers.

"At this point, we'd have to do it anonymously," she said, "I have no idea how we'd go about that."

Silence fell between them for a moment. The man at the end of the aisle was still watching them. Saorla leaned in and tilted her head to whisper in his ear. "I have to confess I feel worse about it than I would if it were merely an overdue library book that I owed a big fat fine on."

Ian chuckled. "They're definitely going to revoke your library card for this."

"Yeah, and that's going to hurt more than you know."

He took her hand. "Come on," he said, leading her down the aisle. A warm tingle spread down her spine; her cheeks were probably blushing.

He let go of her hand. Was it disappointment she felt? Relief? It was getting complicated.

"How are you doing on footwear?"

"I could use a new pair of wellies."

"I was thinking rock climbing shoes."

"What if I told you I'm afraid of heights?"

"Really?"

"Yeah."

"I have a remedy for that."

IAN NOTICED THEM STANDING ON THE SIDEWALK IN FRONT OF THE STORE as he paid at the checkout counter. He swiped his credit card, giving little attention to the price, while he kept his eye on two men in black trench coats.

He gathered the bags, overloaded now, and trekked for the door. "Act normal. Two men on the walk outside are watching us."

"We can slip away," Saorla said. "I know my way around these streets quite well."

"I'll follow," Ian said, though he wasn't sure it would work given all the bags they were carrying.

They exited the store. Darkness had fallen on the city. Maybe that would help.

The two men huddled with their heads tilted down but their eyes veering up at Ian. Saorla increased the speed of her gait; Ian hustled to keep up.

In a couple of minutes, they arrived at a women's clothing shop called Monsoon, went inside, and began looking around. The design of the clothing was exotic, with influences from places like Nepal, India and Afghanistan.

Fifteen minutes later, Saorla explained to the clerk that she wanted to change into one of the items she intended to purchase and leave some of her other packages for safe keeping at the register until tomorrow. The store clerk readily agreed. Saorla paid and then disappeared into the dressing room. Ian kept a close hold on the outdoor gear.

He waited, wondering if something might have happened to her she was taking so long in there. Then, she stepped out. The breath left his chest, and his heart raced. A fuchsia dress hugged the contours of her body to perfection. Her dark brown hair fell softly behind her neck, setting off the beatific vision she'd become. Ian felt his head tilting and tried hard not to gawk. It was no use.

The woman . . . uh . . . the professor was beautiful.

She took a step toward him with her right hand on her hip and the other arm hanging freely at her side, moving like a runway model.

Whoa, I'm in bigger trouble than I thought.

His heart was going to have to be tied up with that climbing rope he'd just bought if he was going to survive this, this . . .

"What do you think?" she asked.

"It's . . . uh . . . you're startling, I mean the dress, it's startling." He gave the thumbs up sign. He guessed she understood what that meant, she was a professor of linguistics after all. A professor? Wait, there must be some mistake; no professor could look like that.

"I suppose it's not bad for not having tried it on before paying for it," she said. "It was the last dress on the rack my size. So, you like it?"

"Are you kidding? It was made for you."

She smiled at the compliment. "I thought I'd wear it to dinner tonight. You know, the one you owe me from the bet we made in the Long Room."

Ian was able to steady his heart rate by taking calming breaths. "I've never been happier to lose a bet. But are you forgetting about our friends on the street?"

She grabbed her coat and pulled Ian through the hallway of the dressing room. "There's another way out on the side of the store."

"I'm not sure that's a good idea," he said, rubbing his nose that was still swollen from the time he'd recently ducked out the back of a pub and got the snot kicked out of him by guys just like the ones following him now. If not for his steady diet of mixed martial arts training over the past several years, he would have been a dead man.

She was already pushing out the door and onto a side street that intersected Grafton. "This isn't an alley. I think we'll be quite safe, if we can meld with the throngs on the street."

After a block of brisk walking, there was no sign of the trench coats. Ian and his suddenly very hot date blended with the crowd, eventually heading down Nassau Street and then up Westmoreland. Ian kept checking over his shoulder; he didn't see any clear evidence they were being followed.

"Think we've lost them?" she asked.

"Could be."

"Losing them seemed too easy."

"I was thinking the same. These guys are better than the goons that have been following us."

"So, what does that mean?"

"They're probably Gardai. I bet that detective that has it out for you ordered the tail."

The words had just tumbled fresh out of his mouth, when he spotted the trench coats. "Don't look now, but we've got company."

"Seriously?"

"Yeah, and now I'm sure they're Gardai," he said. "That's good news in a way. At least they're not trying to kill us."

"Not that we know of. But they are trying to put us in prison for an inconveniently long time."

She had a point. Halfway across the bridge over the River Liffey going north, Saorla stopped and leaned her arms against the stone railing and peered out at the flowing water snaking in from the west.

"All this shopping and walking has made me famished. And *voilà* . . . the Winding Stair restaurant," she said, pointing a couple blocks away in the direction of the buildings on the north side of the Quay.

"Hey, Myrna was supposed to help foot the bill," Ian said in mock protest.

Saorla shook her head, while looking like she was trying hard not to smile. "Another argument over money?"

CHAPTER FOUR

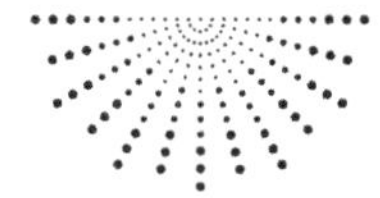

Seated at a candlelit table for two at a window that overlooked the Liffey, Saorla ordered a glass of Merlot made in Bolgheri, and Ian ordered a coke. As they waited for the server to return with their drinks, Saorla's mind ran to the lonely night of her most recent anniversary where she'd set the table for two in memory of her dead husband. Her life had certainly taken a different turn in the last three weeks.

When the waiter finally returned, he set down two wineglasses and poured a serving into each. Saorla sampled hers and gave the approval. He set the bottle of Merlot on the table. "This is on the house," he said without explanation before scattering off to take another order.

"I hope you like red wine," Saorla said.

"Aren't you worried about the wine? On the house?"

"Well, too late now, I've already tasted it. Besides I watched him break the seal and uncork it."

Ian held up his glass. "A toast to the most beautiful woman in Dublin, and the smartest one too, no doubt about it."

Saorla felt her face growing flush, tried to regain her footing.

"Where do you see her?" She craned her head to feign a serious search.

"Ha. I'm looking at her, and you know who you are." He clanked her glass softly with his.

"Your toast is sweet, but I propose a more modest one." She lifted her glass. "To the fellowship of the Patrick quest."

"To the fellowship." Ian tapped her glass. "We're like two little hobbits that God seems to have slipped in to this battle."

She chuckled as she looked into his eyes, all kindness and strength.

"There's so much I've been meaning to ask you," he said, "but we've been running from one extreme to the next. Scarcely had time to breathe."

"Yeah, breathing is essential to survival."

Saorla took a sip of wine; a sweet velvety berry taste refreshed her mouth. "I thought you liked living a hundred kilometers an hour."

"That's the way I'm wired, but so much is changing. These last three weeks have been . . . uh . . . complicated."

"I know what you mean," she said. Life for her had gone from the tangled web of her depression to this—sitting here in a fine restaurant in a fine dress with a fine specimen of a man, on the trail of the most bizarre of mysteries. "You mentioned something once about a place called Mavs you visited the day you got the call from your grandmother and that you were lucky to be here. What did you mean by that?"

Saorla watched his face tighten, then relax.

"Confession time," he said. "Places like Mavs are why I thought I could never be involved in a serious relationship. You don't really want to hear about this, do you?"

Did he view her like that? A candidate for a potential relationship? The questions both scared and confused her. "I asked, didn't I?"

"Where do I start?"

"How about the beginning? The day you left for Ireland."

"You're sure?"

"I have all evening," she said. She barely scratched the surface of knowing this man who had catapulted into her life. And she did want to know him better.

"Mavericks is a place not far from where I live. The waves come in so heavy surfers call them monsters. When Mavs is kickin' after a strong winter storm, the waves can reach over thirty feet. The funny thing is that very few people even knew it was there until around 1990. There was a kid in the 70s' who used to look out the window of his high school English class as these huge monsters rolled in. One day, he paddled out alone on his board and rode one. I always wanted to be like that. Doing stuff that most people would never be brave enough to try. He surfed those waves, mostly alone, eventually with a few friends, for fifteen years, until the world got in on the secret."

"Why is it called Mavericks?"

"I heard they named it in the 60s' after a dog named Maverick. The beast swam out a quarter mile—that's unusually far for a dog—to reach some surfers who were mesmerized by the huge waves they were *not* willing to ride. For good reason too, many people have died out there in the years since."

"So you surfed those waves in the morning on the day you left?"

"*Surfing* would be an overstatement. A buddy of mine was there with me, a crazy dude named Shark. We hooked into a monster and washed around in what surfers call the spin cycle. It was the scariest experience I've ever had . . . at least until Myrna's accident. The amazing thing is that God really used that mishap, and Shark had a conversion experience."

"I think I had a conversion experience," Saorla blurted before she realized what she'd said.

"I can tell something's happened. You're different from when I first met you."

"Please don't remind me of that." Saorla slowly shook her head and looked down at her wine glass. "My behavior was quite abominable, I know."

"Totally understandable given the strange guy with the strange request for your help."

"You're not *that* strange." She flashed a smile at him. "I just had this dark weight on me I couldn't get off."

"You feel it's lifted?"

"I just believe now. And with that, the darkness left. I find myself wanting to please God."

"Can I ask you something I've been wanting to ask since that day in Wexford?"

She shuddered as she recalled that day when she and Ian had found her colleague murdered over the secrets he'd learned about the Book of Kells—that she now knew held a code that could potentially lead them to a treasure of incalculable value. But it was also the day Ian had tried to pry into her personal life for answers she hadn't yet been willing to give.

Saorla took a deep breath. She had an inclination he would bring up Stuart. She wasn't sure she was ready, even now, to go there. She took another sip of wine and found herself saying, "Sure."

"Why did you tell me that you felt guilty over your husband's death? You said it was your fault."

Her eyes burned as the tears started to well. She fought them off.

Be brave like Ian and catch the big wave. You can do this.

"I haven't been able to talk about it. But I want to."

She locked into his kind, blue-grey eyes and decided to trust. "Stuart liked to ride a bicycle, both for exercise and competitively. It was something we did together for recreation, a diversion from the academic life at the college. There was a local race for a good cause: to raise money for some health issue. A short twenty kilometers. We had a couple of kilometers left to the finish. We rode together the entire race, but Stuart wanted to push it out at the end so he sped ahead. I had a terrible feeling that something was about to go wrong. I should have screamed for him to stop."

Tears pooled thick in her eyes, and one escaped down her cheek. She took another sip of wine. "The merlot is perfect," she said.

Ian reached over to place his hand on hers. "I want to hear your story," he said softly, "if you're able. But I understand either way."

A tingling spread down her body at his touch. Her face felt flush but not from the wine.

"Thanks," she said. "I saw Stuart about a hundred meters ahead. He was passing some bikes on a curve, lost control, and landed backwards into a light pole. I don't know what happened to his helmet but he hit his head pretty hard. By the time I got there, he seemed lucid enough. Shaken up to be sure, but he kept brushing off the suggestion that he'd been seriously injured. I should have made him go to hospital, called an ambulance. Something, anything. Later that day, I should have watched him more closely. Before I knew it, he took a turn for the worse. I got him to hospital too late, and they weren't able to stop the swelling."

Saorla dabbed at a tear with her napkin. Ian squeezed her hand, and her eyes dried. Neither said a word for a time.

Ian broke the silence between them first. "Forgive yourself for what happened. It clearly wasn't your fault. Head injuries can be so tricky. Many times people get hit, and it looks really serious but nothing ever comes of it. Then there are the serious concussions and worse. It's hard for people to know what to do. Everything always looks clearer in hindsight."

He was right, of course, but it was just so hard carrying the burden of knowing that if she'd done something sooner, the outcome would have been different. Couldn't God have prevented the accident, despite her failures? If he had wanted to and was good?

"I just don't know why God would . . ."

"Listen, Stuart's accident wasn't caused by God. Trust me on that. I'm an attorney; our creator wasn't the tortfeasor behind what happened to Stuart. It's the thief who comes to kill and destroy. God's desire is for life, that we would have a full pint of it. But He works all things, even the evil that happens, and spins it for good if you are His."

Silence fell again between them; it hallowed out the worldly wisdom whooshing at her brain, while her heart clung to Ian's words. The waiter appeared and asked if they were ready to order.

"The menu's changed since the last time I was here," she said.

"We swap it out several times a year," the waiter said. "The fall menu offers plenty of squashes and pumpkin flavors."

Ian bounced up from his chair and went to the window, probably to see if their tails were still waiting for them outside. He needn't be worried; she had a plan, a way to exit this place without being followed. She leaned back in her chair and felt the stress leave her body.

She handed the waiter her menu. "I'll have the trout pâté, with crispy celeriac, golden beet root and horseradish salad."

Ian made it back to his seat. "Do you have a steak on that menu you can recommend?"

"Certainly. The char-grilled Irish Hereford rib-eye with roasted garlic truffle butter and homemade chips is your ticket. It's my favorite."

"I'll try that."

"By the way, why was the wine on the house?" Saorla asked.

"We pick one table a night to deliver a complimentary bottle. The criteria is very subjective. An older couple celebrating an anniversary one night, or a young couple who looks like they're in love the next."

"So, which of those was it tonight?" Saorla said, as she took the last sip of wine from her glass. It went down smooth and soft. Ian was still nursing his.

The waiter poured her another serving. "Ah tonight, one of our employees in the back said the lady is so beautiful she must win."

The information flummoxed her, and the waiter escaped to another table before she could ask more.

"Maybe you have a secret admirer," Ian teased. "I'm sure you have lots of them."

The night waxed pleasant, and the conversation flowed as smooth as the Merlot. The anxieties of the past couple weeks faded into the far corner of the vibrant and newly expanding horizon of Saorla's world.

Dinner proved to be the *pièce de résistance*. She thrilled to hear Ian declare that it was one of the best meals he'd ever had. Saorla chewed slowly, savoring her last bite of trout.

"I hate to interrupt the pleasant mood," Ian said, "but I was wondering if there's a back door out of here?"

"I know of something better than a back door," she said as she moved closer and drew in her voice to a whisper. "The owner once showed me a secret passageway that heads into the building attached to this one and then leads under the street and comes out on the other side of the river. I asked him about it because I'd read in my research that Michael Collins used the escape a few times during the war."

"So that's why you picked *this* restaurant tonight," Ian said.

Saorla raised both of her hands level with her ears, palms out to Ian in surrender. "If it's good enough for Michael Collins, it's good enough for us."

She was thinking about ordering dessert, when Ian began rummaging through his store bags. He pulled out a couple of headlamps and stuck them in his pocket.

"You ready for an adventure?" he asked.

"Sure thing, Frodo."

"Uh, that would make you Gandalf then," he said, and she laughed hard at that, harder than she remembered laughing for a long, long time.

CHAPTER FIVE

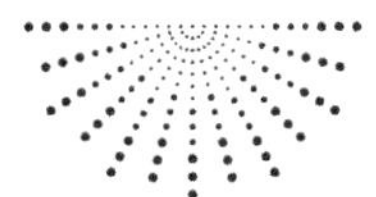

The sun in the eastern sky cast a peachy glow through the large windows of Carly's Rentals. Ian marched to the counter where a young man with a weak goatee greeted him.

A blue Hyundai SUV automatic—equipped with GPS navigation and priced at €93 a day—caught Ian's eye. He would have to fork over a lot more cash than was called for by the list price to convince the guy behind the counter to take cash instead of a credit card. A credit card would place him on the grid. And it was imperative that neither law enforcement—nor anyone else—be allowed to get a lead on where they were going next. Carly's was his best hope; it was futile to think the major chains would accept cash.

"Would you take euros?" Ian asked.

"No. My mom owns the store, and it's against policy."

"What if I made it worth your while?" He tried not to sound desperate.

"Depends on how much we're talking about," the weak goatee said.

Ian reached into his pocket and pulled out a wad of cash and laid it on the counter. "Will this do?"

"Mom's not going to be happy when she hears about this."

Ian reached to scoop up the money.

"Wait!" said the goatee. "You look honest."

"What about mom?"

"She'll get over it."

Ian had just finished the paperwork and held the keys in hand, when Saorla walked through the door. The fuchsia dress was gone, replaced with cargo pants and a sweatshirt, but she was still a vision. She greeted him with a hug at the counter.

"Good to see you," she said, "but seeing you usually means trouble."

Ian grinned. "I could say the same about you, darling."

Through the storefront window, he spotted Sophie pulling away from the curb in her old Volkswagen. He didn't know what he would do without her. A quick call to her last night, and she'd once again come to the rescue, this time snatching Ian and Saorla from the street after they'd submerged from the Winding Stair's secret exit. She'd dropped Ian off at Killian's house in Portmarnock, a small coastal town north of Dublin's city limits, and then took Saorla back to Sophie's apartment to spend the night.

Early this morning, Killian had given Ian a lift to the airport where Ian had frittered away time trying to locate a rental establishment that would take cash, so he was now eager to get on the road. And curiosity was bursting from his pores. He was finally going to find out if the mysterious numbers from their moonlit rendezvous with the Book of Kells were indeed GPS coordinates that would lead to some profound discovery. The more he'd thought about it, the more he became convinced that the numbers had to be coordinates. Nothing else made a lick of sense.

Two and half hours later, they were 230 kilometers south of Dublin traveling N25 along the southwest coast with Ian behind the wheel and Saorla riding in the passenger seat. Ian checked the two GPS devices. Aside from the one on the dashboard of the SUV, they had a hand held one they'd purchased yesterday during the shopping spree. "Looks like we have another hour to go."

"Are you sure we can't be tracked?" Saorla asked.

"I don't think so."

"But you're not *sure*."

Ian clenched his jaw. "It's a chance we have to take."

"Callahan's going to pop a vein if he finds out I'm on the run."

"You're not on the run."

"Tell that to Callahan."

Ian sighed. "I'm more worried about the stiffs from the museum."

Sophie arrived at the Taoiseach's mansion at 10:30 a.m., with thoughts of the professor and her new American friend weighing heavy. As she stepped into the first floor sitting room and prepared to vacuum, she offered up a prayer for continued guidance for both herself and for them. Sometimes a person's life came down to a choice. One poor decision might be enough to sabotage the best of plans. Conversely, one wise decision might set in motion a string of good fortune. Was her decision to become bailee of the Book of Kells the best or worst choice? Were there hazards unseen in a minefield ahead? She prayed for answers.

She'd been a Christian most of her life and knew God would never lead her contrary to his written word. She certainly didn't intend to keep the Book of Kells long, but the timing of its return to the proper authorities would require prudence.

It normally took her about two hours to complete her job at the mansion, but it was one she cherished notwithstanding the prurient advances of the high king who now held all the power by virtue of his new position as prime minister. The grand and ornate rooms never ceased to amaze her, and the grounds at Phoenix Park dazzled her eyes with every color of flowering plant and blooming bush.

On this Saturday morning, however, she was hoping to finish her duties as fast as possible so she could meet Killian for lunch, and then she would have the afternoon to get ready for the big dinner with the prime minister and his wife. She was glad her next cleaning appointment had canceled, leaving the afternoon free.

She made quick work of the sitting room and moved on to other locations on the first floor. While wiping a mirror in a downstairs bathroom, the voice of the prime minister himself startled her out of her reverie.

"There you are," he said. He maneuvered his tall frame into the doorway of the bathroom. "I knew you'd arrived, but I had to search the entire house before I found you."

Sophie scratched an itch on her nose with her shoulder to avoid the cleaning chemicals on her rubber gloves. "I apologize."

"Nonsense," he said, smiling. "The joy is in the chase. How on earth is my favorite immigrant to Ireland?" He gave her that same wink he always gave her.

"Fine," Sophie said. She spotted the prime minister's security detail tucked in behind him.

Braden beckoned her out of the bathroom and invited her for a chat over some tea. Sophie removed her gloves, and joined him in the nearby parlor where a large oval window allowed for a view of the park greens. A rugby game raged on the field in the distance under blue skies.

They sat at a small round table. Tea and crumpets were brought. The conversation flowed comfortably for about ten minutes. Braden complimented her on her English and raved that it had improved every week he'd spoken with her. She replied that when you're at the bottom, there's no way to go but up.

The prime minister's wife, Ann Braden, and her personal secretary, a woman Sophie knew only as Jeannie, arrived and were quickly invited to join the growing tea party. The security agents stood erect and impassive along the wall, seemingly unfazed by the spectacle.

Sophie marveled at Mr. Braden's fascination for her even in the company of his wife. But what would they think if they knew she kept their nation's treasure book tucked away under the covers of her bed?

Probably not a good idea to tell them about it now.

The prime minister's wife asked about Sophie's family and, in particular, her boyfriend. She told them all about her mother and sister and, of course, Killian.

Sometime later, she glanced down at her watch and saw that they had been talking for over a half hour. Her hopes of meeting Killian for lunch would be dashed if this kept up, but she could hardly tell the chief executive of her adopted country that she had more important personal business to attend to.

She needn't have worried, however, because in another moment, the prime minister rose from his seat. "Please do only the most abbreviated job of cleaning this morning. I've already taken up so much of your time."

She wasn't sure what to say to that obvious truth, so she didn't say anything.

The prime minister took his wife's hand and helped her up from her seat, then turned to Sophie. "And would you and your friend Killian do me the enormous favor of moving up our dinner engagement to earlier in the afternoon. A day of golf has been placed on my very tentative agenda for the weekend. The game normally would have been a well-earned respite from my stressed-filled schedule. But I've been given a quite disturbing report of some unusually nasty weather, even by Ireland's standards, that is moving in over the island this afternoon. Consequently, golf will have to be rescheduled for another day, and perhaps the duties of the office would call me away later in the evening. And I really don't want to miss the time we have carved out together."

He gave Sophie a brazen wink, right under the nose of Mrs. Braden.

"What kind of nasty weather?" Sophie asked, still flummoxed by the wink. Her question seemed foolish to her now as she considered that she had witnessed plenty of hard rains over her short time in Ireland.

"Could be quite unprecedented," the prime minister said. "Hurricane force winds and huge rain levels are possible. We are watching it closely. Most of the models show Dublin missing the brunt of the impact, but other parts of the island are sure to be hit hard. If it gets bad, you and your friend can stay overnight in our guest rooms."

There was that wink again. She could sense he quite enjoyed the thought of her spending the night at the mansion.

When tea time was over, Sophie quickly called Killian to inform him of the change in plans. They were now having an early dinner with the prime minister of Ireland, starting at three o'clock.

Killian agreed to swing by her apartment and pick up her dress, her one and only dress, a black sleeveless number, fit for any occasion, hanging in her small bedroom closet. She was adamant that he get the dress and himself out to the residence of the Taoiseach before the severe storm hit.

CHAPTER SIX

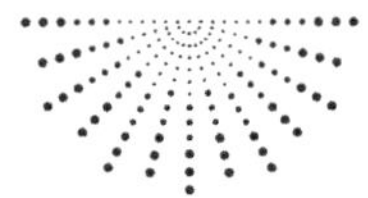

The early afternoon sun splayed the road with warmth, as their rented Hyundai rolled through the hills of coastal southwest Ireland, land of mythic lore. As Ian drove, Saorla became the trustee of that lore, filling his head with stories of goblins, ghosts, and leprechauns.

Although the skies were clear overhead, far out to the west over the Atlantic, clouds were forming on the horizon that were both thick and black.

About ten miles out from the next town, Saorla was recounting the story of Finn MacCool, a warrior-hunter and leader of the Fianna, a small band of Irish warriors. According to Saorla, legend had it that Finn MacCool, also known as Fionn mac Cumhaill, could see the future whenever he sucked his thumb.

"MacCool's unusual prowess," she said, "came about as a result of an encounter he'd had as a boy with a special salmon that was imbued with wisdom."

"A Solomon-like salmon?" Ian asked.

"Yeah, you got it."

"MacCool sounds pretty cool."

"Indeed. Anyway, the salmon was called—quite appropriately—the

Salmon of Knowledge. MacCool inadvertently touched the Salmon of Wisdom with his thumb and that is when the gift was imparted. MacCool became the leader of the Fianna, but that was only after he defeated a fire-breathing demon of a man named Aileen on the high hill of Tara on Samhain."

"Is this a true story?" Ian asked, playing along.

"Well, I certainly think it's as true as any story that old can be." She grinned, showing nearly all of her perfect white teeth and pretty pink gums.

"A lot of people in these parts think it's true. The story has been around since the third century."

Ian rubbed the dense stubble he hadn't had the time to shave before leaving Killian's. "What's Samhain?"

"Oh, that's simple. It's the halfway point between the autumn equinox and the winter solstice. Basically, it's Halloween. Except it was celebrated, mostly by the Druids and ancient celts, from sunset on October thirty-first to sunset on November first. Marking the beginning of the darker time of the year, it was believed to be a day when the boundary between the spirit world and our world could be easily crossed by spirits and faeries."

"I can do without those kind of spirits," Ian said. "My prayer is to be led by the Holy Spirit."

"I want that too," Saorla said.

The resolve in her voice was unmistakable. The transformation taking place in her made him smile. "So what ever happened to old Finn MacCool? I mean, how did he die?"

"Don't you want to know more of how he *lived* first?"

"Who wouldn't?" he said with a chuckle.

She feigned a punch to his arm, and Ian took a hand from the steering wheel to rub it as if she'd really walloped him good.

He glanced over at her to see her grinning at him again. "This is the interesting part," she said. "So, Finn MacCool was out hunting one day when he captured a deer. But it turns out the deer was actually a beautiful woman named Saba who'd been turned into a deer by an evil man she'd refused to marry. When MacCool brought the deer back to his home, she turned back into the woman, Saba. They married, she became pregnant, and they had a son. But then one day, when MacCool was off defending his country in a war, the evil man she'd refused to marry turned Saba into a deer once again. MacCool searched for her for many years but to no avail. He did, however, find their son, Oison, who went on to become one of the greatest Fianna warriors."

She paused from her story to take a sip of Ian's Dr. Pepper sitting in the cupholder. The woman wasn't afraid of his germs. The revelation made his pulse quicken. She flipped her hair over her ear, catching her breath for act two of McCool's story, no doubt. Ian was eager to know the final outcome for Finn.

"So how did he die?" Ian asked.

"Most say he is not dead at all, but sleeps in a cave near the seashore in the area we're going to today."

"You're kidding?"

Saorla giggled, for a moment she somehow seemed younger than her thirty years. "Would I kid about something as serious as this? Legend has it that Finn MacCool sleeps in a cave surrounded by Fianna warriors. Legend says that one day, in the hour of Ireland's greatest need, they will all arise to support and defend her."

Silence fell, except for the rush of the road under their wheels. Ian's eyes watered and his throat tickled as he contemplated what he'd just heard. Were events in the world now moving Ireland toward her hour of greatest need? It seemed like the problems looming before her were beyond human remedy.

"I want to be like the Fianna," Saorla finally uttered.

Ian slowly nodded his head. "I know," he said softly. "And I want to be like Finn."

Ian could have sworn he heard Saorla whisper, "You already are."

They passed a sign telling them they were entering the fishing village of Skibbereen.

"This is likely our last stop before we start our explorations," Saorla said. "It's where Michael Collins, the hero of the Irish independence movement, ate his last meal before he was shot to death in 1922."

"Let's load up on sports bars," Ian said. "If they don't have those, candy bars will do just fine."

"Serious calories easily available for working outdoors?"

"You got it, girl."

"You might not be saying that when you see me climb. Did I mention I'm afraid of heights?"

"Only a hundred times."

"Not going to say it again then."

"Trust me, you'll be fine. We have everything we need, except the snacks."

But there was one thing that now bothered him. It was the feeling that he seemed to be following in the footsteps of Michael Collins ever since he'd taken the secret passageway out of the Winding Stair. And now here he was in the same town where Collins had been shot and killed. Was it bad karma? He shook the thought from his head.

You don't believe in karma anymore, remember? You're in the sovereign will of God now.

Nevertheless, Ian was eager to keep moving, so it was with reluctance that he pulled up and stopped at a stone building, which was freshly painted a bright green. A black sign with white letters read *O'Donnell's Kaleidoscope*. The store sold everything from whiskey and beer to dolls and toy soldiers. Saorla grabbed a few candy bars and some trail mix. Ian opted for beef jerky, a gallon of water, and a Dr. Pepper.

He made his way down the aisle toward the cashier but was stopped in his tracks by a couple of surf boards for sale that were propped against the back wall next to the beer. He was about to meander over for a closer look, when he heard a voice croak from behind the store counter.

"Don't mess with the faeries is my advice. If you step in their blood, they will turn you into a frog."

Ian glanced over his shoulder, hoping mightily that the words were not directed at him.

Hope dashed when he locked eyes with him.

Working the cash register was a small, thin man with big bulging eyes, a scraggly beard, and thin hair that belonged better on the skull of the skeletal remains of a seventeenth century pirate.

"Huh?" Ian managed to mutter.

"I'm talking about the good people, you know, the other crowd, the faeries. You don't want to mess with 'em."

Ian directed his gaze away from Mr. Bulging Eyes in favor of once again checking out the surfboards. Where was Saorla? Probably still in the restroom.

How beautiful would it be to get out back with Shark? Maybe not Mavericks. Santa Cruz would be cool. Someplace where they could ride some *reasonable* waves without killing themselves.

Whoa, where did that thought come from?

Was something in his psychic makeup changing? The unexplainable caution that had just come over him was a new, foreign experience.

Shake it off man. Get yourself back in the game.

The best way to shake it off was to have a look at those boards. He was headed in that direction, when a bony hand patted him on the shoulder.

Ian turned and locked into yellow retinas. Bulging Eyes. "If you keep headin' north up the coast a couple of hours, just before you get to the Cliffs of Moher, there's an excellent spot with big waves."

Now that the man seemed to be talking about surfing, rather than faeries, it didn't seem as necessary to avoid him. But it didn't make sense that Ireland had big waves that could be surfed.

"I didn't know Ireland had surfing yet alone *big* waves," Ian said.

Bulging Eyes let loose with a wild guffaw. "Lahinch is the place. It goes off at least twenty times a year. That's where they went mad and ran off the cliffs. Created the thirty foot waves—"

"Who went mad?" Ian said.

"—from the wild horses. The sprites made 'em crazy."

"Huh?"

"Dad didn't mean to lose you," someone said through the door leading from the back office. A body appeared at the doorway with the voice. She was a brown-haired college-aged girl that had a vague resemblance to Bulging Eyes.

"Daddy loves the old legends. By the way, my name's Mary Margaret O'Donnell."

"Pleased to meet you, MMO," Ian said.

A smile formed on her face, probably at the instant nickname Ian had given her. "When dad talks about the wild horses, he's referring to the earliest inhabitants of the island. They lost control to subsequent invaders, turned themselves into horses, and hid in a cave near Kilcorney rather than flee the island. Then one day the sunshine burst so intense into the cave that they fled north, galloping straight over the Cliffs of Moher and plummeting a thousand feet to the ocean below. But some say they turned into waves when they hit the water. And that's what causes the giant swells at Lahinch. At any rate, it really is a big wave surfer's paradise. People come from around the world to ride them."

"This, I did not know," Ian said with a quick shake of his head. The ache to surf suddenly sent his heart rate elevating.

Get a grip. You're acting like a junkie. There's no way it could happen today.

Still, he couldn't help but ponder how cool it would be to trade his present lot for that of a care-free tourist and surfer.

"Where are you traveling today?" MMO asked.

"Just exploring the coast," Ian said, thinking it best to be vague about their plans. "Probably get as far as Reen before we end up turning back."

MMO raised an eyebrow. "Not much in Reen, a B&B is about it. Otherwise, it's just open country."

Saorla came in the door from outside and explained that she'd been taking a look around town. "You want to see where Michael Collins had his last meal," she asked Ian.

"No way."

The chat with Bulging Eyes and his daughter picked up where it left off, then moved to the topic of faeries, giants, and leprechauns.

This was right up Saorla's table of contents, Ian figured, so he let it go on for a bit. He was just about to bring up some bona fide historical truths about a God-man named Jesus, when Bulging Eyes started to get even weirder.

"The faeries and warrin' sprites are movin' in a big blow comin' this way. They'll be blowin' thru soon, I'm sure of it!"

Luckily, the daughter was there to interpret. "Dad's talking about the storm forecast for this afternoon. It's supposed to be clear for a while yet. But massive storms arrive in the afternoon."

Ian had had enough of faeries and wild horses. They paid for their food bars and drinks and left. "We're definitely going to need the calories if we have to spend time out in foul weather," he said to Saorla as they walked to their vehicle.

Bulging Eyes suddenly yelled after them, "Watch out for the faeries! They're going to bring buckets of tears down on the land. It's not good luck."

"I don't believe in luck," Ian fired back. "I believe in providence."

CHAPTER SEVEN

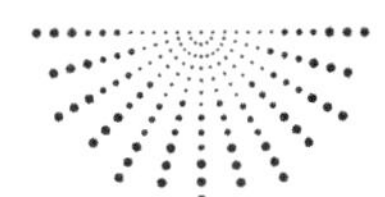

The call came from his red-headed lover around 9:45 a.m. Saturday morning. Professor Claire Curran was proving useful to him in ways that extended beyond the baser elements of his nature. As a colleague and close confidant of Saorla O'Rourke, Red had her eyes and ears in places that even he couldn't crack.

"I just got off the phone with O'Rourke," she said. "They rented a car and are going on a trip to the Southwest."

Lorcan had been sitting on his hardwood floor, meditating and looking through the large windows that circled a room devoid of furniture that was really more of an observation deck from which all of Dublin could be seen. He got to his feet now. "Did she say where she rented the car?"

"I couldn't very well ask her that directly without raising her suspicion. So, I tried it indirectly. She said she was over near the airport."

"Excellent."

"So, I please you?"

"Yes," Lorcan said with a laugh.

"Do you think O'Rourke and the American still have the Book of Kells?"

"I'm sure they have it somewhere," he said. "When we get them, we'll force it out of them."

"Then what happens?"

"We become rich; it's as simple as that."

"I meant what happens to Saorla?"

"She'll go the way of all of those who come to cross-purposes with me, Red."

Claire cooed. "It's a good thing I'm loyal to you."

"Indeed."

"Because I'm good at betrayal. Somehow it's easier than I thought it would be. Turns out I like the excitement. And she isn't the same person she was a few weeks ago. She's become less like me and more . . ."

"More preoccupied?"

"More naive, I guess would be the way to phrase it. She tried to talk to me about faith in God."

Lorcan's mind traveled back to the last time someone had gotten religion around him. He pictured his father now, all wide-eyed, agog, full of new words he'd never used before like *sinner* and *born-again*. He'd been full of the new talk and new-found hysteria, coming fresh from an evangelistic meeting with a famous American preacher—the day before a drunk driver put a permanent end to all that.

A lot of good that new talk did his old man.

"You're really starting to get what I've been teaching you, Red, about the old ways. They are so much better for people."

"I could never deceive you," Claire said.

"It's time I invite you deeper into my life, Red. This year, we're going to celebrate the festival of Samhain together."

He ended the call, and passed the tip from Claire on to his men, directing them to check the independent car rental companies near the airport.

His boys got lucky when a call to Carly's was answered by an employee who had indeed seen a couple matching the description of the professor and her American companion.

Twenty minutes later, Lorcan's henchmen had commandeered the technology used by Carly's to pinpoint the whereabouts of its leased-out vehicles. Picking up the location of the rented Hyundai more than an hour outside of Dublin and heading west on N25 out of Wexford, Lorcan's men sprang into action.

They filled him in on every detail, and he barked back the strategy.

An assassination squad assembled; guns and grenades were loaded. But the orders were clear: the executions were not to be carried out until *after* they had the book. If they spotted the professor and the American in the open, they were to capture them, torture out some information, and then only when they had the book in hand, were they to close the account with no traces left behind.

They left in a black Mercedes SUV. Their arsenal boasted assault rifles, revolvers, pistols and enough ammunition to shoot non-stop for days. Lorcan's two most trusted killers—Hogan Kirby and Torna Mac Vidhir—rode in the front seat. Two other thick-necked men in suits rode in the back.

PULLING INTO SKIBBEREEN, KIRBY BELIEVED THEY WEREN'T MORE THAN forty minutes behind their quarries. The problem was that they'd lost the GPS readout that had been tracking the Hyundai. Skibb, as the town was known by locals, was the last place they'd received a positioning for the vehicle.

Kirby carefully parked the black SUV. As far as he could tell, he was in the exact spot where they'd last received a fix on the coordinates of the Hyundai. "Torna, come with me," he ordered. "The rest of you stay and keep a lookout."

"*O'Donnell's Kaleidoscope,* eh?" Kirby said with a smirk. "A poor choice they've made for their last meal if you ask me."

Torna grunted. "Grand choice."

The two men strutted through the store entrance. A minute later, they were at the checkout counter with a few packs of cigarettes, some cheap cigars, and four cans of Red Bull.

"The sprites love the fags and drinks—"

Kirby leaned his thick frame over the counter and waved with his finger for the old man with the wild eyes to come closer. "Listen old timer . . ." Kirby checked himself and decided to try it again a little more politely. "I mean, Mr.—"

"O'Donnell, Kevin O'Donnell is the name."

"Okay. Mr. O'Donnell, listen, did you happen to see a couple come in here, say maybe forty minutes ago? A woman, late twenties to early thirties, dark hair, real attractive. She was with an American, strong build, athletic look—"

"And why might you be inquirin'? Are they in trouble with the law?"

"Listen, grandpa, I'll ask the questions around here."

"If they're in trouble, the faeries will get 'em. You can be sure." The old man darted his gaze about as if faery dust had just been sprinkled on the whole store.

"You could say they're in trouble with the pow'rs that be," Kirby said, while handing the old man a card that claimed he was an investigator from INTERPOL.

The old man looked over the card. "They did say something about Reen."

"Where's that?" Torna asked, injecting himself into the conversation for the first time.

"About forty to fifty kilometers in a straight northwest shot up the coast. The sprites could fly there in minutes you know."

AFTER THEY'D LEFT O'DONNELL'S SHOP AND GOT THEMSELVES BACK ON the road, Saorla steered down the narrow two-lane highway that wound northwesterly, while Ian watched the green dot that represented their car moving ever closer to the tiny hamlet of Reen. A few minutes later, they passed the town, if it could be called that. The landscape was nearly bereft of any structures of human habitation, and they saw no people. As they moved ever closer to the red dot on the GPS, a butterfly formed in Ian's stomach. He'd missed that feeling.

Saorla turned off the main roadway and onto a tortuous mud road that led down toward the seashore. No tourist trails or haunts to avoid out here.

They parked their car where the road ended, and loaded their backpacks with supplies: water, headlamps, sport bars, climbing equipment, and anything else they might need on the journey. The nearest farmhouse was miles away. The Kenmare Bay churned below about a thousand meters down. From their perch on the side of the hill, it looked to be several kilometers before the bay opened up to the full force of the ocean.

What awaited at the end of those GPS points? Points yet unknown, but points to which they were being summoned by words and wisps from the past.

They huddled and said a prayer together for God's protection and guidance, as the red dot on the GPS blinked like a metronome. Then, they simply started hiking in its direction.

The clouds grew ever darker off on the horizon to the west. Breakers tumbled fiercely onto the rocks at the shoreline.

"No question there's a storm coming," Ian said. "We better get moving."

They hiked a little farther until they came down to near level with the sea. The roar was deafening. Bands of waves hurled themselves, raucous and angry, at the shoreline boulders where they met with inexorable resistance that sliced the water into frothy foam and then oblivion.

Ian pointed to a pathway along the cliffs, which was periodically inundated with swirling white foam. "We have to time our approach just right to get past the water when it recedes. When we get to the dry part behind, I think we'll be in the optimum position to start climbing."

Saorla let out a nervous laugh. "Oh yes, the climbing part. I quite wish that the '*seventy-nine m*' from the Book of Kells didn't mean seventy-nine meters into the sky. I'm afraid I'm going to rue the day . . ."

"Relax," Ian said. "This should be a piece of cake. You can do this."

He truly believed she could, but was he conveying more confidence than he had a right to? If he was completely honest, he couldn't be exactly sure what they would get into just from looking. He estimated the difficulty on the climbing scale to be somewhere between a 5.8 and 5.9. Anything below a 5.8 was fairly easy. With a climb above 5.9, however, even an experienced weekend climber would have difficulty. The highest level was 5.15. Only those who could hang onto a glass ceiling upside down would be comfortable there. Ian had ventured into some 5.11 climbs in his day, which put him in the rarified air of the dedicated climbers.

But what about Saorla? She had no climbing skills at all and had warned him she was afraid of heights. He prayed the climbing would be closer to 5.8 than 5.9.

"You ready to give it a try?" he asked.

"As long as my coach believes in me."

She seemed to infuse confidence into herself by the sheer force of her words. It was a good start, but he would never be able to forgive himself if he let something happen to her up there.

You gotta be on top of your game, dude. No doubt about it.

He studied the sheer rock face jutting up toward the sky. "Beautiful. But this route is a lot higher than seventy-nine meters. Probably a hundred and twenty meters, I'd say. But I see the strangest thing up there."

He pointed to a spot about two-thirds of the way up the cliff face. "At about eighty meters, give or take a few, is a little alcove. I'm just wondering if that's our target, the seventy-nine m?"

Saorla winced. "Only one way to find out."

SAORLA STRAINED TO PULL HERSELF TOWARD A FOOTHOLD ON THE LEDGE just a few inches above her right foot. Her shoulders and biceps were cashed. They felt like the dead earthworms she used to leave for too long in her bait cup while salmon fishing with her father in the hills of Donegal. The extreme effort had made her fiercely hungry, and she desperately wanted to eat the candy bar in her back pocket. But there was no way she could reach it now.

Anything to give her strength. Janey Mac, she'd be tempted to eat one of those dead earthworms she was so hungry.

And thirsty too.

The perspiration poured off her face and dripped nearly two hundred feet to the rocks below. Despite the sixty degree air temperature, it was humid. The system coming in over the Atlantic pumped moisture into her nostrils.

"You're doing great," Ian yelled, no doubt at the top of his lungs, though she barely heard him over the roar of the waves crashing over the rocks below. "We only have about twenty meters left."

Twenty meters? He sounded like it was a walk to the backyard garden. Twenty meters meant she still had a fourth of the way to go. When she turned her eyes up, she could see that Ian was almost at the Alcove. She, on the other hand, was moving even slower now and for the first time she pondered whether she would finish. What if she just wore out right here? Ian could probably get her down somehow. But what if something happened to him?

Well, the birds will eat my sorry carcass, I guess.

Ian had her roped in. Could he pull her to the top if she passed out? He was so strong; he probably could, but it would be dangerous for both of them.

For the first time since she started to climb, she was tempted to look down. She fought the urge, but in the lightheadedness brought on by her hunger, curiosity and weakness overcame her. She turned her cheek to the side of the cliff. Focused her gaze below.

Nothing but air between her and wild swells of water flipping and churning and catapulting into the cliff walls, and then shooting up toward her.

Her vision started to swirl.

She closed her eyes and pressed her face harder into the cliff.

Paralyzed, she clung to the rock as frozen as the statute of the buxom Molly Malone on Grafton Street with her cart of seafood.

"You okay?" Ian shouted. His voice sounded like it was coming from the other side of the Atlantic. But it was enough to startle her out of the spiraling dizziness.

"Yeah," she screamed back, hoping it was true.

A new determination came at the sound of his voice, and she started to strain her way upward once again.

And then it started to rain. Big hard pellets at first. One pellet, followed by two, three, four pellets.

There was no fifth pellet.

Instead, it came in violent torrential walls of liquid.

Her hands gripped into her holds harder. But the supposedly solid rock under her right shoe disintegrated into crumbled flecks of gravel. She screamed out as the panic swept over her.

She grappled, desperate for a new foothold.

A few inches up and to her right, she found it.

Have to breathe.

She lowered her head to prevent water from rushing into her face. She took several gasps of air.

Composing herself by taking long, deep breaths, a new thought suddenly swept into her head, and she felt a fresh current of fear snake down her spine.

The water was scouring the rock. What if the cams and pitons that Ian had hammered into the rock to tether them from falling didn't hold?

She screamed his name into the cliff face, but she knew it was useless to be heard over the many waters. Then she had another idea. And this time she cried to the only one in earth or sky or sea who could possibly hear. "Lord, help me."

CHAPTER EIGHT

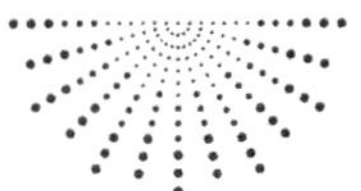

Salivating at the prospect of the hunt, Kirby and his crew bounced down a kidney-killer of a mud road toward the parked Hyundai. Soon after they'd left O'Donnell's store in Skibb, they'd once again began drawing a bead on their targets. Rain pelted them as they exited their vehicle.

It took no more than a moment to select their weapons of choice from their stockpile and to double check that they were fully loaded. In the car ride from Skibb, they'd had a loud argument over who was the most talented marksmen for a job that would initially require wounding rather than killing. Kirby had insisted he was and was eager to prove it. When they finally homed in on the prey, he would show the boys who was the best, especially the recent cocky recruit to Lorcan's security detail named Marcus. The new man claimed to have been a sniper in the British special forces who served a tour of duty in Iraq. But Kirby would show them all why he, Kirby, was the heart, soul and brains of Lorcan's outfit.

Kirby buttoned tight the collar of his coat and grabbed his weapon, carrying it openly. There was no need to conceal out here in the middle of this void.

"Even with this thrashing, I can see a path of sorts with footprints," Torna hissed through the moisture. "Must lead down to the shore."

They followed the path, until they came close to the point where the land was putting up a last-ditch attempt to keep the bay in check. The waves pounded on the rocks to their left so that they could scarcely hear one another as they shouted.

"There's a Dr. Pepper near that rock," Torna yelled.

"So where are they?" Kirby asked.

The rain had eased off a bit, but the wind had picked up and was emitting an ominous howl, which, combined with the surf, caused the men to gather as if in a rugby scrum.

"We know they bought rock climbing gear the other day," Kirby said, "so use your heads. They must be climbing somewhere around here. We'll find them up there like a couple of feral goats in the Wicklow Mountains."

They pulled their heads up from the scrum and began to search the cliffs.

"I see 'em," Marcus grunted.

Kirby silently cursed at the realization that Marcus was the first to spot them. By the time Kirby got a visual, he could see that Marcus was already aiming his rifle.

BECAUSE OF THE WEATHER THREAT AND THE POSSIBILITY THE PRIME minister would be called away, dinner was served at the unusually early hour of four o'clock. Candlelight softened the smaller of the two dining halls where they sat, making for a warm and cozy atmosphere despite the brewing storm outside. It was just the four of them—Sophie and Killian seated across the table from David and Ann Braden. Sophie was determined to make a good show of it to prove that she posed no danger to the prime minister's marriage. He'd informed Sophie that he had framed the evening to his wife as one of getting a different perspective on the world. What better way to do it than dinner with an eastern European immigrant and her well-traveled missionary boyfriend?

Sophie was glad that Killian had made it with her dress before the rain started. Pleased with the way she looked, at least she wouldn't have any concerns about being underdressed. But what about her little secret with the book? How was she going to dress that up and keep her naked heart from being exposed?

A number of courses were brought. The main dinner consisted of scallops, duck hearts, and seaweed soup. The wine was white. Dessert was a trio of chocolates and a crème brûlée served with a port wine. It all tasted like perfection.

The conversation began with the exchange of trite banalities, but after dessert was served the discussion flowed to the political and spiritual realms. Killian and the prime minister seemed to especially enjoy one another's company, although it was apparent they held opposing views on many issues.

A rare lull in their conversation came, and the prime minister asked Sophie about her upbringing.

This she could do. Thankfully, he hadn't asked if she'd done anything exciting lately, and there'd been no mention yet of the story that was gripping the nation surrounding the book's disappearance. The book whose price was too great to have a price.

She recounted her early years in communist Poland and the experiences of her parents' survival in the Soviet-dominated satellite nation that had moved from creeping socialism to communism under Stalin and his successors.

"What was the worst of the oppression that your family experienced?" the prime minister asked. His eyes were eager and attentive.

"My family owned a farm. It was taken away in the mid-eighties before I was born. My parents moved to the city. My uncle? He was thrown in prison. For what? He was artist. That was his crime. Then my father was put in same prison for two years based on rumor that he is for Solidarity."

"That must have been awful."

"I was not alive for this. But later I see paintings my uncle did while in prison. He painted on newspaper, whatever he can get his hands on. They tell story. Skeleton figures and half-human, half-animal. Represent death, bondage, oppression. Government is depicted as dragon tormenting the mass of people that cower. One painting shows man with locks on his lips, eyelids, and ears. Most important about those paintings is that they show contrast between light and darkness. Everything dark about the paintings under communism. Except the one with angel full of light facing firing squad. The angel was all light, but everything else dark. But then change comes. After 1988, his paintings sparkle with hope. One has strong woman holding huge rock over her head. She is covered with light about to crush a small snake. I always think the strong woman represents the people of Poland and the snake is communism. You could say that the seed of the woman crushed Satan."

The confused looks on Mr. and Mrs. Braden's faces only lasted a second because the butler interrupted and asked if anyone wanted more wine. All declined, except Mrs. Braden. The prime minister announced that they would be moving to the parlor shortly where coffee and tea would be served.

Mrs. Braden turned to Sophie. "You seem to be lumping communism and socialism into the same basket. Aren't you overlooking the good socialists do to provide a net of safety for the less fortunate?"

"Is fine if you like giving up your name and identity to become just a number in godless system and if you want to more equally share misery."

Mrs. Braden frowned. Sophie steeled herself for a response, but Mrs. Braden simply picked up her wine glass and took a sip.

The prime minister was scratching his chin and looking up toward the chandelier as if he were giving her words some thought. His eyes sharpened and he turned to Killian. "You've spoken a lot about God tonight. What do you think He thinks of Ireland as a nation?"

Killian looked quizzically at the prime minister as if he'd been thrown off-guard by the question. "Uh, well, I know from scripture that He has a controversy with all the nations, and they've all fallen short. And just because a government claims to be *for the people,* does not mean it can best the sovereign God. There's only one way to have right standing with Him and that's through faith in Jesus."

Mrs. Braden flashed a quick smirk. "If that's the test, then the nations are truly in a quandary."

The prime minister's cell phone buzzed. He answered, listened for a moment, then hung up. "We may have to cut the evening short," he said. "I just received a report that sustained winds clocked at over a hundred miles an hour are hitting the west coast."

"It's like the Night of the Big Wind," Killian said, his voice rising an octave.

"Night of the Big Wind?" Mrs. Braden asked.

"Maybe we should save this story for another time?" Sophie suggested.

"Nonsense," Mrs. Braden said. "I must hear this."

"All right," Killian said. "There was a prophecy in Irish folklore going back hundreds of years that judgment day would come on the church Feast of Epiphany. It was January 6, 1839, when the storm hit. Wind gusts were over one hundred and fifteen miles per hour in the afternoon and by midnight they were sustained at hurricane force. Three hundred people were killed. Lots of property damage. It happened on the Feast of Epiphany. The majority of the people believed it was the end of the world."

"We Irish have always been a very superstitious lot," Mrs. Braden said.

Killian nodded his head. "And sometimes mixed in with the superstition is the true prophetic word."

"But it obviously wasn't the end of the world?" Mrs. Braden said.

"It was the end of the world that day for three hundred. Plus, it was the end of things for the way a lot of people had known them. The potato famine hit some years later and a million people died and another million left the island."

"It will be the end of *my political world* if I don't handle this storm and its aftereffects properly," the prime minister replied grimly. "Especially now that the Book of Kells has vanished on my watch."

CHAPTER NINE

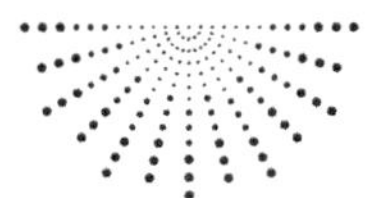

Ian hammered the piton into the rock, yanked on it to make sure it was secure, and then glanced down at Saorla. She was moving slowly but surely now after that shaky stretch earlier when she'd come to an abrupt halt.

Almost at the alcove, Ian checked his GPS for the red dot. It looked like a near match with his present position. A rush of elation hit him at the notion that the numbers from the book really might be GPS coordinates.

A whisk of air rushed past him, tickling his face, followed by a loud cracking sound that echoed from the cliff wall.

What was that?

Then it struck again. The unmistakable crack of rifle fire echoed off the cliffs and cut through the roar of the wind and water.

His body moved on instinct for a higher purchase up the cliff, his hands pulling himself up by a narrow slice in the rock. Within seconds, he'd managed to pull himself all the way to the ledge of the alcove where he found himself looking into a dark opening.

A cave?

The professor.

What was he thinking?

"Saorla!" he screamed. He sprung to his feet, bent low for balance on the ledge, and began pulling her up with the rope. The pump in his biceps ballooned and his shoulder muscles strained against the nylon, ready to tear from his body. Pulling and pulling, he gasped for breath below the saturated and steadily darkening sky.

Faster, dig deeper.

More gunshots pierced the watery air.

It seemed like an eternity, but it couldn't have been more than the seconds he could count on one hand before he'd pulled her to the ledge and she fell into his arms like a scared kitten.

He looked down and saw blood.

"What?"

How? He didn't know. There was no time to check.

Bullets ricocheted off the rocks.

He shoved Saorla to the safety of the cave through a narrow hole in the cliff wall and thrust himself low to the ground.

Over the edge of the cliff, his eyes peered down. Four men. Armed with rifles and who knew what else.

More blood. Coming faster.

His own blood.

A searing pain in his bicep. At least it wasn't his heart.

He slid himself toward the mouth of the cave.

"My goodness, Ian, are you ok?"

"I don't know."

"We have to get off this ledge," she shrieked.

Dizzy and lightheaded, he pushed her toward the darkness of the cave.

"Put your headlamp on," she screamed, "it's dark and narrow through here."

Ian fumbled through his pants pocket, pulled out his headlamp, and managed to affix it around his skull. There was only one way to go now; behind them was death.

But what lay ahead?

CHAPTER TEN

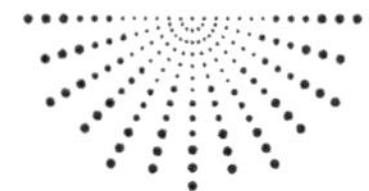

As the afternoon waxed into evening inside of Steward's Lodge at the Farmleigh estate, the home of the Prime Minister, Sophie could hear the constant howl of the wind through the unseen cracks at the windows. Mr. Braden had moved his guests into a warm, comfortable sitting room where they awaited the butler's appearance with tea and coffee. The lights were dimmed. A vigorous fire crackled in the hearth.

With the increasing fury of the storm, Mr. Braden grew more and more agitated. Sophie became convinced he would soon abandon his visitors in order to attend to the needs of the nation.

The comfortable climate inside of Steward's Lodge was a stark contrast with what was unfolding outdoors. Through the large window overlooking Phoenix Park, Sophie gawked at trees bobble-heading so chaotically they looked to be dangerously close to uprooting. The flowers and shrubs became so many miniature flags waving at a street parade. And the precipitation poured in incessant sheets of sheer white. There surely hadn't been this much rainfall since the days of Noah, she thought.

The distracted conversation turned to the nation of Israel. Ireland, like the other Western European countries, was in the process of queuing up to be part of a UN coalition to censure Israel. There was also talk of a future mobilization to march on Jerusalem in response to a global outcry that the city become an international capital with its day-to-day governing authority turned over to the Palestinians.

"My intention isn't to be offensive," Killian said. "But Matthew 25 talks about the sheep and goat nations that Jesus separates from one another on the day of judgment. Many scholars believe these nations are judged over the way they treated Israel in the course of human history, but especially in the last days."

"I know where you are going with this," the prime minister said reflexively. "Nothing has been finally decided by this government on the whole Jerusalem question. However, public support here is overwhelmingly in favor of censure."

"I know the politics," Killian said, his voice more sharp than Sophie was used to hearing him speak. "But I have to tell you this coalition is evil in the sight of God. The Bible repeatedly mentions a time in human history when all the nations will gather against Israel and Jerusalem—"

"How do you know *this* is *that* time?"

"God promised the land to Israel through Abraham. King David established Jerusalem as its eternal capital, and—"

The butler appeared with hot drinks. Killian took a straight black coffee. Sophie and the Taoiseach opted for tea. Mrs. Braden looked pleased to get a refill on her wine.

After everyone was set, Killian grabbed his phone, pulled up a Bible app, and read some scriptures from Zechariah.

"This is a grave situation you have on your hands," he said. "The Lord intends to make Jerusalem a cup that causes reeling to all nations; and when the siege is against Jerusalem, it will also be against Judah. It will come about in that day that the Lord will make Jerusalem a heavy stone for all nations and all who lift it will be severely injured . . . the nations of the earth will be gathered against it."

The prime minister leaned in closer. "Killian, I want to be upfront about something, but you have to promise that you won't leak this to anyone."

Killian nodded. "Of course. You have Sophie's confidentiality too, I'm sure."

She gave a quick nod.

If they only knew the enormity of secret I already keep.

The prime minister took a sip of tea. "The truth is that I had a closed-door meeting with my cabinet yesterday, and we've voted to join the coalition but agreed to hold off announcing it until after the first week in November. Some wanted to wait for the elections in America to see if they are intent on staying the course with their policy, which it looks like they are."

"I can only tell you that this course may prove tragically ill-advised."

"Did you ever consider a career in politics?"

"No."

"You would be quite a conservative voice if conservatism ever becomes *de rigueur* again."

Killian smiled politely. "God's not a party man. Neither am I. And on this issue of Jerusalem, He's clear."

"I admire that about you. Traditionally, Ireland hasn't had a left-right divide as much as other countries. But that has clearly changed. Fine Gail and Fianna Fail are not the only game in town. The extreme leftist from Sinn Fein and Labor are only growing in strength. Clearly more firepower is needed to combat their threat."

The butler poked his head into the room and asked if anyone cared for more dessert. The nay votes were unanimous, and he ambled off toward the kitchen.

Killian returned to his pet subject of Israel by setting forth an impressive case to show that the days Zechariah had prophesied about were indeed just around the corner. Sophie sensed that the prime minister was growing weary of Killian's penchant for international geopolitics as it related to "the apple of God's eye," as Killian referred to Israel.

"One more thing from Zechariah, please, if I may," Killian said, not looking up from the app he had open on his phone. "It says in chapter twelve that the Lord will seek to destroy all the nations that come against Jerusalem."

Mrs. Braden yawned. "How do we know—"

Her words were cut off by an ashen-faced butler, who had swung the door of the sitting room open and had thrust himself into their midst. "Thought you should know, sir, we've been watching the piped telly." The butler gulped a breath of air. "And there's been a most unusual occurrence. An earthquake just hit the southwest coast near Skibbereen. At the same time, they are getting bolloxed up by the storm hitting very hard there. The earthquake, they are saying, is the strongest ever recorded in the British Isles."

Prime Minister Braden's cell phone buzzed. He picked up and listened, his eyebrows furrowing. He ended the call and bowed his head. "It's worse than you can imagine."

The formerly wine-flushed cheeks of Mrs. Braden turned to pale buttermilk.

Sophie thought of the prediction from Father Conlin's book of an earthquake, one that was to occur in the very hour that the code from the Book of Kells is cracked. She also thought of *the cup that causes reeling.*

IAN PLUNGED THROUGH THE NARROW ENTRYWAY OF THE CAVE AND began to crawl. Soon his pants at the knees began shredding to pieces. Knee pads for caving would have been nice.

The small pack filled with his supplies protruded from the center of his back and scraped the rock just above him. If it got any narrower, he'd be stuck. But the cave had to be passable, didn't it? The numbers from the Book of Kells had correctly marked the entrance to the cave and that gave him hope he wasn't in a tunnel to nowhere. And at least it was dry so far.

Warm blood oozed from his arm, and he felt it saturating his sleeve. He would have to have the wound dressed. And soon.

The claustrophobic shaft of cave undulated onward. Every so often the beam of light from his headlamp picked up a fleeting glimpse of Saorla's rock shoes moving like a ghost into the void beyond.

"You see any sign this opens up?" Ian yelled ahead.

But there was no reply, just the intermittent wisp of a shoe.

Ian was panting heavily now. He needed to stop and catch his breath, but there was no telling how soon the thugs would approach from behind. He rested his chin on the cool rock of the cave floor and pressed a button on his sports utility watch. It illuminated his direction—northeast—and a reading of his pulse flickered—way too high at 165.

As he grunted and pushed himself forward still prone to the ground, a wave of nausea hit, and he fought the urge to vomit. The lightheadedness he experienced earlier was back with reinforcements. His cold, clammy skin scraped over the rock. He checked his pulse on the watch again. A whopping 175 beats per minute. Something was wrong.

Yeah, like maybe you're bleeding to death, dude.

Still he pushed himself ahead.

There were no more glimpses of Saorla's shoes, and he realized he must have slowed down.

Stay strong, keep pushing.

He crawled for another fifteen minutes before the shaft opened to a wide cavern. His eyesight was blurred, but he could make out Saorla with a first aid kit already opened. She touched her hand to his face and held it there for a second.

"I swear, Ian, I was beginning to think I was going to have to go back for you."

He blinked away the blurriness and could see the tears welling in her eyes.

"Just dragging a little today," he said, then grunted.

Saorla rolled up his torn and soaked shirt sleeve. "Let me have a look at that."

He managed a feeble smile. "Whatever you say, nurse."

Saorla poked around at the wound, bloodying her hands. "There's no bullet in there. That's the good news. It clipped a capillary in your bicep. I can get the bleeding stopped if I can stitch it."

"I'm not sure we have time for that. They're probably climbing that cliff in a hurry. How soon they get to us depends on how fit they are."

Saorla reached into her backpack. "We have no choice until we get that bleeding stopped." She produced a female sanitary pad and placed it over his wound. "Here, hold this on it. It's the best we have, and I hear they're good for this sort of job."

Ian was too weak to laugh.

She fetched a bottle of Gatorade and a chocolate bar from her pack and forced Ian to drink and eat. In a few minutes, his vision cleared, and he felt his pulse slowing.

"I want to thank you," he said. "For everything. Not just this." He raised his chin to gaze into her eyes. The light from the small lantern from his pack illuminated specks of green and cocoa. "I'm just glad it was me that got hit back there. I couldn't live with myself if . . ."

"Funny thing is," Saorla said softly, the roar of the outdoors a distant memory in the sealed-off solitude of the cave, "when you didn't come out right after me, I thought that I couldn't live with myself if something happened to *you*. And I wished I could have taken your place."

She reached out for his hand, and he took it in his. They locked onto one another without speaking.

"You're one-in-a-million," he finally whispered.

They sat another moment across from each other in silence. Finally, Saorla reached over and took the pad off the wound. The bleeding had slowed considerably.

"I'm going to stitch it up, and you'll be as good as new."

"We should get moving."

"If I don't, it will just start bleeding again, only worse, and you can't afford to lose any more blood."

CHAPTER ELEVEN

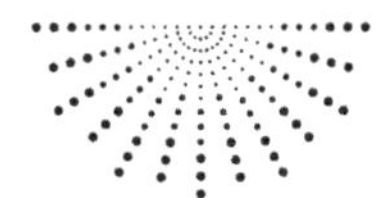

Kirby was furious that they hadn't been able to wound the girl while she hung from the rope. But then again the American had pulled her up incredibly fast. Lorcan wouldn't be pleased if the prey got away. But how would that happen? There was nowhere to hide on that cliff. They were probably tucked away in a crevice near the ledge, shivering their wellies off.

"We got 'em now," Kirby told his crew.

"You know I was the first to plug the American," Torna insisted.

"What?" Marcus howled. "I've heard some crap in my day, but that's ridiculous."

Marcus walked off in the direction of the cliff. The other three continued to argue about whose shot had connected.

The three-way argument was still under way, when Kirby noticed that Marcus was a quarter of the way up the cliff face. The man had strapped his rifle onto his back and had secured his pistol under his belt. The figure moved up the rock like a gecko, a gecko with training in the British Special Forces.

Kirby cursed as he ran to the cliff. "What do you think you're doing?" he shouted up at Marcus.

"Climbing, you idiot."

He had a point. Kirby cursed again. "Let's get going up. We can't let him have all the fun."

Soon, all four men were making their way steadily up the wall of rock thanks to the fixed rope that the American had left in place in his hurry to get the professor to safety.

A little over thirty minutes passed before Kirby, the last of the four and soaked to the bone, had climbed to the alcove near the mouth of the narrow cave entrance. They were all loaded for the hunt, and Kirby didn't plan on coming back empty handed.

IAN WATCHED THE GIANT STALACTITE HANGING FROM THE CAVE ROOF AS if it were an icicle on growth hormones, while Saorla poked the needle through his skin and stitched his wound with the thread from her first aid kit. About twenty yards long, the big stalactite had to be some sort of record, Ian figured. Dozens of others of varying lengths and sizes kept it company.

To avoid thinking about the needle poking his flesh, Ian let his mind drift to the few caving adventures he'd had in the western United States. It was there he'd learned the difference between stalactites, which grow from a cave roof and stalagmites which grow from the floor.

"Do you know the difference between a stalactite and stalagmite?" Ian asked, hoping to stump the professor.

"Both words can be traced to the Greek word *stalassein*," she replied, "meaning to drip. But stalagmite is further differentiated as being from the Greek word *stalagmites*, meaning dropping. So, even though I'm no geologist, I'm guessing that the stalagmites are the ones that spring from the cave floor because they've formed by already having dropped there, while the other is merely in the process of dripping."

"I almost forgot, you're a genius."

"Only with words, love."

Saorla tied off the last stitch and returned the needle to the first-aid kit. A muddled rattle cut through the silence of the cavern.

"Did you hear that?" Ian asked.

"Thunder?"

"Could be voices."

Ian grabbed his pack and thrust his supplies back through the top. "We need to get moving. Now!"

The unmistakable sound of a gun discharging suddenly echoed through the cave. Saorla was already running, and Ian bolted to catch up to her.

Voices behind him. Someone shouted, "There."

Another gunshot.

With the beam of his headlight trained ahead, Ian watched her fly off a ten-foot rock platform to land smoothly in rhythm before she entered an area where the cave began narrowing.

Still weakened by the loss of blood, his lungs screamed for air. He briefly thought of ducking into one of the numerous crevices along the route. Maybe he could surprise them. But there were four of them. Instead he pushed forward to follow Saorla's straight dash through the cave.

He turned his head back. The lights behind him lunged nearer.

More gunfire.

Was it landing close? He didn't know.

He rounded a curve. Should he duck into a nook and attack the man in the lead and get his gun? It would be a huge risk. But would it give Saorla a better chance to escape? Maybe it would if it slowed their pursuers down and provided she wasn't running straight into a dead-end trap. He had to find the right spot for it. And a good lead would be nice.

The cave broadened once again, and they hit an area of stalagmites. Saorla adeptly side-stepped them. The woman's agility amazed him. Must have been an athlete. He'd have to ask her about it . . . if they ever made it out.

Ian's breaths came in heaving bursts, and he nixed the idea of stopping for a bout of hand-to-hand combat. Too weak for that. Running was the only hope. If he and Saorla had more endurance, they'd outlast the thugs, but only if there was another way out.

The cave narrowed to a hall-like tunnel that now seemed to extend into infinity.

Another gunshot. Was it closer or farther away? He kept moving, galloping into the wan light spread by his headlamp.

Sweat poured down his forehead despite the coolness of the cave. The lightheadedness and nausea were gone now, and his muscles responded to a deep cry from within to move faster. Moments later, he was nearly nipping at her heels. They must have traveled at least a couple of miles down this long corridor of the cave.

Their course had alternated nearly evenly between ascents and descents, bursting up long stretches and then back down. Still, he had no guess whether they were high above—or at or below—sea level. Where was this leading? There had to be a way out.

Flashes of gunfire erupted. Bullets splatted in the ground near his feet.

Saorla sprinted, and Ian fell woefully back from her pace.

It was the blood loss, he told himself. And he was going to lose a lot more of it if he didn't suck it up and give it all he had.

Another flurry of bullets skipped by, near his shoe. Perhaps they were shooting intentionally low in order to wound him instead of kill him. What did it matter? Either way, he had to get away.

Saorla had increased her lead on him by about twenty yards. No question she was an athlete. Good, maybe she could escape.

What was he saying? He had to escape too.

He looked back over his shoulders. Lights still bounced and flickered thirty to forty yards back. Saorla was pulling away now thirty yards ahead. Beyond her in the distance he thought he could see the faintest glimmer of light. An opening in the cave?

It couldn't be; it was dark and cloudy outside, right?

It's a mirage, bro, you've lost too much blood.

But it sure looked like a sliver of light at the far end of the tunnel. How far away? He had no idea. He had to get to the light. And he had to get a lead on his pursuers and formulate a plan. He pushed himself into beast mode and sprinted using every last micron of fast twitch fiber he had. They had to be heftily into their third mile by now. Maybe the thugs would start to wear out.

With his new-found extra gear, he closed the gap on Saorla and overtook her. A glance back over his shoulder revealed only a single headlight following. The other goons had probably given up, and the best of them was all that was left. But the best was gaining ground.

Ian bounded over a boulder but on the landing, stumbled over a rock he hadn't seen, kept on his feet though, and continued sprinting full out. If he could get a good lead and found just the right place, maybe he still had enough strength to subdue the one man that still pursued and then force out some information from him. It was time he found out who had tried to kill Papa and who was trying to kill them now.

Ian pushed just past Saorla, hoping to spur her on. She looked to be tiring. "You got this," he shouted.

"Could use a fizzy drink," she shouted back between heaving breaths.

He looked for the light in the distance. It appeared as far away as ever, if it was even there at all. Maybe three hundred yards away, maybe just a complete illusion. There was no way to tell.

Suddenly there was a low rumbling from below that grew progressively louder and then the rock floor below him was shaking.

Everything shaking.

It was like trying to run on a log floating in the water.

He tumbled forward and summersaulted past his head and on to his back. Earth and rock crumbled above him, behind him and to his sides. Forward was clear. He landed with a thud.

"Whoa!" he shouted. "That was a kick in the pants." He couldn't help laughing.

The rumbling continued for another half a minute, but nothing more was falling or crumbling. The hair on his arms was tingling and his stomach swooned like a kid on a swing going too high. A welcomed mixture of exhilaration and terror. The laughter lasted only a second after the shaking stopped.

And then he realized it.

"Saorla," he bawled.

She had been right behind him. But behind him now was a pile of rubble.

"Seer, where are you?"

CHAPTER TWELVE

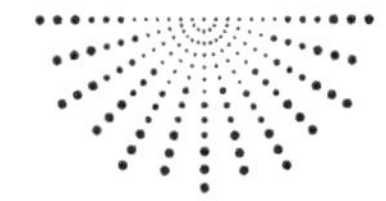

Saorla rose out of the rubble higher and higher into the air. Floating up. She knew she could fly, if she wanted to—and was no longer afraid of heights. Reaching the roof of the cavern about thirty meters from the floor, she came to a halt and surveyed the scene below. Strangely, she could see perfectly despite the former darkness of the cave.

Light from a head lamp flickered near the cave floor, Ian suddenly sprang to his feet. "Seer," he called, "where are you?" Wild-eyed and flailing, he tossed boulders from a huge pile, then moved over to a human leg sticking out of the rubble.

That was *her* shoe on that body.

And the body was hers. But why was she up here?

She watched Ian below. He'd become a mad AI robot, flinging rock debris off her like he'd kicked into super drive and was about to blow a circuit.

Seconds later, he had her clear of the rubble and lying on her back.

"Breathe, Seer," he commanded, as he placed one hand over the other and pressed down firmly on her chest. CPR.

It all came back to her now. They'd been running toward a sliver of light in the distance, perhaps a couple of hurling pitches away, when suddenly the earth shook, junks of cave fell away, and she lunged toward the light. An avalanche of sound and rock swept in on her. A chaotic mess of stalactites and mud pinned her down. And the breath left her chest.

And now she was up here, and her body down there.

"Come on Seer. Stay with me. I love you."

He loves me?

"I love you too." The words were out before she could think them through. Not that she wanted to take them back. But what about Stuart? Ian didn't seem to hear her words from way up here though.

Suddenly, the cave above her opened up to a clear sky.

Where was the storm?

It was a noonday sun all around her. And even brighter when she looked up. She knew instinctively that if she went up toward the brightness, she would see Stuart.

But what about Ian? She loved him now, and he was calling her.

No, praying for her.

All of a sudden she heard a different voice, thundering all around her, from within and without. Audible and inaudible. "You will live and not die. Go back, for there is *a work* that awaits you."

In a beat, she was back down in her body, gasping and panting. Breathing. She sat up, her face inches from Ian's. He placed a hand on each of her shoulders. Tears slid down his cheeks.

She leaned into him. And their lips met softly. She held them there as she felt the blood pumping from her heart, circulating, and warming her body.

"I couldn't leave you," she said quietly and slowly.

Her words rendered Ian mute. He just kept staring into her eyes, amazement animating his face.

Finally he spoke. "Are you all right? Do you think you broke anything? You—"

"I'm okay."

"You must be bruised all—"

"Really, Ian, I'm fine," she said. "I'm just trying to re-acclimate to . . . uh . . . my body. Don't we have to run?" She started to get up. He held her in place with his hands on her shoulders.

"I don't think we'll have to worry about those bad boys that were behind us," he said, looking back at the rubble.

Ian helped her to her feet. She found her backpack and put it on. "I have bruises, I think, and an ache in a couple of them that is a wee bit fierce. But I'll be mobile and ready to give it a lash in a moment. Somehow everything missed my head. I just couldn't breathe, and I think I went . . ."

Her throated clogged up and tears stung her eyes. More time was needed to process what had just happened to her.

"It's going to be all right," he said, while putting his arm around her shoulder.

They had just taken their first steps toward the far-off sliver of light when they heard an awful moaning from the rubble. Ian rushed to the sound and began pulling rocks out of the way. The moaning grew stronger and louder. An arm twitched below Ian. Saorla was helping move the debris now too.

In another moment they had freed the body, a bloody mangled mess, conscious but dying. Ian elevated the man's head over a backpack. "Who are you guys?" Ian asked.

The man simply said, "I'm sorry." The accent hinted of London.

"He's the fast one that was right behind us," Ian said.

Saorla felt for the man's pulse and examined his wounds. "I'm afraid you don't have long," she said. "Won't you tell us who's behind this?"

"Lorcan . . . Duihbur," he managed to rasp out. "He wants the book, the treasure . . . the prophecy he fears . . ."

"The Minister of Foreign Affairs and Trade?" Saorla said softly, trying to make sense of this new revelation. The man gave a slight nod, fought for one last breath, and then died.

The living fell silent, mimicking the quiet of the dead and of the cave.

"So it's the government that's after us?" Ian finally asked.

"I don't think so," Saorla said. "Lorcan Duihbur used to run the

National Museum. He probably still has ties there. That explains the spies you saw, and the interest in your grandfather's artifacts. I'll bet he's part of a black market crime ring."

"At least we know who's behind all our troubles now," Ian said.

"But we need more to go on before we run to the authorities."

"Yeah, there's no way Callahan is going to believe anything we say at this point. And for all we know, he's in on it too, working with this Duihbur dude."

They covered the man's face with his overcoat and headed toward the light. Ten minutes of meandering later, the glimmer in the distance remained as small as when they had first seen it. The crunch of their feet on the stone ground was the only disturbance to the otherwise utter silence of the cave.

Their path narrowed again. Walls of rock constricted around them to the point that they had to walk sideways to continue creeping forward. A maze to navigate now.

The path widened momentarily, but then forked in two different directions. On the rock in front of them, a stone monument hung from the cave wall marking the split in the road, a monument similar to the one they'd found on George's farm.

"What in the world is that?" Ian asked.

Saorla examined it under the beam of her headlamp. "This is incredible."

"What?"

"It's Ogham script. Humans have been in this cave before."

"That means we followed the message from the Book of Kells correctly."

"Maybe."

Saorla was still studying the writing on the stone. "It says, 'Righteous man right, fool left.'"

"Obviously we're supposed to go right," Ian said.

Saorla chuckled. "You must be on the endangered species list—a smart American."

"How diplomatic of you to say so."

She dropped her pack from her shoulders and shook her head in wonder. "I just think it extraordinary that people have been here before. I mean this cave is unknown today. And the vastness of it. There are other large caves in Ireland—even one that extends for over nine miles—but they are all well inland. And to think that we are in the privileged company of the esoteric few that have ever been here is, well, humbling."

Ian took his cell phone out.

"Great idea," she said. "Let's call a cab."

"Sorry, it won't let me do that. But I am able to pull up a scripture verse, Ecclesiastes 10:2. 'A wise man's heart directs him toward the right, but the foolish man's heart directs him toward the left.' "

"You're kidding? That's in the Bible? I guess that settles it then. We go right."

Ian smirked. "So now that you're going right, are you gonna turn in your socialist party card when we get back to civilization?"

She tried not to smile, but they both ended up laughing. "You might be surprised to learn I voted for the Fianna Fáil party in the last election," she finally said, as she picked up her pack, and they headed right.

"Whoa, really?" Ian stopped in his tracks. "The conservative party?"

She turned to face him, the light from her headlamp shone on his chest. "Yeah. What can I say? I've always liked to change things up."

"You really do want to be a Fianna warrior, don't you?"

"We're going to need to be, Ian. If what this dead man said is true, then the corruption that is trying to stop us, take us out, is coming from a powerful source, and maybe it is as you think, it extends to some level within our government."

She turned, and they began to walk. The path constricted again, but after about fifty meters of squeezing through the narrows, it opened to a wide cavern. Off to their right was a huge raised platform of rock about three feet higher than the path and surrounded by a semi-circle of cave walls.

A natural amphitheater.

They paused there. The light from their headlamps shone across the platform and settled on something so profoundly stunning, they fell to their knees.

A treasure trove.

LORCAN SAT IN HIS OFFICE LISTENING THROUGH THE CRACKLE OF HIS speakers to sound transmitted by the listening device of his man in the cave. What had happened? Marcus had been gaining on them. His best marksman and one of his top men. Then a terrible clatter, followed by silence. Then voices; voices of the two mice. They were talking to his man who was injured and dying, and then that man gave away Lorcan's identity to them.

What did it really matter, though, he asked himself? Would his ultimate plans change? No. But even though the plans were basically the same, the urgency had increased. He couldn't take any chances now that the two mice would show up in Dublin trying to expose him.

THE ROCK PLATFORM DEEP IN THE BOWELS OF THE CAVE WAS THE SIZE OF a tennis court. Container after container of golden artifacts glittered as Saorla splayed the light from her headlamp at the site. Treasure trove from the ancient Celtic world seemed to fill every inch of the darkness that retreated with the light cast at it. Saorla was up off her knees now, but her legs were two dead earthworms.

She set up a lantern, then ambled forward to survey the full extent of the booty. The shock of the sight before her seemed to throw off the normal rhythm of her heart, which had already suffered through the terrible minutes she'd been unable to breathe while under the rubble.

"How could this be?" Ian said, his eyes wide in the wan light of the lantern.

Saorla was too awed to reply.

Lying before them were ancient books and manuscripts. Drawings and various forms of artwork. Artifacts of all types. Chalices, jewelry, broaches, Celtic crosses. Diamonds.

And piles and piles of gold and silver coins.

Easily hundreds of billions of dollars' worth of treasure. Perhaps trillions.

A fresh wind of fascination swept over her as she considered that she and Ian were likely the first humans in over a thousand years to lay eyes on what they were now looking at. Come to think of it, few people anywhere at any time had ever viewed such a quantity of wealth.

The questions came to her in a frenetic flurry. Whose treasure was it? When was it placed here? Why? Why was it never recovered? And when was the last time anyone was here?

Her mind raced to Ian's grandfather and his strange dreams of gold coins that became bursting bubbles that sprinkled infectious joy. Somehow she knew there was more to this than an astounding archeological find.

She glanced again at Ian. He was still wide-eyed with wonder. "Do you think this was hidden from the Vikings before one of their raids?" he asked.

"It could be, I suppose. I'm not sure."

"I thought you knew everything about history."

What does anyone *really* know about history? she wondered, as she stared at the treasure.

"You're wrong," she said slowly, humbly.

Ian gently took her hand and drew her toward him. "I'm not wrong about you, though."

She gazed into his eyes, soaking up the warmth they held for her. She took her hand and placed it to the side of his cheek, she leaned her face toward his. Their lips almost touching. A shaking swayed the ground beneath their feet.

"An aftershock?" Saorla whispered the question.

"I think so."

"How are you going to get us out of here?"

"I don't know yet, but if we don't make it out, at least we'll die rich."

"Is that all you Americans think about?" she scolded with a grin and a wink of her eye.

He pressed his lips softly on hers, then drew back. "It's *one* of the things we think about."

"I doubt we'd be able to keep it," she said, her voice cracking a bit. "Treasure trove has lots of complicated legal rules attached to it."

"Complicated legal rules are why lawyers like me exist."

"Unfortunately," she said, still only inches apart from him. He smelled fresh like a pine forest despite the ordeal of the past hours. She fought the urge to lose herself in the forest of him.

She put some space between them, and they walked among the treasure, touching it, taking it all in. Awash in the amazement of it.

Saorla noticed a simple brown pouch set near a large pile of glittering gold coins. The emblem on it stopped her in her tracks. A Celtic cross on a breastplate with a sword across it. The same symbol she'd seen at Dr. Greenwald's and on the items from Ian's grandparent's farm.

"What is it?" he asked.

"A hiero Gram."

"Huh?"

"A sacred symbol. The same one we've been seeing."

Ian stepped near for a better look. "It's his trademark *modus operandi*. Letting us know we're on the right road."

"Whose *modus operandi*?"

"Patrick's, of course."

She put the pouch inside a zip lock bag, sealed it, and stuck it inside a pocket in her raincoat.

She glanced back at Ian. Blood had started dripping from his arm again. "Better let me have a look at that."

She shone the light from her headlamp on his bicep and saw that the stitches were not holding as well as she'd hoped. "We have to get out of this cave, get back to civilization, get you sown up properly."

"Just give me our address, and I'll call for that cab."

Saorla smiled and held out her hand. "Speaking of addresses, give me your GPS. I'll record the waypoints for the treasure."

He handed it to her, and she marked their location.

"What did you name the waypoint?" he asked.

"Motherlode."

"Ha, that's fitting."

Saorla made a mental note of the lengthy GPS coordinates. "Now all we have to do is make it out of this cave alive." She handed the GPS back to him.

"The speck of light we were following was in that direction," Ian said, pointing ahead past the treasure.

They began striding briskly toward the faint light. The path slowly snaked downward. Saorla could tell they were descending because of the pressure on her knees that was required to keep herself from propelling forward too rapidly. And then she noticed something else. A cool wetness in her shoes.

"Do you feel that?" she asked.

"Water?"

"Yeah, it's getting wet."

They projected the light from their headlamps toward the ground in front of them. Water ran over the stone floor and across their shoes.

It was rising quickly. A loud rushing noise swirled from the path above them.

It grew louder, and Saorla began to run.

But there was no place to flee to and no time to do it. A tide of cold sea swept her off her feet, knocking the headlamp free from her head and sending her on a chaotic careening course of least resistance.

She was dog paddling now, trying to stay afloat, but she couldn't see anything in the utter darkness that now swallowed her.

Where was Ian?

She cried out for him but heard nothing.

The force of the current increased with every heartbeat that passed. She reached out a hand to keep herself from careening into the cave walls as she sped along now, expecting at any moment to be slammed into a rock or hanging stalactite.

She had no idea how fast she was traveling, but panic was arcing through her spine. Her elbow banged into a rock, and then her shoulder scraped across the cave wall, while she sped inexorably on the path of least resistance.

"Ian!" she wailed.

"Seer, where are you?" She heard back.

A quick glimpse of light from a headlamp.

But then it went black again, and she heard nothing.

On she floated, trying to keep her head above water. The noise of the rushing liquid gradually increased to a roaring crescendo. The black wall of the cave ahead gave way to the water in thick chunks. Outside now, floating in space, grey wet sky surrounded her for a fleeting second before she landed on her back and began shooting down the rapids of a river.

A new panic seized her while she whisked past the rocky grey shoreline.

Her backpack would flip her face down into the stream if she wasn't careful. But it did seem unusually buoyant. Probably because of the water tight container inside that protected her sleeping bag. She swung the pack off into her hand and flipped it over. A trusty flotation device. She tried to look up into the grey and black, but the horizontal rain was falling in a torrent so hard it stung her face.

Where was Ian?

Before she could call his name, she heard him.

"Seer, you ok?"

She could barely make out his question as the rain spanked the swift current of the cold river. Her body shivered and her teeth chattered in the hypothermic nightmare that now engulfed her.

Ian swam to within a few feet of her. She reached for him but the current of the river kept him from her, carrying them onward. It wasn't for at least another mile that they were able to get a foothold and pull themselves onto the bank.

They collapsed in the thick grass of the shoreline, heaving and coughing.

"Somehow we have to find shelter and get out of these wet clothes," Ian said between coughs as he helped Saorla to her feet.

Water continued to dump from the sky. "Where's your backpack?" she asked, as her shoulders shivered violently.

Ian shook his head. "Probably floating down this river to the next river that turns back to the sea."

"Please tell me you have the GPS?"

"It was in the backpack."

CHAPTER THIRTEEN

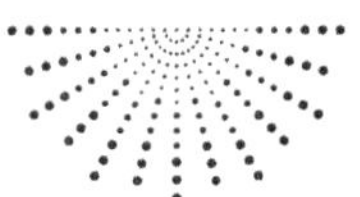

After the prime minister received the bad news from Skibbereen, he'd immediately left for a couple of hours to monitor the crises from his situation room at the mansion. Mrs. Braden had decided to turn in early, complaining of a sudden headache. Sophie and Killian had tried to leave by car but were forced to turn back in the face of a downed tree and a power line that was arcing electricity across the lone roadway out of Phoenix Park. By the time they arrived back at the mansion, the storm had grown so ferocious that Sophie considered it a major victory to have even made it back inside.

Once again in the sitting room, Sophie explained to Killian that she had a growing concern for the safety of Saorla and Ian. And for more reasons than Killian knew. She'd not told him anything about her possession of the Book of Kells or her aid to those who were responsible for its disappearance from the college.

"I dropped them off at car company this morning," she said, warming her still moist hands by the fire. "They tell me they are going to southwest coast today."

"Is there something about those two you're not telling me?" he said.

She turned her gaze from the fire to face him. His eyes were searching hers. When she'd arranged for Ian to spend the night at Killian's home, she'd purposely left things mysterious. Ian obviously hadn't told Killian his secrets she could see now.

"I am not free to speak—"

"Listen, I know something's going on. I don't want you to have to carry it alone."

She knew she could trust him, but up to this point she'd thought it better if he didn't know too much, especially if the Gardai started asking questions. And she sensed there were some bad men involved, given what had happened to Myrna and what she knew from Saorla's recounting of the murder of the professor in Wexford. But the weight of keeping her secret from Killian was going to crush her.

"I know you want to help. I feel it is better if you not know for your own good."

"Your concern for me is touching. But, by now, I think you know I can handle about anything."

It was true, she had to admit. He was as level-headed as any person she'd ever met. Always seemed to know just what to do, and if he didn't, he would pray, and then he would know.

"All right," Sophie whispered. "But you may not believe it; it is so crazy."

"Try me."

"Okay, don't say I didn't warn you. I think they are in danger for lots of reasons. Number one is they find mystery from past. I think it is left by Saint Patrick many hundreds of years ago. He have message for this country, and he gave them clues to find it. They have not found it yet. I think the saint was guided from God to make sure the message makes it into good hands."

"You mean a message like a prophecy?"

"Yes, from what they tell me."

"I can't believe you didn't trust me," Killian said. "I live for this kind of business."

"I know, and I do trust you. And maybe reason why you hear it now is because you care so much."

Sophie quickly considered how much more to tell and decided to plunge ahead a little further. "Number two is there are evil men. I think they are working with the kingdom of darkness to stop the message from coming out. There was a professor in Wexford that was murdered that knew too much, and the professor's assistant at the college was hurt in bombing."

"I read about those incidents in the news, but didn't know the connection," Killian said. "That's awful. You said they were looking for clues. Are they out there now trying to—"

"Yes."

"Not in this weather, I hope. What have they found so far?"

"I'm not sure I should—"

"Please. I need to know how I can pray for them."

"They were given GPS coordinates of a place they say is on the southwest coast. They think they will find big discovery there. Revelations passed down from Patrick's time."

"You say they were given GPS coordinates, how?"

"This is crazy part."

"Try me."

Sophie's words were barely audible she was whispering so softly. "They find a book in the library at the college. They get the clue from the retired professor or somewhere. I don't know. But the book say that there is a message in the Book of Kells—"

Killian gasped, his mouth hung open. "Don't tell me *they* took that book," he whispered.

Sophie just nodded her head.

"They are in big trouble."

"And they need our prayers."

"They have to give it back."

"They don't have it anymore."

"Who does?"

"I do," Sophie blurted.

"My word, you can't be serious. Where?"

"At my place."

The door to the sitting room swung open. It was the prime

minister.

"I do hope you both will make yourselves comfortable tonight," he said. "I've had the guest rooms prepared for you. I'm afraid your rooms are on opposite ends of the mansion from one another though. I hope that doesn't cause any inconvenience."

"No. You are so kind," Sophie said. She knew both rooms were clean and in perfect order from her earlier work. She couldn't say the same for Killian's brain; she was sure she just messed it up with a load of her own dirty laundry.

At least the prime minister hadn't heard what they were whispering about.

He told them to make themselves comfortable in the parlor, while he attended to some urgent business. If they were tired, the butler would show them to their rooms. An hour later, the prime minister returned and spoke with them again. The conversation quickly turned to the spiritual, and the lustful ardor from early in the evening seemed to be gone from his eye. Sophie was in awe of how God had set up the day.

At some point, the prime minister opened up, confessing that the words Killian had shared about Israel and the coalition forming had shaken him up. He admitted that he'd had an eerie sense that he was going down the wrong track, even before he got the news of the disasters hitting the southwest counties. And now reports were coming of serious wind damage in Dublin.

There was nothing he could do about it tonight, he said. They would assess the damage in the morning.

Before the prime minister left the room, Killian bowed his head and began praying. He asked that this *storm of the century*—as it was being called on the news outlets—would stop and calm would be restored to the island.

After Killian finished with his petition and the prime minister left, Sophie peaked out the window for a sign the prayer had been heard. A large oak bowed so heavily from the force of the wind it appeared as if it might snap at any second. The storm was clearly continuing its stubborn rage through Dublin. She glanced back at Killian. He looked peaceful enough. But what was going through his mind now? Now that he was privy to the incongruity of their spending the evening with the nation's most important leader while its most important book, considered by the entire world to be stolen, was tucked away in her apartment.

In the mountainous forest of the Killarney National Park, the rain ceased its assault and the moon poked free from the cover of the clouds for the first time. There was still a fierce wind piercing through the trees, though, and hypothermia was becoming a bigger danger by the second.

"Do you have any idea where we are?" Ian asked Saorla.

"I would if I'd kept the GPS with me," she said.

Ouch. She was probably still reeling at the prospect that they might not be able to navigate themselves to the warmth of civilization, or worst yet, back to the treasure at some future date. There had to be a way he could make things right. He figured he'd start by making sure they didn't die tonight.

"That wall of water kicked me in the pants before I knew what hit me," he said.

"It's all right," she said through her chattering teeth. "You lost a lot of blood."

He knew that was true, and it was undoubtedly the cause-in-fact of his monumental screw-up of losing his backpack with the GPS and the extra food and change of clothes for both of them.

"I did manage to hold on to an extra headlamp though. I see you lost yours. Take this one," he said, as he placed it in her hand.

"Thanks, that's sweet of you. My cell phone survived, but it's low on battery. No reception out here anyway, so I just shut it off. If I had to guess, I would say we are smack in the middle of Killarney National Forest. We must have traveled several miles inland."

"The terrain is sure rugged. Any idea where people are?"

"I really have no clue which way to go. It's all National Park, not heavily traveled. Not likely to be any visitors to the area tonight. We could end up wandering in circles. And you need rest and to keep that arm elevated given we can't get to a hospital."

Ian checked his watch, it was smashed and inoperable. "My compass is broken. I might be able to tell direction by the stars, but there's still a lot of cloud cover, though the storm all of a sudden just fizzled out."

"Yeah that was weird. One minute it was bearing down like a demon from hell, and then—poof—it was gone."

Saorla's shoulders were convulsing involuntarily from the cold, it seemed to Ian that the temperature had dropped a few degrees in the last ten minutes. They had to keep moving to keep warm, and to find shelter. And soon. He felt warm liquid flowing from his arm. The bleeding had returned. He couldn't take the chance of losing much more blood.

"I think we have no choice but to pick a direction and commit to it," he said. "If we find a place that looks like we can take shelter, maybe an old cabin, another cave, whatever, we need to do it. I can try to get a fire going, but I don't know. This is the wettest forest I've ever seen."

They began hiking if for no other reason than to keep warm. The woodland was filled with oak trees and scattered yew; the forest floor was covered with an understory of holly and woodrush. Mosses, ferns and liverworts had attached themselves to the oaks. The dark forest was deadly beautiful in the glow of their headlamps.

Hopefully, it wouldn't turn out to be just plain deadly.

He took a mental inventory of their resources. They had the wet clothes on their backs. Maybe a couple of candy bars in Saorla's backpack. One sleeping bag and one large tarp. A few matches, maybe a lighter, some cheap fire starter product. Not much to help survive a night of temperatures in the low forties with a hefty windchill and extreme moisture smothering the air and ground.

Ian knew of a buddy of his that had slid off a roadway late one night in the Sawtooths of Idaho with his fiancée during a fall snowstorm. Their truck submerged in the Salmon River, and they had to swim for their lives. The only way they were able to survive the frigid night was by peeling off their wet clothes and huddling together for body heat under the cover of a low hanging pine.

Ian hoped it didn't come to that tonight.

But he didn't want to die from hypothermia either. He preferred to wait for his wedding night to be shirtless and pantless with Seer.

Whoa! What was he thinking? He really had lost too much blood, he told himself. Marriage? He didn't just go there, did he?

But what if he did? He could search the world over and over, he knew, and he would never find another woman like Seer. He was in love with her. And she had kissed him so tenderly; she obviously had some kind of feelings for him. But why a louse like him?

They'd been walking about twenty minutes and were both chilled to the bone. Ian could see that Saorla was violently shivering, her body desperately trying to warm itself. But to her credit she didn't complain and kept pressing ahead.

"Do you see that?" she asked suddenly.

Ian looked in the direction she was pointing. There, in the beam of their headlamps, were two eyes staring up at them, low to the ground, maybe two feet above it.

"Wolf?" he asked, before he realized how foolish that probably sounded.

"We don't have them here. It's a fox."

They took a step closer, and it dashed off to the left. They tried to follow it with the light projecting from their head beams, but the fox quickly maneuvered out of sight.

In their gusto to follow it, however, they made an even more important discovery. A large overhang of rock extended out from the side of the hill. Underneath was a perfect shelter from the wind and rain. The area under the ledge had only an eastern exposure and was consequently protected from the horizontal rains out of the west that had bedeviled the island for so many long hours.

Further investigation revealed that someone had recently used the site for a campout. There was fire ring. And more importantly, stacked against the rock wall under the ledge was a large pile of relatively dry firewood and kindling.

Ian thanked God for their good fortune. But grave doubts assailed him—telling him that even with his many years of experience in the outdoors—he wouldn't be able to start a fire with so much oceanic moisture in the air.

CHAPTER FOURTEEN

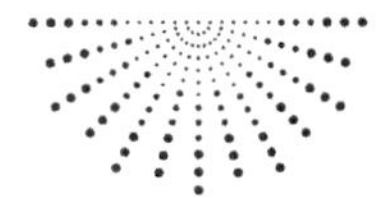

Twenty minutes later, Ian had a fire roaring, and they were quickly warming up. He explained to Saorla that he'd bought some pyro-starter material from the outdoor store in Dublin that worked better than he'd thought it would, and the wood they'd found had stayed dry and protected from the storm.

When Saorla's long sleeve cotton shirt had finally finished drying over a stick she had set up by the fire, she tore the sleeves off to re-bandage Ian's arm. The stitches were holding as well as could be expected, but he looked weak and tired, as they sat together by the firelight.

Peering out from under the safety of the rock ledge, Saorla could see that the sky was clearing and the wind subsiding. The smell of the forest in her nostrils brought back pleasant memories from her youth spent in the hills with her father.

"You use the sleeping bag tonight, of course," Ian said, "I'll be fine under the tarp. We have enough wood to keep us toasty for a couple hours at least."

"Yeah, I think we're going to make it quite comfortably," Saorla said.

"Sure is peaceful all of sudden."

"You know what I'm thinking on a night like this?"

"Coming up with a plan on how to stay alive once we get back to Dublin?"

"Oddly, no."

"That's good; better not to plan for something that serious," Ian said, followed by a nervous laugh.

"I was thinking about Patrick and what it must have been like when he was a shepherd-slave living out every night on a mountain-side much like this, exposed to the cruel elements, praying and singing to his God."

"I've been thinking about him too a lot. Incredible guy."

"I'm starting to see that what made him so extraordinary might not have had so much to do with his own talents, but more to do with the strength he received from the one he was singing and praying to."

"You are on to something there."

"Do you know any songs we could sing? You know, like the ones we sang at Sophie's church."

"Ah, River's in the Desert."

"I'm starting to think it's going to be my church too. That is, if I live long enough to go there."

"You will."

"How can you be so sure?"

"If my grandfather can hang in there this long. Then we've got to do it as well, I figure."

"I'm not afraid to die anymore. At least not after today . . ." Saorla was thinking of her experience in the cave hovering over her injured body as it laid trapped in the rubble.

"We better start praying and singing," Ian said. "Do you remember the one called 'My Heart Sings?'"

"Sure."

Ian started into the lyrics. He still sounded weakened from his ordeal, but he had a nice voice and could keep a tune. They sang a few songs together, and then Ian prayed before he placed another large piece of a dry oak branch on the fire and poked it to life.

He wrapped Saorla in her sleeping bag and laid himself out on the tarp next to the fire.

"I almost forgot about the pouch," Saorla said. She pulled her raincoat over toward her and retrieved the pouch from the pocket. Perfectly preserved. She opened it.

Ian had his eyes closed. He must be really tired she thought. "Aren't you interested in what's inside?"

"Sure."

"There's another piece of vellum with Latin writing. Do you want me to read it?"

Ian still had his eyes closed and didn't respond. Had he fallen asleep already? His chest was rising and falling steadily.

"You won't believe this," she said. "It's a poem in Latin that translates even better to English."

No response. Just steady breathing and then an unmistakable light snoring. At least he didn't snore loud, she thought, because . . .

Because why?

Because she'd like to sleep next to this man for the rest of her life.

He needed the rest now, she knew. Still, she was torn between letting him sleep and rousing him to share in what she was reading because it was nothing short of amazing. It had to be another clue; more was yet to be discovered it intimated. She translated the words aloud in hopes it would wake him.

In the bog of cold and clay
Through the peat of farm and sheep
I've strewn a vision of brighter day
To wake the tired and full of sleep

THE BOOK OF BOOKS LEADS FALSE TO TRUE

Up the cliff to blackest cave
A treasure of dreams for humble few
The land of Eire, Elohim will save

. . .

DOWN PATRICK TO THE FINAL REST
Cold grave opens sky red hue
I pray you pass this signal quest
For Wisdom holds the final clue

SUMMON NOW THE PASCHAL FIRE
Glean the bardic furrow seven
On the hill for all of Eire
Hail now High King of Heaven

SAORLA PONDERED THE WORDS INTO THE NIGHT, WHILE IAN CONTINUED to softly snore. The fire waned from a crackling orange to a smoldering pile of charcoaled hearth.

She could see the presaging outline in the words written on the vellum, telling of the quest so far. Completely consistent with the earlier encouragements, which were now reverberating in her soul: "It is the glory of God to conceal a matter, and the glory of kings to search it out," and "Take the glorious quest."

Their journey had started in the cold peat bog of the Shaw farm with the artifacts they'd found. Had led them to the Long Room, the Book of Kells, and into the blackest cave. But what to make of Down Patrick? And Cold Grave? Or Wisdom holding the final clue?

She thought of the lost GPS and the unknown location of the treasure. If only she could somehow remember those GPS coordinates. She'd had a good look at them and was usually quick at memorization. But it wouldn't come to her. Not with all the stress of the day.

She tried to put it all into perspective. It was the glory of God to conceal the matter. Her times were in his hands.

The stars were out in number now, and as she looked at them, she thought of the greatness of their Maker, and prayed the prayer she had so recently committed to memory.

God's shield to guard me.
God's angels to save me

From traps of demons
From temptations common to man
From all who wish me harm
Abroad and near
Alone and among the people

I summon today power to protect me from every evil
Against every merciless force that may assault my body and soul
Over incantations of false prophets
Over ungodly laws of pagans
Over the false laws of heretics
Over the greed of idolatry
Over the spells of witches, wizards, smiths, and druids
Over every philosophy that corrupts body and soul

Christ to shield me today
From poison and burning and fire
From floods, from drowning, and from wounding
So that I might attain the abundant reward

Christ with me, Christ before me, Christ behind me . . .

With the words of Saint Patrick on her lips, Saorla soaked in the presence of the God she loved, while she watched the man she loved sleep serene near her feet.

CHAPTER FIFTEEN

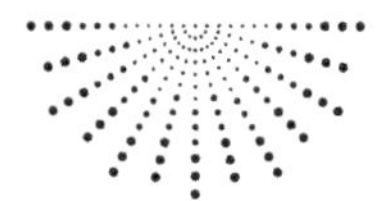

In the power of the Spirit, I take up my pen to write on this Lord's Day. For my flesh it is a day of infirmity, dimness of eye, and dullness of ear. But for my spirit it is a day of ardency and devotion. I have loved the Lord Christ with all my heart, soul, mind and strength since I was a sixteen-year old slave boy, freezing through the nights on the holy hills of Eire. I am an old man of eighty-eight now, and He tells me I am not long for this world.

Oh, that I might already be near His throne. My mind fills of visions of twenty-four elders, casting their crowns at His feet. And He has said to me, 'Come, holy man of God, take your place among them.' I have no idea of what this means, but I will find out in this year of our Lord 580.

The island of Eire is the end of the world. This is what I have always believed. This is what all under Roman rule believe. And I have always believed that my Lord would return in the clouds with great glory when the gospel of His kingdom was preached in this last place, the very end of the world. So I sought earnestly to preach the good news to Eire, a land I believed was the last vestige of the inhabited world. And then would come true the saying that from every tribe and tongue and people and nation, the lamb has purchased with His blood a kingdom of priests for God.

A recent revelation has shaken my understanding. The books must be sealed up for many years to come, the revelation tells me. And your words must be protected from the onslaught of hell that will surely come, and I will prepare my chosen helpers to uncover your hidden words in the Day of Doom. I was shown a picture of the great vastness of this worldly sphere, and multitudes which no man can count, and many generations and many lands that are still unreached as I write. And I saw the people of my own island as a speck of dust, a single sand on the seashore, a drop in the great ocean of humanity, but, alas, much loved by my Savior.

I was shown many generations and many days in the future. A special balm of healing words flow to direct the offspring of my beloved sheep whom I have lovingly guided as shepherd these years. And when I looked into these visions, I saw days, astounding and perplexing. When I inquired, a heavenly voice said, "Prophesy and write; it will surely come to pass."

I hear my disciple coming. His name is Aban. He is thirty years my junior. I will entrust this mission and life's work to him shortly. He will carry out my last wishes. The visions and prophecies I have faithfully recorded, he will preserve. The treasure I have stored, he will hide and others will add to it, before the great invaders come. Great care must be taken that they are hidden and protected for just the right hour. For the last day people of my beloved land. And I will instruct Aban soon what he must do, and I have earnestly beseeched my Lord that His hand would be with my dear brother in all he does.

CHAPTER SIXTEEN

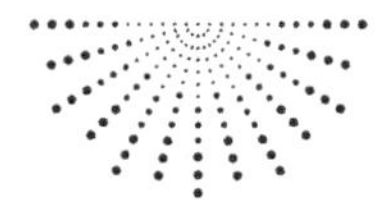

They arrived at the Rivers in the Desert Church and snatched up a bulletin from the card table inside the front door. The service had concluded, but the worship band played softly while a half a dozen penitents lined the front in the space between the lectern and the rows of folding chairs used to seat the small congregation. Most had left, but Ian spotted Sophie and Killian praying for a couple of needy souls. Killian excused himself and made his way toward Ian and Saorla.

Civilization has its merits, Ian thought, as he plopped himself down in folding chair and rubbed his badly injured arm. But at least it wasn't bleeding anymore. He'd awoke that morning reasonably refreshed and had them hiking from their campsite just before sunrise. Traversing the sodden landscape had become progressively easier as the daylight increased. Soon, they'd found a road that knifed its way through the center of the park. From there, they'd hitched a ride from a Good Samaritan who was willing to take them as far as Cork, where they caught the next bus to Dublin.

"You look like you were in a war zone," Killian said. "Or maybe a couple of refugees caught in a storm?"

Ian nodded. Was it that obvious?

"Do you have anyone with a medical background that could take a look at Ian's arm?" Saorla asked.

"I'll call an ambulance," Killian said.

"No. We'd rather not go to hospital," she said. "People are looking for us and—"

Killian held up a hand. "I understand." He pointed at a tall blonde who was singing from a microphone with the worship band. "Jennifer is a nurse. I'm sure she'd be willing to take a look at it. If not, we have a couple of other people in the congregation with medical backgrounds I could call."

Before Ian could thank him, Killian started in the direction of the band.

Sophie approached and hugged them profusely just as Killian left. "I pray for you so hard last night. I am relieved very much to see you."

She took Ian's arm and rolled up his sleeve. There wasn't much to see. The bleeding had stopped for the most part. Dried blood was flaked around the wound. The makeshift stitches still held in place.

"I think he will be okay," Sophie said. "Jennifer maybe can fix him up in the back room."

"You prayed for us last night?" Saorla asked.

"Yes," Sophie said, "and you look like you need it much. What happened?"

"Long story," Saorla said. "By the way, Killian acted strange, almost like he knew everything."

Sophie blushed. "I had to tell him. Don't worry, you can trust him."

"God would probably have told him anyway," Ian quipped.

Killian stood with Jennifer near a doorway and beckoned Ian over.

"Looks like they're calling me for surgery."

In the back room behind the sanctuary, Ian tore off his shirt and laid on the couch, following instructions from his new primary care giver, Jennifer Newsome. The room was a small office that contained a couple of book shelves, a brown leather couch, a small coffee table, and a black leather chair placed at a small wood desk. A large Celtic cross hung from one wall, and a poster of the world showing all of the unreached people groups was affixed on another.

After a trip out to her car and back, Jennifer returned with an EMT kit. Saorla and Sophie were asked to wait outside; to give the patient some privacy, the nurse explained.

Jennifer didn't seem curious to know the details of how Ian had managed to get himself shot in the arm. She did comment on the fresh cut to his lip and swollen face. He simply replied that he had been in some "unlucky situations" lately.

After about twenty minutes of medical attention mixed with copious amounts of small talk, she'd managed to clean the wound and restitch it. She advised her patient to have it looked at by a doctor as soon as possible, but also agreed that her work would likely keep the wound from becoming infected. Ian was lucky, she assured him. The arm would not suffer any permanent paralysis.

After Jennifer left, Killian called in the women waiting outside. He motioned for everyone to have a seat. Saorla sat on the couch next to Ian, and Sophie pulled up a folding chair and placed herself next to Killian.

"Do you want the good news or the bad news first?" Killian asked the women.

"Good news," Saorla said, playing along.

"The good news is Ian will only have to have an arm amputated; otherwise, he'll be fine."

Saorla winked at Ian. "If that's the *good* news, I can't wait to hear the bad."

"The bad news is I'm going to call the police unless you three tell me what's going on. And depending on what you tell me, I still might call them."

Was he serious? Ian searched his eyes and saw he was as earnest as a Sinners-in-the-Hands-of-an-Angry-God sermon.

"You still sure we can we trust him?" Ian asked Sophie.

"He can be trusted to do the right thing," Sophie said.

Ian looked at Saorla. Her eyes said it was up to him. He took a long inhale and then exhaled slowly. "Okay. Either God is in this or he isn't. I'm gonna trust this all works out."

"Good choice," Killian said.

"I was only trying to save you a great burden, friend, by keeping this to myself," Ian said.

"Oh?"

"Yeah. I hope you like adrenaline. It's been a rush and likely will only get more intense."

Killian glanced at Ian's bandaged arm. "It seems to me things have already gotten way out of hand."

Saorla tugged at her dark brown hair and fluffed it over her shoulders. "I think you'll find out what we've already discovered—sometimes the best road to travel turns out to be only a slightly better option than the worst road."

"By 'best road,' you must mean the one fraught with danger and hardship, and by 'worst road,' you must mean the one that leads to certain defeat," Killian said.

"Something like that," Saorla said.

"Only God knows what road is the better of two seemingly bad roads," Killian said. "It helps me to remember he controls our times."

Saorla nodded at Ian, and he proceeded to sketch the whole picture for Killian, beginning with George's mysterious dreams, his dire medical condition, the artifacts they'd found on his property, the call to *take the glorious quest*, the murder of retired professor Greenwald in Wexford. He then moved to how the clues had inexorably led to the need to take a look at a certain page of the Book of Kells under a midnight moonlit sky, and how that misadventure with the book had gone terribly wrong, leading to Sophie's possession of it. Ian then moved to the connection between their discoveries and the historical Saint Patrick, who seemed to be communicating with them through the centuries, via the strange clues they were finding that had led from one amazing discovery to the next, culminating in the incomparable treasure they'd found in the darkest of caves, as Patrick had called it in his poem. But even stranger—and potentially more important than all the wealth in Ireland—was the possibility that there was a hidden prophecy from Saint Patrick himself, which he'd addressed to a generation far removed from his own.

Ian also included a detailed account of the dark forces opposing them, and Saorla's increasing ability to tell when something was amiss or when harm was about to befall them. Ian noted that there seemed to be a strange connection between the National Museum and their troubles. And then he told him of the dying declaration of the man in the cave that had implicated the Minister of Foreign Affairs.

When Ian finished his recital, Killian was silent and had a far off look in his eyes.

"What do you think?" Ian asked.

"You expect me to believe that Saint Patrick—the legendary apostle, miracle-worker—was also a prophet trying to communicate his message to the twenty-first century, and you two are the lucky snoops hot on the trail."

Ian turned to his partner in crime. "That about sums it up, wouldn't you say so, Seer?"

She nodded. "It's almost like we're getting to know Patrick. He's become . . . I don't know . . . a friend and a tutor leading us closer to something very special. At the same time, we're getting closer to the God he served."

"So what do you think we ought to do?" Ian asked Killian.

"Call the police, turn yourselves in, return the Book of Kells, expose the minister of foreign affairs."

"You can't be serious." Saorla said. "Nobody would believe us."

"It seems like the right thing—"

"We've no interest in depriving the rightful owners at Trinity College of the book," Ian cut in. "We just had it out for a look and couldn't get it back. Technically, we're not really guilty of any crime."

"Then you shouldn't run into any trouble when you give it up," Killian shot back.

"You must know that to hand it over to the police under the present circumstances would look very suspicious," Ian said.

Wrinkles gathered on Killian's forehead. "And how do you think not giving it back looks?"

He had a point, Ian realized.

"I have a solution," Killian said.

"You do?" Ian asked.

"Yes. Give *me* the book, I'll take care of everything."

"Whoa. What?"

"Relax, I'll take care of it. I can make this work."

"Care to share your plan with us?" Ian asked.

"It might be better that you don't know, at least for the time being."

"So we're supposed to just trust you?" Saorla asked.

"That's what friends do," Killian said calmly. "Besides, it isn't right that Sophie has to be saddled with it."

"This is so much bigger than just the Book of Kells," Saorla said.

"And we haven't really known you that long," Ian said.

Killian nodded. "All true, but I say we put everything on the table. Even the main thing of what to do next. God gives wisdom to those seek it from him."

"So you actually believe us?" Saorla asked.

"I believe in the two of you. And it certainly seems plausible that there is a legitimate Patrick prophecy. Why wouldn't he care about the future descendants of his people?"

Saorla emptied her coat pocket, pulling her cell phone out and the old leather pouch she'd found in the cave with the treasure.

She placed the phone on the coffee table in front of her, opened the pouch, and took out the ancient vellum script. "I found this in the cave," she said.

She handed it to Killian. He touched it gingerly and examined it carefully. "Amazing. It looks like you brought it straight from a museum. I know some Greek, but not much Latin. What does it say?"

He handed it back to Saorla, and she translated all four stanzas. When she finished, he had her read the last two stanzas again, as he leaned back in his chair and closed his eyes.

Down Patrick to the final rest
Cold grave opens sky red hue
I pray you pass this signal quest
For Wisdom holds the final clue

Glean the bardic furrow seven
On the hill for all of Eire
Hail now the High King of Heaven.

"Seems like the first half, the cold peat, the cave, etcetera, has already happened from the story you told me," he said. "And now it's just a matter of walking out these last two stanzas."

Saorla nodded. "Wisdom holds the final clue."

"We should wait on the Lord together for a few minutes." Killian bowed his head and prayed a short prayer.

And then they waited.

The church was quiet now, no more instruments playing or voices lifted in song. The last stragglers must have gone home or off to Sunday dinner. Ian tried to clear his head, and he silently asked God to speak to him. At first, he couldn't get past the thoughts of men in black coats chasing and shooting at him.

He continued to pray, and then he saw himself with Saorla in a small coffee shop and bookstore. She held an old book in her hand, and the shopkeeper—an older woman with grey hair piled up in a bun—came up to them and mumbled words Ian couldn't make out. Then he heard her clearly ask, "Shall I set you up on the sofa with some tea?"

The vision ended, and it was back to men in black raincoats shooting at him.

When about five minutes of silence had passed, Killian asked, "Has anyone received anything."

"The word, *Tara*," Sophie said. "Nothing else. I do not know what this means, this *Tara*."

"That is very interesting," Saorla said, "because I've been meditating on Patrick's poem. There are references to the 'Paschal fire,' 'the hill,' and 'the high King'… These are all allusions, I think, to the Hill of Tara and the legend surrounding Patrick."

"I know where you are going with this," Killian said, leaning forward his seat.

"I'm the only one completely in the dark," Ian lamented.

"You forget I have no comprehension either," Sophie said.

Saorla reached over and touched Ian's knee. "Sorry. I should have explained. For the ancient Celts and druids, the biggest events of the year were Samhain and Beltane. Bonfires were lit at these rituals, and the hill of Tara was the most sacred place in all of Ireland for these ceremonies. It was the site where the high king was crowned, important rulers were buried, and key councils were held. The fires were thought to protect one from evil spirits and bring fertility to the land. Some say human sacrifices were originally a part of this; they would use criminals, prisoners of war and the like. Some think it was like Baal worship."

"Evil," Sophie said, shaking her head.

Saorla gave a quick nod. "The rituals eventually evolved to where they would just *pretend* to burn someone in the fire, and that person would have to be as though they were dead for a few days. There is some indication that the ritual evolved still further to the sacrificing of a lamb."

"Makes me think of how Christ is the lamb of God," Ian said.

"That's an interesting correlation," Saorla agreed. "And with the feast of Beltane, anyway, it appears to have evolved still further, to people driving themselves and their cattle between two great fires, where the goal was to get the smoke and ashes over them as protective power from the forces that would do them ill."

"Why does it speak of the Paschal fire in the poem, isn't 'Paschal' a word that has to do with Easter?" Ian asked.

"Yes," Killian said, "Easter or Passover."

Saorla leaned back in her chair. "Beltane was likely held on the halfway point between the spring equinox and the summer solstice. And so corresponds roughly with Easter. On the other hand, Samhain, is the fall ritual that corresponds exactly with Halloween and All Saints' Day, it represents moving to the darker time of the year."

"Halloween is coming up in a few days," Ian said. "Do people still celebrate it at the Hill of Tara?"

"There are actually some," Saorla said. "They call themselves Neopagans, and they gravitate to Tara for some festivities."

"Did you say *Neopagans?*" Ian asked, remembering the gang he'd encountered in the Castro district that were responsible for so many problems in his professional life back at home.

"Yes. Why?"

"Long story I don't need to talk about now."

"Perhaps, sometime later," Saorla said. "Neopagans are mostly harmless unless—"

"I was more interested to hear how you think all this relates to Patrick," Killian said.

Ian found it all fascinating, but he had to admit that the sooner they got to the bottom of all this mystery the better. He prayed a silent prayer that his grandfather would be able to hold on longer.

"Well, as I said, the pagan Beltane feast falls near Easter. And it has to do with the great bonfire. Tradition had it that all fires had to be put out for the feast and had to be relit from the high king's bonfire at the Hill of Tara. Patrick lit his fire to celebrate the Easter resurrection of His King, the Christ. The druids of the time warned the high king of Ireland, Laoghaire, that if Patrick's fire was not extinguished, it would consume the whole kingdom. And that's just what it did!"

"Whoa, that's courage," Ian said. "But I'm still confused. Where did Patrick have his fire? Tara?"

"No, he had his lit in advance of the king's at the Hill of Slane. It would be clearly visible from Tara, though, to the southwest. Both are in County Meath."

"Why didn't the king just have Patrick's fire put out?"

"Some say he tried, but couldn't because it was a supernatural fire. He summoned Patrick, who may or may not have converted the king, but he gave permission for Patrick to spread his Christian teaching. Patrick was then allowed to literally start the king's bonfire, with his own Easter fire."

Saorla's cell phone suddenly vibrated to life on the coffee table. Ian looked down at it by instinct. It was Claire Curran. Saorla let it buzz.

"It sounds like you need to make a pilgrimage to Tara," Killian said.

"Another thing that happened recently was that I had a life-changing encounter after I met a woman. Guess what her name was?"

"Tara?" Killian asked.

"You got it."

"I would definitely add the Hill of Tara to your agenda then," Killian said.

"Another thing I find interesting is the reference in the poem to *Down Patrick* and the *cold grave*," Saorla said.

Killian rubbed his chin. "I'm guessing you find it interesting because that is the supposed burial site of Patrick, right?"

"Correct," Saorla answered. She turned to Ian. "It's a city in Northern Ireland."

"Add Downpatrick to the list of places to visit," Killian said, as if dictating to a secretary keeping the minutes of a meeting. "And, in particular, his gravesite, which I believe is marked by a monument in a churchyard at Down Cathedral."

"Right again," Saorla said.

"Does anyone have any insight about the rest of the writing?" Killian asked.

Silence fell over the room.

Finally, Saorla said, "The rest is a mystery, particularly the part about 'Glean the bardic furrow seven.' "

Killian asked if the Lord had spoken anything else to any of them during the waiting time. Ian thought about the motion picture in his head of the old woman in the bookstore asking him if he and Saorla wanted tea. He decided it was just his overactive imagination, not anything that needed to be shared with the group.

Saorla's cell phone buzzed again.

This time it was Detective Callahan.

CHAPTER SEVENTEEN

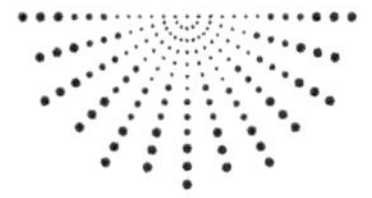

The next morning, Saorla sat at her office desk at Trinity College grading test papers. A busy day now awaited her. She needed to arrange for someone to take her classes for the week, which would likely lead to an unpleasant talk with Dean Grady about being out on personal business for a few days. Then, she'd meet Ian in the early afternoon.

Their plan that spawned after the meeting with Killian was to go on an informational treasure hunt. With their noses to the wind, they would first venture to the Hill of Tara. Maybe they could sniff out their next move there. Second on the agenda was a visit to Ian's grandfather, George Shaw, at his home in the Antrim Hills on Northern Ireland. The man continued to drift in and out of consciousness, but perhaps he could tell them one last tidbit of information that would break them free to solve the puzzle. Finally, a trip to Downpatrick was also being bantered about as a possibility.

The constant fear for her life that Saorla had felt last week had muted after the experience she'd had watching Ian pull rubble off her listless body, followed by the thundering voice telling her to go back. Still, she didn't want to die, and she knew she would have to be fiercely circumspect if she wanted to survive the week.

When Callahan had called her cell the previous afternoon, she'd told him as much as she could about where they had been for the last twenty-four hours. They'd rented a car, had a cliff-climbing adventure that went wrong, and were forced to bivouac overnight because of the storm. Callahan didn't appear to buy any of it, but she couldn't worry about that now.

The detective's learning that she was back in Dublin was a mixed blessing. The constant tailing resumed, but the added benefit was that Saorla was able to get overnight protection at her home. With Myrna out of the hospital but still needing a lighter load while she continued to recover, the two slept peacefully last night knowing that the SDU was watching the perimeter of the house.

Now that she was alone in her office and able to garner a rare moment of quiet, her mind strained to grab on to the lost GPS coordinates. She knew she could make her way back to the cliff where they'd entered the cave. Their rental car was probably still parked nearby. But the way to the treasure was now blocked by a million pounds of rubble and debris. And where was the location where they'd catapulted out of the cave? It would certainly make things easier if she remembered those coordinates. Why didn't she hang on to that phone instead of giving it back to Ian?

Ian.

He was the other crisis simmering. Had she really touched her lips to his—kissed him eagerly—and then woke next to him by the fire? She could scarcely think of anything else.

She had so many questions. What if he loved her too? She suspected he did. Hadn't he said so when she was out of her body? What would it mean if he did? They lived worlds apart but had been thrown together into a winding gyre of emotion and adventure. How would it work if ever the currents around them stopped swirling?

Maybe she should just be honest and tell him exactly how she felt about him.

And then there was her new love for God. With Him she knew she had all things in One. She took out a Bible from her handbag and laid it open on her desk. A copy of "the Lorica" tumbled out. She closed her eyes and prayed the words she'd committed to memory. "I arise today . . . Christ with me, Christ before me—"

She suddenly saw numbers in her head. The GPS coordinates. She quickly began scribbling them down on a piece of paper.

There was a knock at the door.

"Come in," Saorla said out of habit. She was still writing when she glanced up and saw Claire standing in front of her desk.

Saorla finished with the last number and nonchalantly slipped the paper into the desk drawer.

"Hi stranger," Claire said with a smile.

"Oh, hey, sorry. I should have called. Things have been . . . well . . . crazy."

"Wanted to make sure you were all right."

"I'm fine. What's new?" Saorla asked, trying to get the focus off herself.

"Same old, same old. Grady's still breathing down everyone's necks. I wish he would just make the cuts instead of letting a bunch of us die a slow death every day."

"You don't sound *that* worried about it anymore, though," Saorla said.

"You've always been perceptive."

"So, I'm right?"

"I have some things in the brew. I think I'll be able to work some magic. If not here, I have some other cauldrons to stir."

"Sounds like you have it figured out."

"I try. If I were you, though, I wouldn't worry about a job."

"Really?" Saorla blurted in surprise, unnerved by the sudden thought that Claire might have somehow discerned that she'd undertaken a pursuit that was eclipsing even her professorship.

"Yes, you're too popular with the students for them to let you go."

"Are you serious?"

"As a grand mal seizure. Now, what about you and the American?"

"Not too much to tell."

"You know he left a note on my door around the time he hired you. Very sweet really. I would have taken him on in a heartbeat. I bet he is quite the lad with the lassies. His note gave me that impression anyway."

Saorla felt her mouth drop open. "What—"

There was another knock on the door, and Myrna walked through.

"Hey kids. I am so keen on getting back to work after being held up in that hospital. Not one male doctor the whole time. Can you believe—"

"Excuse me," Claire said, "I've got a meeting I have to get off to." She gave Myrna a quick hug and walked towards the doorway, then turned back.

"Saorla, love, I was serious about what I said. I really think you'll make it through the budget cut. Me too, I suppose, which is some consolation, seeing as I didn't get a chance with that smooth-operating American."

Smooth operator? What did she mean by that?

After Claire left, Saorla spent more than an hour enduring a long bout of Myrna's loquaciousness. Saorla was finally saved by the bell tower ringing in the noon hour. Bobbing up from her chair, Myrna excused herself, saying she had to limp off to her next class.

Finally left alone, a wave of paranoia flooded over Saorla at the thought of being the sole custodian of the coordinates of the treasure. What if something happened to her? The coordinates would be lost forever unless she passed them on to someone she knew who wasn't likely to be with her if she ended up a victim of foul play.

She couldn't call or text Ian with the numbers. He'd lost his phone and didn't have a new one yet. Furthermore, whatever fate awaited her likely awaited him as well.

What about Killian? Now that she'd made the decision to trust him with the Book of Kells, it was an easy leap to trust him with the location of the treasure.

She texted him the numbers and the following message: "Location of blackest cave. You are my back up plan." She returned the slip of paper to her drawer, stuffed her phone in her purse, and left her office, making double-sure she locked the door on the way out.

Claire moved catlike down the hall of the third floor of the Art's Building. She slipped the key into the lock and turned it.

Voilà.

The door clicked open, and she slid silently into the office of Professor O'Rourke.

She'd had to wait an hour before receiving the call from Kirby that Saorla had left the campus and was making her way toward Grafton Street. The key she'd purloined from the replacement sets kept on hand in the Dean's office, which had gone unmanned while the staff stepped out for lunch.

She opened the top desk drawer and drew out the piece of paper she'd seen her colleague stuff there earlier. There were two series of numbers. GPS coordinates no doubt marking some discovery of great significance. Lorcan would be delighted with the information, especially if it yielded some choice fruit, and that in turn meant he would be delighted with her. Together they were on the rise, and no one could suppress them now.

Ian walked out of the store on Grafton Street with a new phone all set up just as a long lunch-hour queue rapidly formed at the entrance behind him. His sixty-euro-a-month plan would allow him to be in touch with the world again. His old phone was probably still floating down an unnavigable stream in the Killarney National Forest, or maybe it had washed out to sea by now. Oh well. He'd learned a long time ago that the loss of good equipment was often the price to be paid for an epic adventure, especially when it involved a good mullering.

As he walked down Grafton, the sun poked around the clouds, flooding him with warmth. It felt good after suffering near hypothermia over the weekend.

He opened his email account and saw he had about thirty unread messages. Two of them were from his secretary, Joan, and two from Jarvis Read, all sent since he'd last checked his account on Friday afternoon. He decided against reading those messages from his co-workers, however. His office on the 42nd floor with Horowitz, Dunlap & Connor seemed a zillion lifetimes in the rearview mirror. He could wait a little while longer to get back to that world.

There was another message from Shark sent Saturday afternoon. He clicked on that one and read it. When he finished, he wiped a tear from his cheek.

Why was he so sensitive all of a sudden? Probably the stresses of the weekend. He sighed.

Man, I'm glad the Shark is moving with you, Lord.

He stopped amid the bustle of the wide sidewalks of Grafton Street to type a reply back to Shark. Ian's new cell phone began playing Timba. It was Cheryl Miller, the flight attendant.

"Hello," he said proudly into his new phone.

"Hey there, 007. You have time for lunch today?"

"Uh, maybe, why?" he asked, caught off guard.

"Because I'm hungry, because you're the only one I know in Dublin, and because who wouldn't want to have lunch with 007."

Ian laughed. She had a way of making him do that. He didn't have to meet Saorla for an hour or so, and there was a ghost-like rumble in his stomach. Still, he hesitated. "I dunno, I have to be somewhere in a little over an hour."

"Perfect. Plenty of time to get in and out of Cornucopia."

Ian laughed again. "An offer I can't refuse."

"How long will it take you to get there?"

"I dunno, ten minutes maybe."

"Cool, I'll walk with you."

"Huh?"

"Turn around."

Ian twisted to the side. Cheryl stood in front of him with her cell to her ear. She placed her phone in her coat pocket and threw her hands in the air. "Turnabout is fair play," she said, grinning ear to ear.

SAORLA MET MYRNA FOR LUNCH AT A SMALL SANDWICH PLACE CALLED Angus and Cheddar, located on the Quay to the south of the River Liffey. Saorla ordered the shop specialty—melted brie on chorizo with peppers and tomato. Myrna opted for the sliced pastrami with gorgonzola cheese on a spinach salad. Their orders came up in a matter of minutes, and they took them to an empty booth by the front window.

Saorla snapped down on a large bite and churned the flavors in her mouth. "Can't believe this is so good. I'm quite famished."

"You look like you lost weight," Myrna said. "Not that you needed to, of course."

"That's what happens when you spend an entire day running for your life. I need to replenish for sure."

"Make that two of us. It should be a crime to serve the food they give at hospital."

"I've heard it's bad," Saorla said, as she watched Myrna devour her spinach salad. "I'm so sorry that you had to—"

"It's over now, and I just want to forget it happened. Tell me about you and Ian. I want details and not those of an archeological variety. Is he hooked on you yet?"

Saorla felt her face growing hot. "Maybe we should talk about something else. Like, how was your salad?"

"So, he *is* hooked on you."

Saorla couldn't see any reason not to be transparent with Myrna. They were essentially roommates now. Like the younger sister she'd never had. And she'd become even more dear to her after the bombing incident. "I think so, but more important I'm hooked on him."

Myrna gasped.

"Don't look so surprised," Saorla said.

"But you've only known him how long? Two, maybe three weeks at most?"

"I just know, plus we've been together non-stop."

"Still, what do you really know about him? And what did Professor Curran mean when she said, 'I bet he's quite the lad with the lassies.' "

"You know that's just Claire being Claire."

"Maybe, but that doesn't mean she might not have a point. Did you run a background check on him? You even google his name?"

"Did they give you suspicion-inducing medication in that hospital or what?"

"I'm just saying."

"If it'll make you happy, I'll google him right now."

Saorla took out her phone and searched for Ian Shaw, San Francisco Attorney. A number of recent newspaper articles came up. Most of them about a lawyer who was disbarred last Friday. As Saorla read, her world shifted to grey.

"What is it, dear?"

Saorla barely heard Myrna and didn't answer.

The details were vague. Something about an assault that occurred last July in a San Francisco park. Assault?

She tried to find more clarity, but couldn't get any specifics. Just the simple fact that an assault had been committed, for which no charges were brought by the police. However, a California lawyer's commission hearing the matter decided it was conduct unbecoming an attorney that required the most serious of sanctions.

She found one other article on him, basically describing how paramedics were called out to a place called Half Moon Bay to treat a couple of out-of-control surfers that had needlessly risked their lives. The article identified one Billy Williams and one Ian Shaw, as suffering life-threatening injuries.

"You look like a ghost," Myrna said.

The words knocked Saorla from her trance. "I feel like I've been working with a ghost."

CHAPTER EIGHTEEN

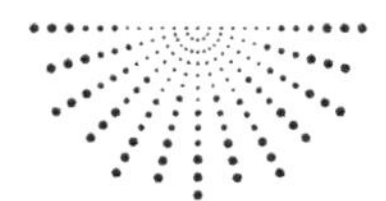

Saorla trudged her way down Trinity Street toward Wicklow Street where she would connect up with Grafton to meet Ian at a bus stop. She was sure she'd lost her tail, but her heart suddenly wasn't in the gamesmanship.

They'd agreed to meet at 2:15. The public bus would take them to within a few minutes' walk of the Hill of Tara, an ever-popular must-see stop for foreign sightseers. It would be better than driving, and cheaper than paying for a tour bus. They intended to meet Ian's grandmother at the grounds and then ride home with her to the farm in the hills of Antrim.

As Saorla drifted down the sidewalk, she kept telling herself that there must be some explanation. Some perfectly good reason why Ian had not shared the news she'd read about him.

She had herself half convinced that there was nothing to worry about, when she glanced through the window of Cornucopia to her right.

A tall brunette stood next to a man that looked like Ian.

The breath fled from her chest.

It couldn't be.

Moving a few steps closer, she peered through the window.

It sure looked like Ian. Ian and a tall brunette with cover-girl good looks and the figure to match.

She had to be sure. Positive confirmation was needed. She drew her face closer to the window.

The brunette tugged on the man's right arm. His injured arm. She reached her head up to peck him on the cheek with her lips. The man, whoever he was, maybe Ian, was at the counter paying for something. The brunette trekked for the door and then skipped past Saorla smiling.

The clerk at the counter handed the man a bag of food to go. The man tossed the clerk a bill. He was leaving a tip. It had to be him. He turned toward the door and began to walk.

It was definitely him.

She had to get out of there.

She bolted west on Wicklow, heading toward Grafton. Sprinting now, the shops whizzed by in a blur. Get away. Anywhere.

With the air drained from her lungs, she stopped somewhere on Grafton and began heaving heavily.

When she finally caught her breath, she realized she was at a bus stop.

Their bus stop.

A tear splashed down her cheek.

Calm down. Think.

She stepped on the bus and took a seat in the back.

IAN HAD LOST HIS TAIL EARLIER IN THE DAY, WHETHER THEY WERE THE goons or the Gardai, or both, he didn't know, and he was cautiously optimistic that he could remain unseen until he escaped town on the bus to Tara with Saorla.

The food his second time at Cornucopia was as good as the first, and he was now well-prepared to make it through the afternoon. Cheryl had been her usual gregarious self. Her airline was suspending flights to Ireland now that the prime tourist season was over. She could probably pick up the same Dublin route come next May. She looked forward to flying trips to Cabo San Lucas to escape the bitter winds of the Chicago winter looming large in her world.

Ian had wished her luck. She asked him to call if he ever made it to the Windy City. He assured her it wasn't likely. She gave him a brother-sister peck on the cheek and vacated his world.

A couple of vegetarian egg rolls and some brown rice filled a to-go bag he held in his arm. He was thankful to have it in case Saorla hadn't had time for lunch, at least she wouldn't starve. Ian arrived at the bus stop with five minutes to spare before departure.

No sign of Seer.

As he waited, his thoughts continued to fixate on her. The beautiful smile. Her sense of humor. The tender way she'd kissed him in the cave. He had scarcely been able to think of anything else. Hunting treasure trove and ancient artifacts and wisdom from the ages was certainly a thrill. But he knew that the real treasure in all this, if he was honest with himself, was Seer.

But how would it work? She had her world here, and he had his back home.

At 2:15 p.m., there was still no sign of her. He made a frantic search up and down Grafton and saw nothing. No glimmer of the intelligent beauty and grace he'd come to adore.

The driver of the coach told him it was the last call to board. Ian wouldn't go without her, of course. About to walk away, he suddenly had an idea.

"Please, one second, let me check the bus. I'm supposed to meet someone and—."

"Of course," the driver said.

Ian leapt aboard the bus and bounded into the aisle. There, in a back row window seat, he spotted the familiar black-brown topknot.

Ian floated down the aisle to her.

She'd been crying, or at least it appeared so.

"Hey there," he said as he slid into the seat next to her.

She didn't speak.

"Had a bad day I'm assuming? Want to talk about it?"

No reply.

"I brought you some lunch in case you didn't have time to eat," he said, as he placed the bag from Cornucopia on her lap.

She didn't acknowledge Ian or the food for that matter.

The bus pulled away from the curb, headed down Grafton, and made its way to the north.

Forty-five minutes after leaving Dublin's city center, the bus was lumbering on about ten kilometers out from the Hill of Tara according to a sign that flashed into Saorla's line of sight. She'd kept silent the whole trip, not trusting her emotions. Mercifully, Ian hadn't pestered her but instead had given her space to ruminate, allowing her head to calm and clear. She decided that her best tact was to put on an air of amicable professionalism. She would finish the job she'd signed on for, learn what she could, and be thankful that the whole affair had brought her out of the shadows of sorrow and into the clarity of a relit faith in the God of her fathers. After her work concluded, she would move on. Ian would go his way, she would go hers.

With her emotions now in check to the point where she could trust her voice, she turned the page to finishing the mission at hand. "I think you will find the trip here peaceful and insightful," she finally said, not yet ready to look over at him.

"I was beginning to wonder if you had been struck mute," Ian said.

"No, just a wee melancholy today. I get like that sometimes. Although it hasn't happened since I started the job for you."

"I totally understand, given the passing of—"

"Don't," she began more sharply than she meant to. She tried to soften her tone. "I'm all right, really. We need to focus on why we're here."

Ian didn't respond, and neither one said anything until the bus slowed and pulled off to the side of the highway.

"This is our stop," she said stiffly. "The bus goes on to other locations, and we've a wee bit of a walk."

Saorla's words were confirmed by the driver who announced that those passengers going to Tara should disembark, while the rest should remain aboard, as they would continue on shortly to Navan.

Saorla grabbed her purse and overnight bag and followed Ian off the bus. They were the only ones that stepped off. The sky had been clear earlier, but it was quickly greying. Saorla thought she felt a sprinkle hit her face. At least it wasn't tears. Hopefully, she was past that now and could move forward with her work.

THE PACE OF HER GAIT WAS FASTER THAN NORMAL, AND IAN MADE THE extra effort to keep up. Long green grasses covered the earth as far as the eye could see. The rural nature of the area surprised him. In a few minutes, they arrived at a small visitor center and bookstore that had been converted from a church.

Saorla was speaking to him again after the odd silence on the ride out, but her voice had an uncharacteristic tone of detached competence. He had no idea what had caused the sudden change. He vowed to get to the bottom of it before the afternoon was out, but then decided that whatever it was that was bothering her would come out naturally in its own good time.

He decided that it probably had something to do with the fiercely stressful events of the past couple weeks. Not many people would have coped as well with the constant surveillance, not to mention the attempts against her life after witnessing a gruesome murder scene. And then there was the stress of the Book of Kells, and their recent decision to entrust it to the care of Killian, who they knew little about. Although he'd come into their world with high commendation from Sophie, a woman they both trusted implicitly, there was still reason for concern. The man had been unwilling to tell them exactly what his plan was for the book's return.

They spent some time mulling around the bookstore. Ian kept a close eye on his surroundings. Surely he'd be able to recognize the goons who'd been placing his life and limbs in jeopardy if they showed up out here. But he saw no signs of danger so far.

On their way to the top of the hill, Ian asked a few questions about the site, and Saorla readily provided the answers, albeit in a professional, almost robotic, manner. He learned that the Hill of Tara was multi-faceted: a spiritual and ritualistic holy ground, a dwelling for royalty, a place of natural beauty, a scenic overlook, a burial and coronation site for kings and a strategic military high ground. According to legend, the name *Tara* came from the Spanish princess and goddess named Tea, who had asked to be buried on the most beautiful hill in Ireland.

It took less than ten minutes to reach the top. Ian peered in all directions at the surrounding countryside. Green hills stretched on forever no matter which way he glanced. A good wind was already blowing and seemed to be picking up in intensity. There was plenty of cloud cover, but off to the west he could see the sky clearing and something like a rainbow to the south.

"I can see for eternity, and yet it doesn't seem we're very high," he said.

Saorla shrugged. "The hill is only about one hundred and fifty-five meters. But because it sits at the periphery of Ireland's central lowland plains, it allows for viewing of miles of landscape to all points of the compass."

The robotic voice was going to continue for the indefinite future, he could see.

He strolled about the hill, trying to get some sense spiritually of why they were led to come here. He felt nothing and could not think of a single thing that he'd learned so far that could be of significance to their quest. The only exceptional item of note in the vicinity was a large stone that was maybe six feet high and shaped like a giant thumb sticking up from the ground. To be sure there were other stone-like monuments on the hill, but nothing remotely approaching the curiosity level of the giant thumb, which also looked like a giant something else in Ian's estimation.

"That's the *Lia Fail*," Saorla said in a drone-like manner.

"Translation?"

"It's also called the Stone of Destiny. Literally, *Lia Fail* means the 'stone under.' It was believed to screech and roar when the true high king touched or even approached it."

"What was the purpose of that?"

"Other than identifying the rightful king of Ireland I'm not sure what its purpose was. Its phallic nature is obvious. Legend has it that all true high kings entered into a ritualistic marriage with the Goddess of Sovereignty before they could rule. The high king would then have access to entreat the goddess for good crops and blessings to secure the continuation of his reign."

"Strange place," Ian muttered.

"Yeah. Under our feet is the Mound of Hostages."

"What's that?"

"Ritual and burial site," she explained, "the hostage part comes from the fact that the kings sometimes took hostages from other jurisdictions to help secure their reign."

"I thought they relied upon the goddess for that."

"That was plan A for sure. There are different personifications of the goddess in Ireland. Here at Tara it takes the form of Maeve or Mebd. Did you ever hear of the *Tain Bo Cuailgne*?"

"No."

"How about the *Cattle Raid of Cooley*? It's the same story."

"No again."

Saorla laughed for the first time since Ian had been with her today. "Medb was the outsized warrior-queen in this story of a couple of lovers arguing over which of the two was greater and ending with Medb stealing a prize bull from Ulster to prove herself superior. The spoiler alert is that her hubris caused it to end badly. You have really got to get yourself on a good reading program."

Saorla's laughter was a welcomed sight to Ian's eyes. "I'm waiting for my instructor to provide the list."

"My list would be like a full-time job for you, Mr. Attorney. You'd have to give up your law license just to—"

She stopped there, and the smile and laughter faded. Ian finished the sentence for her. "Just to get through the list."

"I guess *you* wouldn't have to actually give up a license at this point," she said, but then abruptly clammed up and walked on.

Ian caught up to her to ask a few more questions about the hill. But the drone-like demeanor was back with a vengeance, as they covered some of the same ground of the previous day about Patrick and his Paschal fire.

"Which direction is it to the Hill of Slane where Patrick's fire was kindled?" Ian asked.

Saorla pointed to the southwest. "Twenty kilometers away," she said, but then closed up again.

"Can we pause a minute to pray for guidance," Ian asked.

Saorla nodded her agreement. They each took a turn praying, and when they were done, they both admitted they didn't have any leading.

Ian's cell phone buzzed to life in his pocket.

It was Aryana, his grandmother. She was waiting for them down by the visitor center.

CHAPTER NINETEEN

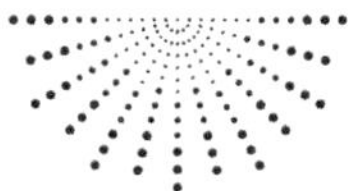

Ian drove his grandparent's truck up the gravel approach to the house. Saorla had been quiet during the ride, giving one-word answers to Ian's questions and only becoming animated when conversing with Aryana.

The sun had set. The big dipper, the northern star, and a thousand other luminaries sparkled in the cloudless, inky-black sky over Antrim. Yeats and Lance, his grandfather's dogs, bolted to the truck and placed their paws on the driver's side door. Ian let down his window, and Yeats stuck his head through to lick Ian's face.

A white SUV rental was pulled off to the side of the drive next to a small blue compact.

"Visitors?" he asked his grandmother.

"The white one is your father's rental, and the blue car belongs to the home nurse."

Thinking of his father's presence set his teeth on edge. "When were you going to tell me about Rory still being here?"

"I didn't want you to worry because worry only drains your strength and doesn't prevent tomorrow's pain."

Ian grunted. "I guess."

Ian and Saorla settled themselves in their respective guest rooms before joining Rory and Aryana near George's bedside to begin a vigil waiting for the old man to wake. From across the room, Ian's eyes met his father's for the first time in years. Immediately the stresses of the past were back. Rory was still the imposing figure Ian remembered with the fierce look of determination in his greenish-brown eyes. His rugged red hair was now slightly thinning and greying, but his strong posture made Ian think the man would have made a good general. As Ian looked the man over, he was surprised by his father's kind smile, though neither made any effort to bridge the distance with a hug or even a handshake.

"Hey, Ian," Rory said.

Ian looked down at the floor. "Hey."

"He's usually conscious for a bit around this time each evening and then again in the early morning," Aryana said, breaking up the awkwardness.

The group sat and waited. Remarkably, the conversation remained pleasant; soccer was not mentioned at all. Saorla regained some of her allure in the company of Ian's grandmother and father. She fielded a whole array of quirky odd-ball questions with humor and delight.

As the vigil continued into its second hour, Aryana suggested that Ian and Saorla turn in for the night as they obviously had had a long day. There was no guarantee George would awake, and if they got some sleep now, they would be well rested if he awoke in the morning.

"I feel melatonin flooding my brain," Ian said. "I think I'll get a few hours and be up by three or four to watch him."

"I'm sort of a night person," Saorla said, "Usually stay up quite late. I'd love to read for a while and keep watch."

Ian's grandmother and father both said they weren't tired yet either and would like to wait a while longer. Ian rose to his feet with a yawn. He looked in Saorla's direction. "If he wakes up, ask him what we should do next."

"Yes, boss," Saorla said flatly.

Ian trudged down to his guest room. He closed the door, sat down on his bed, and took off his shoes. Leaning his torso back on the bed, he closed his eyes. He was almost asleep, when he remembered his unopened emails.

He clicked on a message from Jarvis. It was sent 10:30 a.m., last Friday, San Francisco time.

Hey Ian,

Just to give you a heads up. The Disciplinary Court is set to rule soon in your case. Rumor is out that they are going to go hard on you. Wish it wasn't so. Part of it is they are ticked at your decision to stay away from the proceeding forcing them to proceed in absentia. Too bad because I'm sure the oddsmakers in Vegas had you as the favorite to make partner—over me—until this.

TRULY YOURS,

Jarvis Reed

Whoa. This was all going much faster than what he would have thought. Where was the due process? And how in the world could they rule the way Jarvis was suggesting when Ian was clearly not at fault? No arrests were made. And if there had been, clearly the police would have arrested the criminals in the park, the Neopagans or whatever they were calling themselves.

Ian quickly clicked on the next message in the queue he hadn't read earlier. It was from Joan, his secretary. Short and to the point. Ian had been disbarred by decision of the Disciplinary Court handed down about 3 p.m. on Friday. Joan's tone was one of it all being a *fait accompli*, but she sprinkled it all with a dose of compassion: *I am truly going to miss working with you. You were one of the good ones. Please stay in touch.*

Ian slammed his fist onto the bed.

He would appeal, of course. He'd have thirty days to file one. That was enough time to get all his t's crossed and i's dotted. But what was he going to do for income in the interim? The temporary legal-aid job he'd taken here in Dublin didn't pay much at all, and it wouldn't be long before he'd be forced out of that job if they got wind of his disbarment in California. And his mortgage was past due. He'd probably have to miss a second payment now on the condo. Foreclosure loomed on the horizon after that. If he didn't get his license back, he would lose the place for sure. He'd be out of legal work for at least a year before he could even apply for reinstatement.

He had to come up with a plan. Get his license back. He wasn't sure he wanted to work back at his old firm though, not even if they offered to take him back with a partner's salary. In fact, he knew he would never return there. Maybe he'd get a job at another firm or hang up a shingle as a solo practitioner. But it was his law license that was the key.

And that's when it hit him.

Saorla knew about this.

It had to be why she'd been such a frozen trout all day. And it explained her odd comment about it obviously being unnecessary for him to give up a law license to get through her reading material. Followed closely on the heels by her freezing up even more. Obviously, she was thinking he *used to be* an attorney. How else to explain it?

Ian read the two articles online about his disbarment. Both ended with the parting shot that Mr. Shaw was unavailable for comment.

Oh yeah, well, he hoped to have the opportunity to comment soon enough. But for now he had to keep his focus on the main thing.

And the main thing was to survive the trial he was going through right here in Ireland.

SAORLA TALKED INTO THE NIGHT WITH ARYANA AND RORY BY THE firelight of the living room hearth to one side and the death bed of a frail old man to the other.

"Ian had supreme talent, but I messed him up," Rory was confessing. "I should have given him more space. I see that now."

Even though she'd never been a fanatic over football, Saorla found the conversation interesting. It wasn't every day that one was honored to talk sports with a bona fide national legend.

"What do you mean by supreme talent? And how did *you* mess him up?" Saorla asked.

"If he would have stuck with it with real drive, he would have been the kind of player that would have made the difference for a small nation between being utterly mediocre and winning a world cup. And I don't think I'm exaggerating. But Ian was always different. He had lots of interests, loved the outdoors, and was always taking the most outrageous chances with some or another dangerous activity."

"I think he seems to be mellowing in that regard, son," Ian's grandmother corrected. "I know he wants to be responsible as he can be. But he's wired different. And he comes by it honestly, dear, just look at yourself."

"No question I've made some big mistakes. But I'm realizing I need to do what I can to set the biggest ones right so far as that's possible. I know I need to repair things with Ian. And with his mother too. I haven't told him, but I'm in the process . . . I plan to spend the off-season in Seattle. There's been a lot of hurt there . . . she still has an open heart. We're going to work on patching things up."

"But tell me about you," Rory said to Saorla. "I'm told that Ian talks about you all the time. I can certainly see why."

Saorla felt her face growing warm. "He must have had so many girlfriends over the years."

Rory laughed. "Actually, from what I know, he's never had anything like a real girlfriend. He spends all his free time outdoors trying to—"

"That's true," Aryana cut in. "You're the first he's ever talked about. And let's just say he's not risk-averse when he's out on one of his adventures, but he moves slow as molasses when it comes to matters of the heart."

"I noticed that about him with the adventures. We went cliff climbing last weekend and . . ." Saorla looked down at her lap and shook her head.

"You weren't caught in the great storm?" Aryana asked, looking worried.

"Yeah, and something happened today that made me think he's a ladies man who likes to play the field," Saorla blurted.

Aryana chuckled. "What gave you that idea? Ian's always been a gentleman, a faithful confidant, and if you befriend him, you're a friend for life. He'll always be there for you. He doesn't play the field."

There was a rustling from the bed. George's voice croaked out a weak, "That's right." The nurse who had been quietly knitting in the corner was off her feet now and propping a pillow under the frail man's gray head.

"How about some water?" he asked.

The nurse held a small cup with a straw to his parched lips, and George took a slow sip.

"Come here," he said to Saorla beckoning her with a single wan finger.

Saorla was by the old man's bedside in a second, holding his hand.

"It's good to see you again, my dear. Is Ian all right?"

"He's in the guest room sleeping."

"Good. What time is it?"

"Little after midnight."

"Yes, of course, right," he said, trying hard to shake off the confusion.

"What have you learned?"

Saorla recounted as much as she could think of, trying to squeeze it all in before he fell unconscious once again. She laid out for him their finding of the cryptic message in the Book of Kells, but left out the derring-do inherent in escaping that night, and then moved on to the surreal discovery in the cave of the treasure and the poem.

"We believe that Patrick is, was, communicating with us," she said softly. "But I just can't escape my doubts that we'll ever be able to crack the last of the mystery dealing with the poem."

He asked her to read the poem, and she pored over it with him. He assured her with a weak grin that she was doing marvelously, but there was definitely more and to keep looking.

Saorla squeezed his hand. "We need to go faster, I know, for your sake. You deserve to know everything that can be known—"

George held up a limp hand. "Don't worry. I may yet turn out to be a Simeon who will live to see the Lord's consolation, and then I can depart in peace."

Saorla tilted her head, perplexed over the reference to Simeon. She knew George was referring to a biblical passage, but wasn't sure about the context. She felt a sudden shame at her mammoth knowledge of Irish history and mythology compared to her picayune knowledge of scripture and Theology.

"Luke, chapter two, you can look it up later."

The old man smiled and closed his green eyes. Asleep again.

THE TWO SAT IN THE HOT TUB ON THE OUTDOOR PATIO OF LORCAN'S penthouse suite at the top of the thirty-seven story building. Lorcan tipped a bottle of champagne to fill Claire's glass.

"You did well," he assured her.

"You still haven't told me if your men found anything at the site of the coordinates. And you promised you would. *Before the night was out,* I believe you said."

"I haven't told you?" Lorcan teased.

"You know you can trust me?"

"Hmm."

"So are you going to tell or keep stalling?"

"Maybe."

"They did find something significant though?"

"That is why we celebrated so lavishly tonight."

"So, what was I celebrating?"

"All your dreams coming true beyond your wildest fantasies."

Claire cooed with delight. "I knew there had to be something of value there. Not that I care about wealth for myself, of course."

"Of course not, but we will be rich beyond belief, though. All is safe in the cave. I've instructed my men not to touch so much as one coin or trinket. Any disobedience on their part would be unthinkable.

They know it. The only other people cognizant of the treasure's existence will be dead shortly."

"So, it's a treasure."

"Yes. Unfathomable, I believe was the adjective my expert on the ground used."

"So, why leave it there?"

"Patience, madam. I want to see the whole lovely site as it was found. Take it all in. I will do that as soon as I finish with some other very important business that goes right along with this."

"What could be more important than—"

"Samhain, of course. There's going to be a great turning back to paganism. It's the vanguard of a great spiritual movement. The reason I've even been allowed to find such a treasure is because of my decision to please the Goddess. No one can rule a treasure like that without her favor."

"A special Samhain?"

"Like a high king, I'll relight the pagan fires to spread across the isles."

"History reversed through magic. I see where this goes. Will you allow me to be with you?"

"We'll pass through the fires and smoke together, invoke the blessing of the Goddess, then seize the resources from the cave."

"What about the prophecy and the Book of Kells?"

"I haven't forgotten about the book. I'll destroy it, along with anyone intent on unearthing a hidden prophecy. But remember the power is in the blessing of the Goddess that comes from the sacrifice."

"It sounds positively exhilarating."

"I see you are coming around nicely."

CHAPTER TWENTY

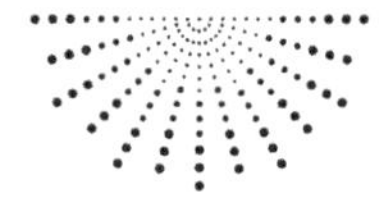

The alarm on Ian's cell buzzed him awake at 4 a.m. He forced himself out of bed and ventured into the family room to find Rory sleeping in a recliner. Papa George was asleep too. Saorla was gone now, probably turned in hours ago. He took a seat in the chair next to Rory and began softly flipping through pages of a Bible, looking for some early morning spiritual nourishment.

Rory began to slowly rustle awake. He rubbed his eyes, and tried to focus them in Ian's direction. "Hey kid, up already?"

"A little military discipline never hurt anyone you always used to say."

"Aw, you remember that?"

"Of course. Who doesn't remember their drill sergeant?"

"I guess I was harder on you than I should have been."

Ian thought of a few choice sarcasms, but quickly chased them from his mind. He'd never been off-the-hook disrespectful to the man, and he wasn't going to start now.

He decided to change the subject. "Has Papa been up at all?"

"An hour or so after you went to bed. He talked to your girl."

"She's not my—"

"Don't be naive son. I can tell. Although she's on the wonkish side, she's beautiful and you'd be crazy not to . . ."

Wonkish side? Ian gave a quick tilt of his head. His dad hadn't seen Saorla run. If he had, he'd be trying to make a soccer player out of her. She was marvelously erudite, but not wonkish, no way.

"You know how I am," Ian said. "Never had the time . . . Or maybe it's the fact that it just doesn't fit with my . . ."

"Sometimes you have to make sacrifices for love."

Love? It was a concept, nothing more, to his father. "Not getting attached is a sacrifice. And what do you know about love?" Ian fired back.

"I'm trying to make some amends. For the way I treated you and Wendy."

"Leave mom out of this," he said loudly, suddenly shocked at himself for shattering the peace of the early hour.

"That's what I wanted to talk to you about," his dad said in a soft, pleading voice. "I'm sorry, Ian. I really am. For being gone so much, for pushing you so hard when I *was* around. For not being a better husband and father."

Rory's eyes were watering. "I know it's probably too little, too late," he said. "But it's all I've got, I can only do the best I can from now on."

Ian didn't know what to say. He'd never seen his father so contrite about anything.

"I'm going to reconcile with Wendy. I'm going up to Seattle for the off-season on into the summer. I'll be done coaching soon. A year or two more, tops. I want to grow old with the mother of my son."

The warmth of the words poured through the wall of ice Ian had erected between his heart and his father. The syllables on his tongue choked back into the silence of his throat.

The two sat quietly together. Minutes passed, and Ian finally said, "That's great, Dad."

His father nodded.

But why? Ian wondered. What had caused the change? He hoped his dad hadn't also gotten some bad news from the doctor. "Why now?" he asked.

"I don't know how to answer that. Other than I just can't shake the feeling something is missing in my life. And when I took a good look, I realized what it was. I'd hurt those who should have been closest to me."

Big changes were underway, and Ian suddenly felt ashamed he'd been too bitter to seriously pray for his dad. It now looked like God was answering prayers he wasn't even praying, while declining to help on other matters he was praying about, like his law license and his grandfather's health.

"So what did Papa say while I was out?"

"A bunch of nonsense about being like Simeon in the Bible who wouldn't die until something big happened."

Ian doubted that his father's rendition of the conversation was accurate. Some things in his dad's life were changing for the better, and other areas still needed work.

"What if he's right? Are you prepared to take note?"

His father grunted out an indecipherable inanity and laughed. Ian laughed too, but at the ridiculous thought that at least this really was his father and not an imposter that had taken over his body.

Grandma Aryana served a late breakfast for her guests at nine-thirty. The sun, rising as it does relatively late in October in Ireland, had only crested over the horizon a little over an hour ago.

The table contained a smorgasbord of eggs, sausage, fried potatoes, and something called rashers—a thick bacon-like country ham. Scones, toast, and tea were also a part of the mix. Ian watched Saorla pick at a single piece of toast and sip tea. She'd obviously lost the healthy appetite he'd always known her to have.

Rory, on the other hand, was a boy again eating his mother's cooking after ten hours of soccer practice. He was halfway through an enormous plate of eggs and rashers before Saorla had managed to nibble a quarter of her toast.

"Sleep well?" Ian asked her.

"Yeah."

"Hungry?"

"Sure."

The same monosyllable responses to his attempts at conversation were in play again today. How long would this go? They needed to have a real talk, and soon. When Rory asked about her family and her father in particular, Saorla came alive like she was Yeats or Lance hearing a car come up the gravel drive.

After a long update on her family, Saorla said to Rory, "My father would have loved to meet you. He's a big fan of Irish football and follows the leagues in America too."

Ian could only sit back and listen, flabbergasted at Saorla's ability to turn her mood from melancholic monotone when addressing him to robust amicability when addressing others. Ian's bewilderment, was interrupted by a feeble, "Hello," coming from the other room.

The nurse sprang into the kitchen. "He's awake and asking for you," she announced.

Ian rocketed to his feet and was at his grandfather's bedside in less time than it would take a professional soccer player to deliver a penalty kick from his cleats to the net.

SAORLA REMAINED IN THE KITCHEN STARING FIRST AT HER TOAST, AND then at Ian's mobile. What would be the harm in having a quick peak at it? She picked up the phone and slid the bar at the bottom, jump-starting it to life. She told herself she was just checking out the man's mobile, you know, to see if she might like to get one like it. But that was a tall tale bigger than the *Cattle Raid of Cooley*, she knew.

Curiosity would curdle her insides if she didn't have a wee bit of a look. She pulled up his email and saw one from his secretary and one from a co-worker named Jarvis. They seemed to be sympathetic to Ian's plight and thought he was a good lawyer. Okay, maybe he was being treated unfairly in his professional world. But what about his personal world—his relationships?

And what about his hook-up with that brunette yesterday on Grafton Street?

Saorla tapped open his text messages. One caught her eye immediately: Cheryl Miller.

Great to see you yesterday! Thanks for the Good Times!

The good times? Cheryl was also kind enough to text a picture of herself. In a bikini no less! Over the caption: *Cabo San Lucas here I come.*

It was all just as she thought. Saorla was the hired help, and Cheryl —the successful knockout American model—was the real love interest of Ian Shaw.

She put the mobile back on the table and joined the gathering in the parlor. George was talking about where he wanted to be buried. Something about the way he was fighting so hard to get his words out told Saorla the topic was really important to him.

"I don't want to be cremated. If ye were to do that to me, I'd come back to haunt your every waking hour," he said with a mischievous grin.

"Of course not, honey, we've been over this," Aryana assured him.

"Just making a point," he said, his breathing labored and his voice weak. "The resurrection of the dead, it's more than a doctrine to me now. It's an act of faith to make mention of your bones. Just look at the patriarchs. There's more written about where they were buried than there is about so much of the other things church people fuss about these days."

Saorla hadn't considered the theory George was proposing. She would have time to search out the scriptures on a whole array of matters as soon as she finished this job for Ian Shaw and for this dear old man.

He locked eyes briefly with Saorla but then struggled to keep his eyelids open. "My family descended from Scottish Presbyterians. Came here in the 1680s. Stayed loyal to God and Crown. We've been hard at it a long time on this land. Have the funeral at the Presbyterian church in town. Bury me under the big oak where you found those treasures."

His eyes shut and he appeared to be asleep, but then he mumbled, "Put up a stone that mentions I loved God."

CHAPTER TWENTY-ONE

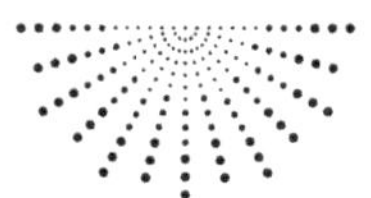

The churchyard at Downs Cathedral in Downpatrick, Northern Ireland, was not normally a place that could escape the rampant footfalls from throngs of tourists, as it was considered by many to be the final resting place of the great patron saint himself. On this Tuesday afternoon in late October, however, Ian and Saorla had the site to themselves.

They maneuvered through the well-manicured grounds, and identified a large grey granite boulder marking the supposed gravesite. Ian stretched himself out on the boulder, lying face down. Saorla wondered if the cold-shoulder routine she was giving him was causing him to crack up. Or perhaps he was still touchy over the conversation they'd had on the ride to the gravesite. Ian had asked, "Do you know about my license?"

"Yes," she'd admitted.

"I'm going to get it back. It isn't what you think."

"What should I be thinking? You have an anger problem that cost you your job?"

"That's your assessment of me?"

"I don't know."

"If you read the articles, you saw I wasn't available for comment.

You might have noticed that I've been pretty busy here these last weeks. So busy I haven't been able to defend myself against some clearly bogus allegations. It's just a default judgment that was entered quickly when I didn't appear."

"You must have done something?"

"So, you believe everything the media writes?"

"They don't disbar people for being a *good* barrister."

"I defended some Christians in a park, is all, who were under assault. I got messed up in the middle of something. What happened after that is pure persecution."

Saorla had decided to let him think that the flap over his disbarment was all that was bothering her. She was going to walk the fine line between giving him a rugby stiff arm and coming on so warm that she'd be in danger of him thinking she was still romantically inclined toward him. She decided that Ian might well be right about his law license. But her heart was going to be a closed door from here on out nonetheless.

Ian laid on the stone slab so long Saorla thought he was sleeping. "You still awake?"

"Yep."

"Why are you laying there?"

"Did you ever read about the bones of Elisha?"

"Not sure where you're going with this," she said, thinking that there'd been a lot of talk about bones already today. They'd already both agreed that George's odd instruction about the merits of Christian burial over cremation was surely about more than an old man's outlining of his final wishes. God must speaking to them through George's words, they both sensed. They'd broken down the lines of the poem that seemed to speak of the gravesite.

Down Patrick to the final rest
Cold grave opens sky red hue

From this and from George's words, they'd determined it was time for an immediate visit to Patrick's putative grave.

"Don't feel bad," Ian said, flipping over to lie on his back. "I've just been reading about the life of Elisha since my grandfather started talking about burials and funerals. I'm a work in progress too, as far as being Bible literate."

"You are further along than me," she acknowledged.

Ian still lay looking up at the sky. "Elisha was the understudy of the prophet Elijah, who was the one that called fire down on the prophets of Baal. He also prophesied judgment on King Ahab and Queen Jezebel."

"So what's this have to do with Patrick?"

"I'm getting there. Patience."

"I'm not sure your grandfather has time for us to be patient."

"It's a fruit of the Spirit," Ian huffed. "As I was saying, Elisha was the understudy. Elijah promised the young wannabe that if he saw him when he was taken up to heaven, the young Elisha would get his anointing to do the work of a prophet, even a double portion compared to Elijah's. So you know what happened?"

"I'm going to study this, so you better get it right."

"Yes ma'am, I mean yes, professor," Ian said, grinning. "So, Elisha was there when Elijah was taken to heaven in a chariot of fire. And then Elisha took up Elijah's mantle, his cloak, and asked, 'Where is the Lord God of Elijah?' And guess what happened after that?"

Saorla gave a slight nod that Ian didn't seem to notice. She was starting to remember the story from her childhood.

"The Spirit of God came on Elisha," Ian continued, "and he got a double portion of the anointing that was on Elijah. And after that Elisha went out and did twice the number of miracles that Elijah did in his life, except in one area."

Ian was laying on his back now and had suddenly stopped talking. He seemed to be staring up at the sky, deep in thought.

"Sky red hue. Like the poem."

"Huh?"

"The poem, the sky right now—I feel like I'm living a vision."

Saorla hadn't noticed the firmament until now. It was giving off a bold magenta-red flare, as the sun arched lower in the heavens toward the scattered cirrus at the horizon. A tingle snaked down her spine, and the tiny faint hairs on her arms stood erect, like she'd read about survivors of lightning strikes saying they felt shortly before impact. It wouldn't be dark yet for a few more hours. But the day had the eerie feeling of twilight to it.

"So what was the one area that Elisha was short in?" Saorla asked.

"It was in the realm of raising the dead. They were tied one-to-one when Elisha passed. But you know what? He gave specific instructions about his bones too, just like Abraham, Isaac, Jacob and Joseph. So specific that one day a company with a wounded man was riding near Elisha's grave. When they realized the man had died, they threw the corpse on the grave of Elisha. And Whammo! The guy came back to life when his body came to rest near Elisha's bones."

"This is strange stuff," Saorla said. She would have to study this out. Gladness suddenly hit her at the thought that she'd buried Stuart and not had him cremated. But she figured that even if his body had been reduced to ashes—like her life had been the day she'd lost him and then again the day she'd learned about Cheryl—the God who created the universe was more than able to make amends.

"You asked me why I'm lying on the stone, and that's my answer why. If this is Patrick's grave, who knows, what Patrick carried, the gift . . . the anointing, whatever you want to call it . . . may still be present."

"If you get the anointing, you can take it with you to Cabo San Lucas," Saorla blurted out before she could take the words back.

"Huh?" Ian grunted. He catapulted himself up to his feet to face her.

Saorla felt the blood spiking through her veins. She was out on the limb and saw no harm in sawing it off now. "You and Cheryl can celebrate in Mexico together. I'm sure you'll be very happy there."

"Cabo San Lucas? Cheryl?" Ian asked, words forming slowly.

"See! You know what I'm talking about!"

"Actually I have no idea—"

"The American model—"

"You mean the American Airlines flight attendant."

"I'm talking about the gorgeous model you had lunch with at Cornucopia."

"So this is what this is all about. Giving me the cold shoulder, making me go crazy these last thirty-six hours, making me think I was spending time with one of the Stepford wives or that old man O'Donnell had sprinkled some faery dust on you at his store."

"That doesn't change what I saw."

"Look, Seer, you might as well know it," Ian's voice was full of calm resolve now. He took her hand in his. "I love you. I'm crazy about you. Have been from the moment I first laid eyes on you. And I don't know what to do about it."

Saorla didn't know what to say so she just stood there holding his hand. He was looking into her eyes. She saw only honest sincerity there. But she wasn't ready to cave yet.

"So who's Cheryl?"

"How do you know about her?" Ian said, rubbing the stubble on his chin.

"I saw you with a beautiful woman yesterday, and then I saw the text message. I'm sorry I looked at it, but I had to know."

"Cheryl was my flight attendant on the way out here. She was kind to me—"

"I bet she was—"

"And a few days after I arrived, I ran into her by complete accident while I was preparing to take a tour of the National Museum. The next time I ran into her was yesterday, again by complete coincidence."

"So you saw her more than once."

"No . . . I mean, yes . . . Just the three times I've said. But it was nothing but lunch."

"So you don't have a model in Mexico?"

"Not even close. I bet that text message is the last one I ever get from Cheryl. Her airline is discontinuing flights to Dublin out of Chicago until spring. It was a fluke I bumped into her again."

Ian let go of her hand and took his mobile out of his pocket. "Did you listen to this message?" he asked.

"I didn't listen to any of your voice messages," Saorla said, the shame at reading his other messages now covering her like a thick fog.

Ian played a voicemail from Cheryl where she wished him luck on his endeavor in Ireland. Just before ending, Cheryl noted how Ian had raved over his friendship and budding romance with the professor, and said that she was truly happy that he had met someone so special.

Saorla looked about the churchyard. Maybe there was a rock big enough for her to crawl under and hide.

"I'm sorry," was all she could manage to say.

"Does this mean that we can get things back to normal?"

"I . . . don't know. This all happened so fast. I've been living on a knife's edge these last weeks. I think I need to take a step back and—"

"I understand."

"You do?"

"Yeah. Let's just figure out what we have to do next."

"I haven't a clue. How about you?"

"Nope. But I think coming here was somehow a profound piece of the puzzle. If only to clear up the misunderstanding between us . . . and under such a sky."

Saorla looked up at the magnificent red hue. The hair on her arms was sticking up again.

Cold grave opens sky red hue.

"It's uncanny."

Not knowing where to go next, the two sat atop Patrick's gravestone and prayed for guidance. When they finished, they still had no idea.

"Do you know that this stone wasn't placed here until 1900?" Saorla asked.

"You're kidding?"

"No, an engineer lobbied for it."

Ian shook his head. "Do you think Patrick is really buried here?"

"Why not?" she answered. "Nothing would surprise me after what we've learned." Her appetite was back, and her stomach was calling for food. "How about we go into town and see if we can get some chips and a fizzy drink?"

"Sounds like a plan. You only picked at your toast this morning."

"I had a lot on my mind."

TOMORROW NIGHT WOULD BE THE MOST SPECIAL SAMHAIN IN THE history of Ireland, Lorcan thought, as he sat meditating by the shore of a remote eighty-acre lough in the mountains of Wicklow. He'd taken a rare day off to prepare himself mentally and spiritually for the solemn and magical occasion.

Intent on teaching Claire his spiritual secrets, he'd brought her along for the day. At his insistence, she'd traipsed her way through a long meditative trip in the forest and was now meandering toward him, hugging the shoreline to his left.

His mobile device suddenly began playing a wispy strain from an Irish flute. An incoming call. It was Kirby. Lorcan had given strict orders that he was not to be bothered by his men unless there was some dire emergency or they had located their quarry.

"We've spotted them."

"Where?"

"Downpatrick. Both the professor and the American."

Lorcan gave instructions to swiftly get the essential assets in place. This time they were to finish them off without any questions asked. He would thank them for being such useful idiots after they were dead. There was simply no need to keep them alive any longer. The idea of the existence of an important prophecy from Saint Patrick would die with them. Lorcan had everything he needed. Enough treasure to secretly finance ten thousand political campaigns and to buy influence in every capital in Europe and beyond.

But what about the Book of Kells?

Lorcan had no use for it now that the world's greatest personal fortune was within his easy reach. But it still needed to be found and destroyed, and it would please the Goddess immeasurably, he knew, if he could sacrifice it in the Samhain fires along with that beautiful maid the prime minister had been so intent on bedding.

It was time to wrap everything up into a neat package without any residual mess. This was way too important to sit out and let his security team handle, he realized. He would see to it that the troublers of his new world order were silenced. And he would see to it even if he had to get his own hands dirty in the process. A little dirt wouldn't matter at this point. He had no more political ambition himself; everything he needed to accomplish from here on out after the Samhain could be done behind the scenes with the wealth he was about to amass.

He hailed Claire's attention, and they made a quick departure from the serenity of the mountains.

"Excellent," he chanted repeatedly, as he steered his Mercedes north on R115 headed for the small town of Rockbrook just on the other side of the mountains. There, he would order a helicopter to take him to Downpatrick.

He pushed the pedal toward the floor, and smiled at his ability to rearrange the world around him. He would be in Downpatrick in less than an hour.

CHAPTER TWENTY-TWO

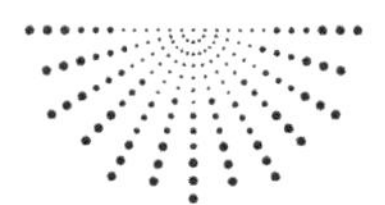

Motorists drove on the right side of the road in America. Saorla therefore couldn't imagine how difficult it must be for Ian to drive on the left and have the traffic whiz by on the right. They'd had more than one close call with him behind the wheel. So it was with relief that she'd successfully persuaded him to let her drive the short trip from the hill at Down Cathedral to the town square in Downpatrick.

She squeezed into a hobbit-sized parking space on Market Street. They exited and began exploring the town. With a population of ten thousand, it was a quaint departure from Dublin's half-a-million souls. Saorla searched for somewhere to grab a bite to eat, all the while keeping her eyes and ears open for Heaven's leading. She still hadn't a clue where to look next on the trail of Saint Patrick and was more than a little disappointed that something hadn't turned up at the gravesite, other than the "red hue."

She marveled at Ian's ability to remain sanguine. He seemed thrilled over finally learning the truth about what had been bothering her, commenting more than once that the whole trip was worth it just to clear the air. She, on the other hand, just wanted to get on with the quest. They were close to something big, she could feel it.

They turned into a place called the Brick Hearth Grill and ordered a couple of sandwiches. Saorla settled on a corned beef on rye after Ian ordered one.

Thirty minutes later they found themselves wandering down Market Street, passing the facade of a small bookstore and coffee shop with large windows.

"Wait a minute," Ian said.

"You need a coffee?"

"No." He was looking down at the sidewalk like he was trying to remember something important.

"You need a book? Don't tell me you want to get started on that reading program I suggested?"

"Something like that." He took her hand and led her inside through a glass door with green-wood trim.

"Did you notice the sign on the door?" he asked.

"The Bard's Wares?"

"Yep."

Puzzled, she was about to ask another question, when she saw the potential significance. "*Glean the bardic furrow seven*. I'm not sure—"

"It's worth a look."

Saorla shrugged her shoulders.

The store smelled musty from the large quantity of old weathered tomes on offer, but it was the kind of place where Saorla felt right at home. There was a small reading area to the front near the till, with a sofa and a couple rocking chairs. Meandering down the aisles, she parted from Ian's company momentarily. She selected a volume of Celtic poetry and lost herself for about ten minutes in the glen's and dales of the land.

Ian startled her back to the shop with a tap on the shoulder. "You notice anything about the layout of the store?"

She shook her head. "Other than it's small, and there's a lot bookshelves for the space, no."

"There's two sets of four rows. And the rows are numbered one through eight."

"So?"

"So I say we look in row seven, or *furrow* seven."

It couldn't be that simple.

"Okay," she muttered.

They searched through the shelves for about twenty minutes for anything that might catch their eye. Praying all the time for guidance, they hunted for some thread of connection to what they'd learned so far. It was like trying to meet up with a friend without a mobile inside Croake Park when it was filled to its eighty-five thousand-seat capacity.

"I don't know, Ian, this is maybe a silly goose chase."

"Don't think so. I've been here before."

"What? Why would—"

"In a vision. Sunday, when we were praying, waiting on the Lord with Killian."

"You never mentioned—"

"I'd never had a vision before so I didn't know what it was until . . ."

"Wow. We should keep looking then."

They continued on down the aisle, Ian hunting on one side and Saorla on the other with their backs to each other. A few minutes later, Saorla picked up an antiquated title called *Little Known Legends of Saint Patrick* and started perusing it.

Suddenly, the same awful foreboding was back. The same feeling she'd had at the National Museum. The same mix of terror and dread before the bomb-blast had nearly killed Myrna and before the shooting started when she was on the rope at the cliff.

"Ian, I think we should—"

"You found something?"

"—get out of here."

Saorla handed off the book to Ian and began looking scattershot around the store. Everything seemed to be in order. Nothing out in the street or lurking behind a bookshelf.

But still the dread increased.

"Look at this, Seer. On page seventy-seven, line seven of the book. It starts talking about St. Patrick's church at the foot of the Hill of

Tara that we saw yesterday. Says here, the current church was built in 1822 on the site of a previous church."

The crouching doom refused to subside. Instead it grew stronger. "Yes, there has been a church at the site going back to a charter dating to 1190 AD."

"And it says that something very important is buried beneath the tile floors."

Ian handed her back the book; she sped through it. Such tales would have been flagged as nothing more than hagiographic hogwash a few weeks ago in her world. But now she was not so sure.

Pure dread was encapsulating her in ever-increasing waves. A cold sweat blanketed her forehead.

We have to get out of here, now!

"Watch this," Ian said, pointing to an old woman with a grey bun walking down the aisle toward them. "She's going to speak to us about tea and sitting on a sofa," he whispered.

The woman approached, mumbling something that couldn't be deciphered, stopped and then said, "Will ye be buying the book now, or shall I set you up on the sofa with a cup of tea."

The surprise she felt at Ian's foretelling of the woman's conversation was overshadowed by the growing anticipation of terror.

"We'll take the book," Ian said.

"No, we have to get out of here immediately," Saorla bellowed.

The old grey bun frowned.

In her mind's eye, Saorla saw the windows of the storefront shattering to pieces as bullets riddled the store. The old woman was down and bleeding. Shrill shrieks of panic filled the air. This imaginary world faded to white before Saorla reemerged in the real.

SEVERAL KILOMETERS OUTSIDE OF DOWNPATRICK, THE WHITE AND BLUE Eurocopter EC 155 pulsated northward. The craft was captained by Lorcan's personal pilot, A.B. Wilson. Lorcan sat in the co-pilot seat, even though he didn't know the first thing about flying. He had ordered the craft into the air over the pilot's protestations that it was low on fuel. Claire lounged in the roomy thirteen-seat passenger compartment.

Lorcan took a call from Kirby just as they were about to land at a nearby heliport for refueling. Kirby informed that his team had located the elusive duo at a bookstore on Market Street and were closing in for the kill.

"Bloody excellent news!"

"They've run out of luck. We're finally going to get them, boss."

"Shoot to kill, clean up, and get the boys out of there before anyone can figure out what happened."

"We got this."

"I'm on my way. I'll follow from the air."

Lorcan ended the call and turned to the pilot. "Don't take it down. We're going back up."

"But we only have about twenty minutes of fuel left."

"Won't need that much."

In a few seconds, they were hundreds of feet in the air and making a straight line for DownPatrick.

"WHAT'S THE RUSH?" IAN ASKED. "YOU KNOW WE NEED THAT BOOK."

"No we don't," Saorla shouted, grabbing his arm.

"What's got in to you?"

"I'm having one of those feelings."

Ian's eyes grew wide.

Saorla shifted her gaze to the front of the store.

"Not already!" She pointed at a couple of men getting out of a black SUV across the street, each brandishing an AK47. "Look!"

Pulling his arm now, Saorla dropped the book to the floor and dragged Ian to the back alley emergency exit.

In a blink, she pushed open the door and barreled out to the alley.

Nobody there. She inhaled, then took off sprinting.

"What about the book?" Ian yelled.

She could hear his shoes slapping the asphalt pavement behind her. "Excuse me, I'm trying to save your life," she yelled back.

"But the clue—"

"I know where it is."

"You do?"

"Yeah, I'm a fast reader."

"Not as fast as you run I bet." He finally pulled up even to her with his lungs heaving. They came to the terminus of the long unimpeded draw of the alley before it crossed the east-west arterial that intersected with Market Street.

"Let's head down the alley one more block and double back to the vehicle," he said.

"I don't know."

"You got a better plan."

"No," she acknowledged, before starting a full-out sprint once again down the alley, trying to see how far ahead she could get before he caught her.

It was halfway down the next stretch of the alley when she first heard the wap-wap of a helicopter. Probably evacuating a sick kid to the hospital. It would make a splendid distraction when they came out on Market Street.

He caught up to her before they reached the exposure of the next street. "Let me have the keys," he said.

"You're kidding, right?"

"Trust me. I can handle this."

"But I'm a better driver and—"

"Remember Queen Medb," Ian chided with a nervous chuckle, "you don't want to end up like her."

Saorla handed him the keys without a fight.

The helicopter hovered two blocks to the south in the direction they'd just come from over near the bookstore. "Let's get out of here," Ian said. "The chopper is hunting us."

They were almost at their truck when they saw the black SUV speeding their way.

She grabbed the handle of the passenger door of the truck. It was locked.

She swiveled in time to see Ian fumbling the keys. Dropping them to the pavement.

The SUV was squealing its tires, bearing down on them. Maybe a hundred and twenty-five yards away. Now ninety.

Seventy-five.

Their doors clicked unlocked. And she flung herself into the passenger seat, gasping for oxygen.

In another second, Ian was behind the wheel and had the vehicle started. With their truck now pinned between two compacts, she was suddenly not as enamored with her own parallel parking skills as she'd been earlier.

Ian wrenched the vehicle into reverse, slammed the car behind and then clipped the one in front as he pulled out onto Market Street. He crunched the accelerator to the floor. The SUV was barreling down on them.

A game of chicken.

The other side wasn't blinking. Neither was Ian, traveling on the wrong side of the street. Going too fast.

Saorla poised for the head-on collision. The SUV swerved first, slightly to Saorla's left. Ian swerved the truck to the right. The truck scraped the SUV and flipped around to face the same southerly direction the truck was traveling.

She heard a splat of gunfire. Tires screeched. The truck's engine roared as Ian gunned it.

The helicopter had a visual on them now and hovered to their rear about thirty feet overhead. The SUV had recovered and was gaining ground. Ian had both hands firmly on the wheel, grimacing as he tested the old truck's horsepower.

Saorla strapped on her seatbelt. "Are they the same knackers that were after us at the cave?"

"Do you want me to stop the truck and ask them?" Ian said, as he took a hard right and semi-circled back to the north.

The SUV was gaining now. A thick man with a dark suit leaned out the passenger window and aimed a weapon. Saorla ducked and screamed. She heard a loud crack of gunfire and bullets dinging into the exterior of the truck.

"Should I call 999 for the police?" she asked.

"Not unless you want to go to jail." He had a look of pleasured excitement on his face, as if he were blowing out the candles on a cake for his eighth birthday. He also seemed to be an incongruous study of calm focus.

"I might settle for not being killed," Saorla screeched.

"I'm going to get us out of this."

The helicopter drew itself to the passenger side of the vehicle. A man aimed a rifle out the opening.

"Ian!" she screamed.

He hit the brakes and darted the truck down a narrow street. The buildings on either side prevented the copter from getting a bead on them. But the SUV had recovered and was now on their bumper.

More gunshots.

The back window of their truck shattered; glass landed in Saorla's hair.

"Give them the Thunder and Lightning," she screamed.

"Huh?"

"It's a naughty child's game. You knock like thunder and run away like lightning."

More gunfire rocked the town's normally mundane environs. The helicopter prowled overhead and then lunged into their field of vision when further down the roadway.

Ian opened the truck's engine to a steady hum. He took his right hand off the wheel and flashed Saorla a Shaka sign with his thumb and little finger extended. "Hang loose!" he roared.

The truck hurled over a bump and caught a few feet of air before the tires slammed onto the road and careened like a bobble-head toy. Ian gripped the steering wheel harder and kept the beast on tract.

But they were still coming. "Ding-dong ditch," he finally sputtered out. "That's what we called it."

Saorla nodded her head in recognition, even though she was doing her best to keep low in the seat and out of the line of fire. "Every country seems to have had its own variant. You were one of the miscreants who indulged in the States, I see."

"So let's play," Ian hooted as he made a sudden curve to the right to get off the main highway. He was on Strangford Road now. He punched it till the speedometer registered 160 kilometers per hour.

Despite Ian's evasive driving maneuvers, the SUV caught them again and was tapping the truck's bumper. Ian twisted through a turnabout, the tires skidding to keep a grip on the pavement. With one tire leaving the road, Saorla could sense they were about to roll. She silently prayed.

Christ on my right, Christ on my left—

IAN MADE A QUICK CORRECTION BY JERKING THE STEERING WHEEL TO the right and kept the truck from rolling. They steamed up the narrow highway to the east, which was bordered on both sides by ubiquitous waist-high grey-stone fence.

He could see the SUV in the rear view mirror. Closing fast.

And then . . .

Whack!

It rammed their back bumper.

Have to keep them pinned behind.

The bad guys were desperately trying to outflank him to the side, where they would no doubt let lose a barrage of firepower at point blank range.

The SUV lunged hard to the right, and Ian swerved to meet it a second later. The same maneuvers were repeated to the left. The pattern held for a few minutes.

The SUV finally switched to a new strategy of putting the pedal to the metal to drive right through the truck. Ian was thinking of slamming on the brakes to see what would happen when he noticed an arduous curve and embankment ahead.

He made a quick drift to the left and let the SUV think it could sneak by on the right.

This had to work, or they were toast.

The SUV took the bait. And Ian could now see the driver's face to the right. A buffaloed-neck man with a crazy hammer-shaped scar in the middle of his forehead. The same man he'd seen at the museum and at the cliff.

"Have to end this now," Ian said, but doubted Saorla heard it over the constant drone of the chopper.

The suit in the passenger seat leaned over the driver's chest. Aimed a weapon through the open window.

Ian lurched the wheel. The truck veered quickly to the right, smashing the SUV's side against the embankment. The shooter was flung back against the passenger window.

Ian glanced at his speedometer. His truck slowed to one hundred kilometers per hour.

Have to speed up. Have to cripple the goons.

The copter, however, was relentless. It continued its harassment by flying dangerously close to the truck's windshield. Ian now worried he would be shredded to death by the blade.

What kind of psychotic was up there?

Ian continued to grind the SUV against the stone for a split second longer.

Saorla had her cell phone in hand.

"Time to call the police?" he asked.

"Past time."

"I thought you were having fun."

"I'm suckin' diesel."

"Huh?"

Saorla punched at some numbers on her phone. "Means I'm having a good time."

Ian shrugged. "So much irony in these Irish idioms—"

"Hello, I'm in an emergency. Men are shooting at me from a black SUV," Saorla said into her cell just before a percussive blast hit her window. Glass fragments splattered everywhere. Ian veered his truck to the left, releasing the vice on the goon's vehicle.

Saorla was all of a sudden in high dungeon, talking breathlessly into her mobile. "Where am I? I'm in a white Nissan pick-up truck heading east on Strangford Road. I need help—"

Another crack of gunfire. Then, the SUV's right headlight clipped a piece of stone fencing. And this jolted it into a wobbling lame-duck status.

Ian looked over and noticed that Saorla's phone had disappeared. She was picking shards of glass out of her hair. "What happened to your mobile?"

"They shot it out of my hand."

A new level of panic shot through him. "You weren't hit were you?"

"Just by flying glass. Relax. No blood . . . yet."

With the goon's slowing considerably, Ian was able to put some distance between them.

The helicopter, on the other hand, was an entirely different matter. Whoever was commanding it was either rabid-dog mad or fiercely determined to see Ian dead, or maybe it was a lot of both. "Who is that guy?" Ian blurted.

"It's Lorcan Duihbur," Saorla said. "The prime minister has come to kill us himself. He can't take the chance that we have enough to incriminate him."

Ian continued to plunge the truck forward even though it appeared that any second the skids of the helicopter would land on the truck's hood or the blade would chop the cab in half. For several miles, he continued to command the truck like it was a triple-crown race horse spinning out of the final turn.

It was a game of nerves. But neither side was relenting. All the while they were heading further northeast, toward the coast and the sea.

Yet they wanted to head south. Get back to Dublin.

The SUV behind them guarded the way back. And was gaining

ground again. There was no turning around. And there seemed to be no other roads that would get them off the one they were on.

A sign ahead read *Strangford Lough*. "I'm afraid we're headed for a bit of a dead end, dear," Saorla said, with an amazing amount of calm in her voice.

"Any roads cut back to the south?" Ian yelled over the roar of the chopper.

"I think there is one ahead. If you miss it, we'll be trapped."

"Got it. The lough blocks the way north, and straight ahead to the east is the Irish Sea."

"If you don't mind a good swim, we can jump in and start stroking to the Isle of Man."

"Ha! How far is that?"

"A wee fifty or sixty kilometers of open sea. A healthy swim."

"We need a better plan."

"Becoming fish food isn't a good strategy?"

Ian laughed as he glanced over at her. He took in the perfectly formed white teeth contrasting with luxuriant black-brown hair and soft peached-colored lips. If he was going to die, he wanted that to be his last image.

"Did I ever tell you I love you?"

"Yeah, you said that today."

"Just wanted you to know in case we don't make it. Even if we do—"

"Oh no!"

"What?"

"We just missed the road to the south!"

"SIR, WE ARE DANGEROUSLY CLOSE TO RUNNING OUT OF FUEL," THE pilot said.

Lorcan couldn't believe what he was hearing. He had them trapped. His Eurocopter was nearly directly on the truck's hood, impairing its visibility and making life generally miserable for the driver. Kirby and the boys in the SUV had recovered from their earlier mishap and were again riding the back bumper of the truck. In another mile or so, it would be the end of the line. The Strangford Lough and the Irish Sea would trap their soon-to-be captives at the small port town of Strangford.

"How could you be such an idiot, Wilson?"

"We have enough to get to the nearest heliport. That's all—"

"Keep after them."

"But boss—"

"Shut up. I don't care if we have to put this down in a field somewhere."

Realizing that the fuel situation must indeed be dire if the pilot dared to bring it up, Lorcan quickly sorted through his options.

"Keep pursuing," he finally said.

"But—"

"Tell me when we're ten seconds from falling out of the sky."

"How can I know that?"

"Guess."

"We probably have no more than another couple of minutes."

"Keep going! We'll have them in less than a mile."

THE TRUCK WAS STRAINING AT NEAR PEAK CAPACITY. IT WAS EVIDENT TO Ian that the maximum speed of two hundred kilometers per hour at the far end of the speedometer was nothing more than a pipe dream. Nonetheless, the truck had somehow managed a fifty yard lead on the SUV. But the helicopter was still a demon from the netherworld, as it maintained a haloed cacophony over the truck.

Strangford City Limits, the sign read as it flashed by.

"This is the end of the road," Saorla yelled.

Ian didn't know what else to do so he kept going. Maybe he could pick up a police tail in town.

Even though Saorla had made an emergency 999 call earlier, Ian saw no sign of a police presence as he careened through the main street of town that led toward the dock.

The dock!

The dock where the Strangford Ferry departed every hour on the hour for a crossing of the lough to the town of Portaferry on the other side. To the east was a hundred miles of open sea to Scotland.

They were bearing down on the dock, and there was nowhere else to turn.

The ferry was just pulling up shop and getting ready to depart.

Ian punched it up the last small hill and onto a ramp. They soared, airborne now. Floating toward the ferry. Flying over the gate toward the long parking deck.

"Run like lightning," Ian hooted.

The truck hit with a thud, and Saorla screamed. Ian slammed and locked up the brakes. The truck skidded violently, the wheels snaking back and forth. Hot smoke wafted from the pavement atop the ferry. The smell of burning rubber filled the cold humid air over the lough.

The deck was relatively empty, and the truck clawed the pavement for about thirty yards before slamming into a Toyota Prius. The air bags deployed, and Ian felt the hard jolt.

He instantly realized he was unhurt. But the air bag was covering his passenger. And he couldn't see if she was moving or even conscious. "Seer!" he yelled.

No response.

His way to her was blocked by the air bag. He jumped out of the truck and circled his way around the outside of the vehicle to get to her.

The chopper was above him, rocking and swaying. He didn't care if they shot him. He had to get to Seer. As he latched onto the handle on the passenger door of the cab, the chopper was hovering above him, and then it wasn't.

Instead he heard a steady thumping that grew progressively more distant. Ian craned his head up and paused to watch the chopper fleeing to the south.

A relative calm settled in for a second, except for a gentle swaying from below. The ferry had departed from the dock.

And then there was a loud crash. The black SUV had gone airborne and slammed into the side of the ferry.

After a few seconds, the squatty man with the scar on his forehead emerged, shaken from the wreckage of the SUV. He stood in the shallow water by the dock and pulled out a rifle. With shaking hands, he aimed in Ian's direction. Ian was already out of the range of fire, but he could swear that he heard the thick man yell, "We'll collect your carcasses on the other side."

CHAPTER TWENTY-THREE

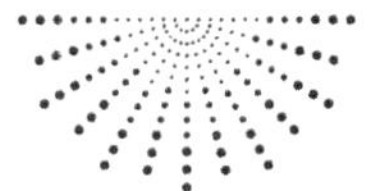

The chopper made its way back to the heliport in Downpatrick where Wilson was forced to lay down the craft just short of the designated landing spot. Lorcan cursed the incompetent pilot for a whole string of failures, beginning with his not having the chopper fully fueled.

But there was no use berating the poor slug any further, he finally decided. With a little luck they would yet see the success of their mission. The traveling distance between Strangford and Portaferry by road was approximately seventy-five miles and would take about an hour and a half by car. The ferry, however, could make the trip, which was less than one nautical mile, in under ten minutes. He couldn't take the chance of exposing himself further by refueling and taking the chopper back up for pursuit.

Lorcan dialed Callahan and reported that his international sources had informed him that the Art of Death was now in the country and actively pursuing the professor and the American in the vicinity of Strangford Lough. What he didn't tell Callahan was that when the PSNI recovered the SUV from the shoreline, they would discover that it was registered to a businessmen from Turkey with ties to the Art of Death. It would all fit seamlessly with the narrative he was developing. The PSNI would detain his quarries on the other side of the lough at Portaferry, question them, and when they didn't find the Book of Kells on their persons, they would presumably release them. At that point, he would track them until he could finish what he had started.

WHEN IAN SWUNG THE TRUCK DOOR OPEN, HE FOUND SAORLA WITH HER eyes closed, mouthing words of a prayer. "Thank goodness," he said exhaling. She didn't move her head to look up at him, but kept on praying. Ian—speechless by the sight of her uttering muffled words into the airbag—stood frozen.

"I rise today through the strength of heaven . . . through God's strength to chauffeur me."

He finally touched her arm. "Hey, you all right?"

"God's shield to protect me," she prayed, ignoring him.

"Uh, he sent an airbag for a shield, and I was your chauffeur by the way."

Saorla cleared herself from the airbag, opened her eyes, and sniggered at him. "You were just a prop in God's hands. He's the one that got us out of that."

"Well, we're not out of the water yet; no pun intended."

A small crowd had gathered around them. Ian eased Saorla out of the truck. The few ferry passengers on the boat were now gawkers that clapped softly at the site of the attractive female passenger emerging unscathed from the wreckage.

Ian apologized to the group for disturbing their evening. A man yelled back that it wasn't everyday he got to watch *Fast and Furious* in real life, real time. Ian simply nodded, but momentarily entertained the thought of taking a bow for his successful landing. Instead, he quickly led Saorla to the back railing on the southwest side of the ferry. He was already thinking about what awaited them on the other side: it was either the authorities mustering to detain them because the ferry operator had called ahead or else the thugs would be there. Either way it was bad; they couldn't afford to lose the time in police detention, and they didn't have enough evidence yet of the minister of affairs' involvement to sound convincing.

Out in the distance where the lough met the opening to the Irish Sea, a small fishing boat cut through the channel in their direction. The sun was setting low in the sky to the right. There'd been a time change the weekend past, with the clocks turned backwards an hour, and nightfall was coming much earlier now. A cool breeze chilled the autumn air.

"Wait here," he said to Saorla.

He jogged to a storage cabinet marked, "Emergency" and took out two life jackets and a flare gun. When he returned to Saorla's side, he handed her a life jacket.

She was shaking her head. "No way."

"It's our only option."

"You ever heard of the Loch Ness Monster ?"

"You can't scare me with that. Besides, you have to pick your poison. The thugs have probably called ahead and more of them are likely waiting for us on the other—"

"You ever heard of hypothermia?"

"We've been there and done that. Besides we're close to civilization now, and a hot bath will be waiting at shore."

"This isn't Half Moon Bay where you can be saved by paramedics like you and Mr. Williams were."

"What do you know about that?"

Saorla frowned. "I looked you up and read about it. I hope that your surfing friend has forgiven you and—."

"When did you become the suspicious type?"

"When I saw you with that American beauty, of course. But you never answered my question. Did your surfing friend ever forgive you for almost killing him?"

"As a matter of fact, I think he would say it was the best thing that ever happened to him, but you'll have to ask him yourself someday when you come to California with me." Ian flashed a playful grin.

Saorla blushed and fell silent.

That's when they heard the distant thump, thump, thump coming over the horizon. "It's the chopper," he said loudly. "We don't have a choice."

They both put their lifejackets on. Ian hoisted himself up over the rail. Saorla followed suit. They stood on a narrow strip of decking with nothing between them and the water.

"We really are going to be fish food!" she said.

"Isn't there something in that 'Breastplate' prayer about not drowning?"

"Yeah, Christ protect me this day against poisoning and drowning and wounding."

"That should cover it. Pray. And jump!"

He took her hand, and they catapulted together into the chilly grey waters of Strangford Lough.

LORCAN CAREFULLY MONITORED THE POLICE COMMUNICATIONS FROM the helipad near Downpatrick. The PSNI had conducted a careful search of the skiff and from their interrogation of its passengers had concluded that the two curios had jumped ship in the middle of the dark waters of the lough. The sun had just set in the sky, and it would likely be impossible to find them now. Maybe they would turn up at shore, weak and hypothermic. More likely, though, they wouldn't survive the chilly waters.

But if they had survived, which side of the shore had they chosen? East or west? Strangford or Portaferry?

Lorcan left Kirby and a couple of men to hunt the Strangford side, and he sent the pilot Wilson to Portaferry, where Wilson observed a full-blown search being conducted by the PSNI at the shoreline.

An hour later, Lorcan called off his men when there was no sign of the two fugitives. The swimmers had either drowned or escaped, and only time would tell which of the two had occurred. If they had escaped, they would turn up soon. There wasn't much room to hide on the Emerald Isle.

As the dragnet was running its course, Lorcan's curiosity was suddenly piqued about something he now realized should have drawn more of his attention throughout the day: the Patrick Prophecy. He had to know that it would never be revealed. And he now wondered what the couple had found so interesting in the bookstore in Downpatrick. If he could determine where they would look next for the prophecy, he could be there waiting for them.

A few quick orders and twenty minutes later, Lorcan was on Market Street at the Bard's Wares bookstore. Closing time was six, and he'd just made it inside. An old, abysmally plain woman greeted him with a weak smile.

"I'm afraid we'll be closed soon," the old hag said.

"What I'm after won't take long."

"You know the title you're looking for?"

"No. But some friends of mine were here earlier. A couple about thirty. They were in a hurry. Perhaps they bought something—"

"I'm afraid I don't give out information that could compromise the privacy of our patrons."

Lorcan had had enough of the old wench. He would have loved to have just shot her on the spot, but of course that was not practical and he wouldn't get any information.

Instead Lorcan pulled back his overcoat to allow the woman to see the pistol tucked at his belt. "I'm SDU and working on a case that's taken me through the north today. Now, I don't need much, and I was hoping you would cooperate."

"Yes, of course," the old woman gushed. "I remember the couple well. Acting very odd indeed. Left in quite an anxious dither."

"Were they looking at anything in particular?"

"Oh yes, they most certainly were. They left in such a fluster they dropped a book on the floor. I had to bend over with my bad back—"

"Do you recall the title of that book?"

"It's so bad I can't straighten up anymore. Going on five years since—"

"Look, grandma. Do you remember which book?"

"Most certainly do. Nothing wrong with my memory. Just the

back, you know. My late husband used to take a little Jameson for his—."

"Enough," Lorcan said. His head ached. He fingered the pistol at his waist. "The book?"

"Had to restock it myself."

"Then ring it up. You've just made your last sale of the day."

"Yes, of course," she said, limping slowly away. "Aisle seven, book was called *Little Known Legends of Saint Patrick*."

"Excellent," Lorcan said. He would have some reading to do this evening. He wasn't looking forward to indulging himself in Christian myths, but he smelled an opportunity to finally get one step ahead of the game. The professor and the American had come to this bookstore and had looked at this particular book for a reason. And he was almost certain that reason had to do with the final location of the Patrician prophecy. And it would be just in time for tomorrow's Samhain celebration. He could feel it all wrapping up nicely. It was only fitting that his quarries should die on such a big day for him.

CHAPTER TWENTY-FOUR

The fishing boat was an older model twenty-foot trawler built for six with a small bridge house. Captain Finn Hooligan called her *Gaelic Dawn* and had a been commanding her out on the Irish Sea for more than thirty years now, managing to avoid both shipwreck and detection by law enforcement, despite his and the boat's sketchy past. His two grown sons, Kevin and Pete, were his regular crew, along with a deckhand named Danny. Mackerel, cod, pollock, salmon, and sea bass were the staples that kept their marginal business afloat.

During his long tenure on the seas, Captain Hooligan had witnessed a steady decline in the fish populations, except for the sea bass which had actually become more numerous. Strict quotas on catches had done nothing to reverse or even stabilize the problem. Scientists, predictably, were blaming the changes on global warming. Hooligan was a skeptic, but couldn't deny the impact on his bank account.

It was past twilight now, and Saorla and Ian owed their survival to Captain Hooligan. His sharp eyes had spotted them plunging into the water in the wake of the ferry as it glided its way toward Portaferry. Within minutes, the captain was in the vicinity to scoop them from the sea. With its newfound cargo safely on board, the ship quickly disappeared like a ghost into the cool darkness of the northern regions of Strangford Lough. It turned out the chopper Ian had heard in the distance was not the one that had been chasing them earlier. Rather, it was two choppers—one bearing a local television news logo and the other bearing the initialism PSNI.

Ian and Saorla crouched next to the captain in the bridge of the boat. The fishy scent of sea bass and cod on ice permeated the air.

Out of their wet clothes now—Saorla in a white bath robe and Ian wearing an oversized raincoat that reeked of fish—they were both still dripping salt water.

"Not that we're picky, but where are we headed?" Ian asked the captain. "And, I gotta say, you look familiar."

Finn Hooligan stroked his long grey-white goatee, which matched thick hair that feathered behind his shoulders to give him an eagle-like appearance. "Greyabbey," the captain replied. "It's a few miles up on the east tongue of the lough."

The captain was eyeing Ian suspiciously now like he was trying to place him. "Ian?" he finally asked. "Ian Shaw, grandson of George Shaw?"

"Yeah," Ian said, a light was switching on for him too. "You're my grandfather's friend, the fishing boat captain. You were out at the farm some weeks ago."

"Right. How's he doing?"

"Not good."

Captain Finn shook his head. "Sorry to hear that. You must have had a terrible fright or a fierce dose of stupidity to jump off that ferry."

"Definitely a case of fright," Saorla chimed in.

Ian nodded in agreement. "There are some awfully bad men after us."

The captain's face grew serious. He nodded toward his sons. "Boys, take the dog watch on deck. I need to confer alone with our guests."

After the boys left the bridge, Captain Hooligan turned to Ian.

"You must have something they want, or else you know secrets that they can't afford to have you know is my guess."

"Something like that," Ian admitted.

The captain reached over to an old wood cabinet on the wall. He took out a revolver and began loading it. He grabbed a few packages of ammunition.

He handed the gun and ammo to Ian. "Here. You can take this Webley Revolver. Standard issue in the UK until 1963. I used to run guns through these waters for the IRA. A man needs protection in times like these. But you've got to clean this gun before you use it or else it'll probably jam up. We can maybe clean it later tonight."

"I can handle it," Ian said.

Saorla's lips turned from red to white to blue, and her face lost what little color it had. "You were a weapons smuggler for the IRA?"

"Yeah, but if I were you I wouldn't tell anybody." The captain made his hand into a gun and pretended to fire a shot at Saorla. "Bang." He let out a loud guffaw.

Ian held the gun and ammunition at arm's length as if to give them back to the captain. "Sir, I don't think I could impose—"

"Take it, you're going to need a fighting chance, lad."

Saorla shook her head. "Not a good idea, Ian."

"It will have to do until a better one comes along," he said, as he nestled the weapon in his hand at his side.

"She's a bold one," the captain said to Ian, while pointing with his eyes at Saorla.

Saorla felt a hot flash of anger snake down her spine. "A gun smuggler? How much blood must be on your hands?"

The captain shrugged his shoulders. "Someone had to do it. Pay was good . . . while it lasted. Most all of the weapons were eventually turned over and decommissioned in 2005 when the IRA agreed to stop hostilities; adopt peace."

"If you were IRA, how'd you befriend a protestant like my grandfather?"

"That's a long story."

Saorla turned to Ian. "I don't have a good feeling about this."

"Another one of your premonitions?"

"No," Saorla admitted. "And I wouldn't call them premonitions. A premonition sounds, I don't know . . . untethered from God. It's God's spirit warning me when I get that unexplainable dread."

The captain's eyes narrowed. "I've had a few of those in my life. Kept me alive through some dangerous times."

Ian didn't seem to find the conversation about gun-running appalling. Another reason for her to tap the brakes at the possibility of a future relationship with him.

"So what was your most harrowing encounter?" Ian asked.

"There's been a few, but one stands out."

"More about guns, I bet," Saorla sniffed.

"Don't vex your noggin, missy. You and I will get on like a house on fire in no time if you just relax."

Saorla huffed.

"So you had one that stands out?" Ian pressed.

"Gloucester, thirty-five miles north of Boston, we loaded a shipment aboard the *Gaelic Dawn*. Twelve coffins, with real corpses, dead Irish expatriates who'd wanted to be buried in the soil of their ancestors. Only underneath the bodies was a five-ton arsenal. Bombs, machine guns, rifles, pistols, bullet-proof vests. One stop in Philadelphia for more explosives and grates of oranges. Another stop in the Mediterranean. The trip across the Atlantic was uneventful for the most part, but the closer I got to Ireland, the worse this feeling of disaster got. The weather went from bad to worse. A real lashing. Then I had the Irish navy wanting to board. I knew a mole had given us up. We made a run for it. The weather got so bad we nearly sunk her. But alas, we escaped. Lucky for the storm."

"How long ago was that?" Ian asked.

"Let's see." The captain started counting with his fingers. "More than eighteen years ago," he finally said. "That was one of the worst storms ever. But couldn't hold a candle to the one we just had, I'm told. Happy to say we missed it. Me and my boys were on an extended voyage to the south, thank goodness. Brought in a great batch of swordfish and tuna off the coast of Andalucía. Got some cod and sea bass on the way back. Missed the winds, just a good lashing that's all."

"Ever have any regrets?" Ian asked.

"About missing the big storm?"

"No, I mean about your life in general and gunrunning in particular."

The captain hung his head for the first time. Tears welled in the corner of his eyes. "Yeah. Remembering back, I can see that not much was accomplished. I look at my boys now, and I realize some fathers are not so fortunate. Maybe my actions . . ."

"Did you ever ask for forgiveness?" Ian asked.

"Aw, that's not an option for me."

"Why not? Christ forgave the Apostle Paul, who murdered Christians."

"That's what I got the regret over. Likely some died by the guns and bombs I brought in."

For the next twenty minutes, Saorla watched in rapt fascination as Ian and the captain discussed God's forgiveness and mercy. Suddenly, the trawler came in to dock. They'd made it to Greyabbey, no doubt.

As Captain Finn's sons busied themselves with the haul of fish, Ian and the captain bowed their heads and prayed. Saorla was now ashamed over her earlier thoughts about Ian. Why was her opinion about him oscillating so wildly? She realized it all started with Claire's visit to her office that had laid the seeds of suspicion. The same Claire that had been pumping her for information about her work with Ian. Was the woman somehow involved in the opposition Saorla was facing?

THE CAPTAIN'S THREE-BEDROOM COTTAGE SAT ON A HILL ABOUT A hundred yards up from the dock. The sons had their own homes and families but had sent word ahead that they'd had a lucrative haul that demanded a celebration commensurate with their catch. The captain's oldest son, Kevin, explained to Saorla that they'd make a half year's wages on this one outing. Thus, the whole extended family was gathered at the cottage for the party. The job of attending to the fish and making haste with them to market fell to the captain's youngest son, Pete. He'd return in a couple hours to join the festivities.

Strains of guitar music wafted from the direction of the cottage toward the dock. The party was already underway it seemed. Captain Finn invited Ian and Saorla to spend the night and help celebrate the good fortune. They eagerly accepted, having run out of other options a long time ago.

An hour later, with their clothes washed and dried, they found themselves in the family room of the cottage listening to folk music. The captain's descendants, including his grandchildren and his daughters-in-law, were more than adequate musicians. All of them could play something—flutes, violins, guitars, and kettle drums were passed around with each new song. As Saorla watched Ian singing along to the familiar songs that were her heritage, she couldn't help but think what a surprising, and dare she say, uniquely complicated and special person, Ian Shaw had shown himself to be.

She considered her recent treatment of him and feared that he would soon want nothing to do with her, if he hadn't already come to that conclusion. She didn't deserve a guy like Ian, as she hadn't deserved a guy like Stuart. The least she could do was help him to help his grandfather. Ian had checked in with Aryana, and the report was not good. George's vitals had taken a turn for the worse. He hadn't been conscious since they'd last spoken to him over twelve hours ago. For George's sake, Saorla would screw her head on straight and keep her focus on the main goal—the Patrick prophecy.

Later that night after the violins and flutes fell silent and were tucked away, Saorla discussed strategy with Ian alone in the family room of the cottage. "Tell me you remember the book in furrow seven," he said.

"Yes, right, the book plucked from row seven."

"You remember, good."

"Have I let you down yet?"

"Can I exercise my right to silence?"

"Not unless you want a punch in the arm."

He grinned. "I'll take the punch."

Saorla flashed a smile. "You're insufferable. The bottom line is the book speaks about the hidden prophecy from Patrick that we've been on the trail of all along."

"Sure sounds like this is it."

"It could be," Saorla agreed.

"So where do we go?"

"The Hill of Tara."

"You're kidding, right? We were just there."

"I know, but now I think we have the leading we were looking for."

"And that would be what exactly?"

"Go to the high point of the hill at sunset on the Eve of All Hallows and—"

"Huh?"

"That's tomorrow on 'All Hallows Eve,' as it says in the book, or as we call it now Hallo-ween."

"Gotcha. I remember your tutorial about All Saints Day and Samhain."

"Good. So tomorrow we queue up on the top of the hill, find the sunset, and pace off one hundred steps of a 'long man,' as it says in the book, all in the opposite direction of the disappearing sun, and *voilà*, we have our spot, where the prophecy is promised to be buried."

Ian sighed. "Can this really be it?"

"It better be for the sake of your grandfather."

"What about Lorcan Duihbur and his thugs?" Ian asked.

"They'll have no idea where to find us now. Once we find the prophecy, we can come out with everything, including the Book of Kells. Share everything we've found with the authorities, and tell them what we heard in the cave about Lorcan. People will have to believe us then. It will all be so overwhelming."

A noise suddenly came from the hallway around the corner. It sounded like a cup dropping. "Is someone there," Ian asked as he leapt to see.

It was Captain Finn. "I'm afraid I'm not above eavesdropping in my own home."

"Why?" Saorla gasped. "How much did you hear?"

"I'm acquainted with this Lorcan. I mean, I really know him, in a manner the public doesn't. I ran some guns his way about twelve years ago. I know a killer when I see one, and his associate too, a man with a scar. You're going to need my help."

CHAPTER TWENTY-FIVE

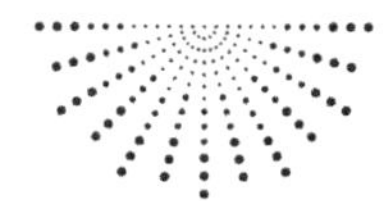

Halloween was a day best spent in prayer, as it was more prone to being seized by the powers of darkness than most days. Killian wasn't going to let that happen on his watch. Awake and out of bed before six, he listened in his den for the still small voice or for the thunder. However his Lord chose to speak was fine with him. Hearing nothing, he opened a Bible and read from the Book of Daniel about the prophet's counsel to King Nebuchadnezzar. Killian admired the ancient prophet like a twelve-year-old Dubliner might admire a star player on the national rugby team.

A couple of hours passed in prayer, but the heavens seemed like brass. A call on his mobile interrupted. It was the secretary at the Taoiseach's office. From what Killian could gather, the prime minister wanted to set up a special interview with him. He was being considered for some sort of position as an unofficial advisor and spiritual confidant to Mr. Braden.

He thought about his reading from Daniel, and the counsel the prophet had given to the king. Was God giving him a chance to have real influence on the government? There was simply no adventure on earth that could compare with walking with God and being led by him.

A few hours later, Killian was ushered into the prime minister's office. He quickly relaxed as he shook Mr. Braden's hand. The Taoiseach displayed a warm smile, and the two settled into a comfortable conversation that belied the relatively recent acquaintance. Theirs was quickly becoming a relationship more reminiscent of old friends. They covered a wide range of topics that included the Mediterranean bailouts, the coalition aligned against Israel, and Mr. Braden's reelection prospects.

Finally, the prime minister brought up the missing Book of Kells and the deleterious effect it was having upon his poll numbers. The public was antsy for some progress in the investigation. The book simply had to be recovered. Killian saw his opportunity.

"What if I told you I could get it back?" he said matter-of-factly.

"I'd say you were a miracle worker," the prime minister laughed.

"I'm being serious," he said, locking eyes with the most powerful man in Ireland.

"Wonderful, who has it?" Mr. Braden's tone was almost mocking.

"What if I told you it was me?"

Mr. Braden chuckled. "I'd probably have you arrested for high treason and robbery. Send you to the gallows."

"Capital punishment has been abolished."

"I'd make an exception."

"Bring back the old ways, eh?"

"Joking aside. The theft of that great book is one of the most serious crimes that has ever been committed against the nation. The public would demand fierce retribution for the guilty. I have no doubt about that."

Killian's smile faded, and his brow furrowed. A bead of sweat formed at his forehead. "What would you think if I said it's Sophie who had it, and there is a very innocent, logical explanation?"

"Impossible."

"But, if it was found, and there was no harm to it, it would help you politically, no?"

"Yes."

"So what if you guaranteed a pardon to any and all who were

responsible for the book going missing if they returned it by a certain deadline? What if you got the offer out there for the next news cycle?"

"You can't be serious."

"Look, you can set a deadline for its return. Imagine the electricity it will create. The press will lampoon you . . . for a short while. As the hours go by, your offer will look crazy. People will have another chance to be reminded what a national treasure the book is. You'll become a pathetic, but no less sympathetic a figure, who is just trying to do something. Until—"

"Until nothing happens, and I get impeached."

Killian shook his head fervently. "No, the book *will be* returned. Then, you are suddenly a genius."

"And you can guarantee the return of the book?" Mr. Braden smirked.

"Yes."

"Even if you could, it would be a big risk. I'm not sure I can use the political capital on that right now."

"But if it worked. It would be worth it, no? If the book comes back unharmed and the perps are pardoned, you haven't lost anything. And you'll get a big return on that investment of political capital."

"True. But there's not the slimmest chance—"

"Look, I can guarantee it. Trust me. The book is going to be returned. The only question is whether you will share in the credit for its return."

"I need to have more to go on."

"All right, what if I told you that I know the professor at the university who took it? Quite innocently just to have a look at it. Was unexpectedly prevented by alarms from getting it back and has, all this time, been looking for the opportunity to set things right."

"Pure fantasy. But tell me more."

"The professor was on to something so important that it was worth the risk to get the book out for a look."

"Like what?"

"Something so astounding I know you won't believe it."

"Try me."

"There's a secret prophecy for Ireland that will change the nation forever. That's what the professor is after."

"Now you're telling me the book of Kells has a prophecy in it that nobody has ever noticed before?"

"No. There was a clue hidden within the Book of Kells that leads to another clue that—"

"You expect me to believe—"

"I can also tell you that there are some very bad people on the professor's trail, from the National Museum and one from your own administration. They certainly believe it. The bombing on the Quay was proof of that."

Mr. Braden was nodding his head now. "I know about the bombing, and the suspicion centered on the professor."

"The Gardai are going down the wrong road on this, I can tell you that much. Look, why would the professor have a bomb detonated that injures her own grad assistant in a car she too was about to get into?"

"The SDU tells me that there is a string of suspicious activity circling the professor."

"I can tell you who is at the bottom of this, and it's not the professor."

"Who then?"

"It's Lorcan Duihbur and his men from the museum. They are after a big payday on the black market. There needs to be a new direction in the investigation. The book needs protection. And so does the professor and her friends."

The Taoiseach was silent for a long moment. Killian could see that he was losing him. "I'm sorry. I just need more information to go on and that's my—"

"Look," Killian cut in, realizing he would have to take a risk now. "I have a way to verify that what I'm saying is the honest to goodness truth."

The Taoiseach checked his watch. Killian was definitely losing him.

"Go ahead. I'm listening, but you'll have to make it quick. I've another appointment."

Killian cleared his throat. "I have GPS coordinates of a cave on the southwest coast. If you send men out today to take a look, they will find a treasure. It's beyond shocking, I'm told. When they find it, everything I'm saying will be confirmed. And you should have no trouble taking action. You could even get a secret, shadow investigation rolling of Mr. Lorcan Duihbur."

"Why not bring the book in now, if you have it?"

"It all needs to be presented together for our story to make sense. We shall, perhaps, have the last piece of the puzzle very soon."

The prime minister walked to a window to look out at the greens of Phoenix Park. A minute passed before he turned to face Killian. "Give me a list of those that need to be pardoned."

"You got it."

"I'll think it over," the prime minister said while rubbing his chin. "I could have men out to the cave in an hour. If it checks out and if I do decide to go with it, I could get the offer of a pardon out in the news cycle this afternoon. It would drive the press crazy."

Killian grinned. "Probably be a feeding frenzy like we've never seen."

"What do I have to lose? I stand for reelection in less than half a year, and I'm suddenly unpopular in the polls. It's past time to shake things up."

LORCAN HAD ALREADY GIVEN ORDERS TO BRING THE POLISH GIRL INTO captivity by late afternoon. He'd had her phones wiretapped and her apartment bugged yesterday in order to keep an eye on her.

Sophie Zaworksi is going to be the perfect sacrifice for the Goddess, he was thinking, when his cell phone rang.

It was one of his contacts at the museum. From their monitoring of the activities at the prime minister's office, they now had some news to leak to Lorcan. The prime minister had met with a man named Killian Murchu, a businessman and lay church leader, who'd told the prime minister that he had in his possession the Book of Kells. The other piece of news to report was that their subsequent surveillance of Murchu revealed that he was picking up Zaworski at her apartment later in the day to take her to the Hill of Tara to meet the professor and the American there.

Excellent. They would all come to him.

Lorcan now changed his orders to allow Murchu to bring in the sacrifice. There would be plenty of opportunity in the hours ahead to ask the man about the Book of Kells before they killed him.

"YOU CAN TELL ME EVERYTHING YOU KNOW, OR YOU CAN SPEND THE night in a jail cell," Superintendent Callahan said simply. "The choice is yours."

"Even if I knew something, your threats wouldn't scare me," the young grad assistant said.

"You might feel differently after you see your cellmates. I can assure you a parade of horribles."

Callahan had brought in Myrna Cahdan for questioning out of desperation. His investigation had gone cold. He had to warm and stir the pot.

"Stop playing around. You know something, and it's time I break this case."

"I have rights." She looked as if she would spit in his face if he ventured any closer to her. She sat handcuffed in a chair across the table from him. They were at a covert building the SDU sometimes used just a few blocks off from their main Harcourt Street location.

"Save it for a judge," Callahan said.

"You're some kind of a fascist—"

"Look, missy. I know you like to talk. And you're going to start singing like a lark."

"I'm no songbird. But if I was, I'd be a crow, and that's just what you'll be eatin' if you continue to violate my rights."

"Calm down, little sister. I want to turn a deal with you."

The girl flipped to silent mode, her face impassive.

"I know what you want," Callahan said, more softly this time. "You have applications out there to Berkeley and Stanford. You have goals and dreams, right? You want to go places."

"You've been violating my priv—"

"Am I right about your plans?"

She just stared at him.

"It would be a shame if those dreams got messed up over trouble with the law. I can make that go away in exchange for a little information. I might even be able to arrange some financial help to get you out to the Golden State as part of our witness protection program."

She had a look of utter disgust. "You're asking me to make a deal with *you?*"

"An extra ten grand a year in your pocket and an alias to get you started out on the Pacific Coast."

"A deal?"

"Sure. Why not? I'm not a bad guy. Just trying to solve cases and bring—"

"You can shove that deal up—"

The woman's words were interrupted by the ding of a cell phone that sat atop the table. Callahan had had it removed from the interrogee's coat before the start of the questioning. He picked it up now over the young woman's protestations and looked at the message.

"What do we have here? From Saorla O'Rourke: *Myrna, please meet us at the Hill of Tara at sunset; we will put together the final piece of the puzzle there.*"

Callahan felt a rush of cool relief. This was the break he was looking for.

There was a quick knock at the door a second before it opened. Jumbo stuck his head around the corner. "You won't believe this."

He'd told him no interruptions. "What is it?"

Jumbo beckoned Callahan to the doorway. "The Taoiseach has offered a full pardon from prosecution for anyone connected to the Book of Kells caper if the book is voluntarily returned in the next seventy-two hours. And rumor has it the book may very well be returned."

Callahan reeled as if he'd been kicked in the chest. Time would be of the essence now if he was going to receive full credit for solving the case.

"You and I leave for the Hill of Tara within the hour," Callahan barked to Jumbo. He turned and glowered at Myrna. "Have the boys take Ms. Cahdan to the station. We'll hold her till she decides she has a melody for me."

CHAPTER TWENTY-SIX

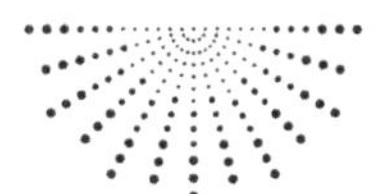

With binoculars in hand, Lorcan stood in a small clump of trees on a lesser hill about a mile from Tara. He'd been lying in wait since four in the afternoon with Claire and Torna at his side. The mice were about to come to the cat. The high Hill of Tara was the bait.

Lorcan had tasked Kirby with the important mission of tracking Killian Murchu and making sure the lovely sacrifice arrived from Dublin. Tonight was the night it would all come together; the night Lorcan would eliminate those that could unmask him. But he wouldn't just kill them, he would sacrifice them all to the Goddess. A fragrant offering to the resplendent Queen Maeve. Abundant provision would be the overflow of her pleasure toward him.

The crux of the matter was that the professor and the American would be dead. The threat they represented would be over. But not until he let them uncover one final artifact—the great Patrician Prophecy, inspired words from the one the people referred to as Patrick, the Patron Saint. It was not something he would ever attempt to convey on the black market. No, he would destroy it. Nobody would ever see a single sentence. And he would use some of his great fortune to see to it that Patrick's legacy was recast to the point where he would be known henceforth as Patrick, the Patron Con Artist.

Little else hardly mattered now, he knew, other than the final blessing. Now that he had the GPS coordinates to the treasure he would be rich and irrepressible. His men had assured him there was more wealth in that cave than he could ever spend.

So there was just this one last important detail to attend to: gain the imprimatur of the High Queen and release her favor. He had the fires ready. The evening was young. A new course would be forged.

THE BURNING CARNELIAN SUN SINKING BELOW THE SCATTERED CLOUDS to the southwest turned the sky lavender just above the dark verdant mounds of green in the distance. Ian peered out in rapt attention from his position on the Hill of Tara with Saorla and Sophie at his side. He had shovel in hand. The Webley Revolver gifted to him by Captain Finn was wedged at his waistline under his coat. It had taken a lot of persuasion to convince Captain Finn that Ian had everything under control and didn't need help.

Ian and Saorla had borrowed an old, rusty van from Captain Finn, who'd called the rig a "people carrier," before saying his good-byes and telling them he was in no hurry to have the van back. After leaving Finn, they'd driven it to a roadside cafe near the tiny hamlet of Skryne where they'd arranged to meet Sophie and Killian. Killian had driven Sophie up from Dublin, but had remained behind at the cafe, insisting he needed to pray. Ian wasn't about to argue. He'd been knocking his head against an invisible ceiling all week. He knew he was close to something he couldn't explain. An ancient message from Saint Patrick? Hope for the future? A last consolation for his grandfather? He wasn't sure exactly. But he realized he needed all the spiritual help he could get and that included Killian's prayers.

The more he thought about what he was about to do, the more stoked he became. He sensed he was about to catch the fiercest wave of his life, bigger and tougher than the monster he'd hooked into at Mavs that had nearly killed him and Shark.

Was he finally about to get some resolution for his grandfather? He prayed it wouldn't be too late. Even if Ian uncovered something so epic that it stunned the world, it would be a hollow victory indeed if Papa wasn't alive to experience it.

So Ian watched and waited with his new friends for the exact moment the sun would touch the horizon. They waited to both uncover and make history. When the positioning was right, Ian would trudge along, marking off one hundred paces in the exact opposite direction of the solar contact point. Hopefully then, he would be standing over the spot that promised a wisp from the past that would connect the present with a fusion powerful enough to mold the future.

"Is very beautiful, don't you think?" Sophie asked Saorla, as she peered out at the sinking sun.

"Sure is."

"This land has become home," Sophie said, the tears forming in her eyes. "I have much love."

"You came, but so many have left," Saorla said.

Ian realized she was referring to the mass emigrations from Ireland through the centuries, including the one sparked by the great potato famine of the 1840s. There was also the present day trends that saw numbers of young people exiting the country because of poor job prospects and the high cost of housing.

"True, but I have hope," Sophie said slowly.

Saorla's face seemed to suddenly fill with a rush of optimism. "I know the future will be bright because you're here," she said, her tone full of nothing but warm love.

"I hate to interrupt the admiration fest," Ian said, "but it's time for the *dusk* patrol."

The sun was just about to clip the horizon. They quickly agreed that Saorla would maintain her position at the top of the hill while Sophie ran down to position herself at the bottom in a spot that looked to be in line with Saorla and the sun.

When everyone was in place a dozen seconds later, Ian began pacing off his steps. Every ten paces or so he checked to see if the girls were motioning to correct his position. After a few course corrections and Ian having covered about ninety paces, he stepped over a clump of stones about three feet high that appeared to be the remnants of an old wall.

Ian completed his steps and looked back up the hill to Saorla. His eagle eyes could see she was holding both palms out toward him, as if to say no corrections were necessary. She then flashed the thumbs up sign and bounded down the hill.

He let out a sigh of relief when he realized he was a few feet shy of the church's western exterior. Somehow he'd expected to have to enter the church, which in recent years had been converted to a visitor center run by the government. The prospect of having to break into publicly owned property gave him the shivers. He simply didn't have the stomach for another dubious nighttime raid.

He already had his shovel moving and was yanking dirt from the X-spot with Sophie looking on when Saorla joined the two of them. "At least we don't have to break in," she said. "I guess the mission doesn't call for Ireland's most infamous cat burglars to come out of retirement."

Ian looked up. "You're a woman of many talents," he said, smiling, before swinging away another shovel load.

Saorla set up a battery-operated lantern. It was still too early to know how much light it would put off. "I'll take over if you need me to," Saorla said, "but I'm not sure you get fatigued unless you've been shot or nearly drowned."

Ian grinned and kept shoveling. An hour later, he'd hallowed out a good three feet of dirt from a ten-foot radius, and decided to take a short break. When he resumed, the very next jab of the iron shovel sounded out a promising clank.

"Hit something solid?" Saorla asked, stating the obvious.

She focused light from her flashlight on the broken earth. The lantern didn't offer much illumination after all. Ian probed with the shovel and then began scraping dirt with his hands from the hard surface he'd struck. The object was a hexagonal pattern about three and half feet in diameter.

"The shape is odd," Saorla said. "Almost like one of those creations from the Giant's Causeway."

"Yeah right, you told me that Finn McCool character from your legends was responsible for those. Maybe he put this here too."

"It's not Mr. McCool whose been communicating with us," Saorla corrected. "I have my heart set on hearing from Patrick."

Ian continued to dig around the sides with the shovel. The object appeared to be some sort of stone container that was tubular in shape.

As he continued to dig, he noticed two things. First, Saorla had grown extremely quiet. Second, the object appeared to have a cover at the top like a giant, stone bottle cap that was perhaps two inches thick.

"Are you all right?" Ian finally asked.

She didn't say anything.

"I said are you all right, Seer?" This time his voice was louder.

"Not sure," came the tepid response.

Ian dropped the shovel and stared over at her. Her face had turned a shade paler. Otherwise she looked near normal.

"What is it?"

"It's probably going to be fine."

What did she mean by *probably*? Was this another episode of her dead-on discernment triggering? He was so close to finding something. This couldn't be happening again, could it?

"It's a container down there, and I think it has a lid on it," he said.

Saorla was quiet again.

"I'm going to see if I can pull it off," he said.

He bent down and heaved at the stone lid, which perfectly sealed the hexagonal tube upon which it laid. It was heavy, but it moved, a little.

He would have to use more muscle. In one great heave, he dislodged it from its seal and lifted it so that it perched askew atop the tube.

Ian was about to ask for the flashlight, when Saorla said, "I think we should go now."

"You're kidding, right?" he asked, even though he knew she wasn't.

"I'm dying to know what's in there," she said. "I don't want to leave, but the feeling's back."

Her face was ashen.

"Are you sure?"

She started to shake now. "It's unmistakable."

KILLIAN SAT ALONE AT A TABLE IN A ROADSIDE CAFE THAT WAS EMPTY but for the young female employee cleaning up behind the counter. There had been only one other customer in the last hour. A thick man with an ugly scar on his forehead—or maybe it was a tattoo, Killian wasn't exactly sure—had ordered an espresso to go. The man spoke in a low voice and had his back turned to Killian most of the time. After the man left, it seemed harder to pray.

Killian sipped a black coffee and alternated between prayer and entertaining the cacophony of thoughts that swarmed his head. The plan he'd pitched to the prime minister was proceeding on course. Shortly after the Taoiseach had made his announcement about the potential pardons, Killian had managed a phone meeting. He'd agreed to turn over the Book of Kells within the next twenty-four hours with a list of names to be included for exoneration and full pardon.

The Book of Kells, for now, sat an arms-length in a locked brief case at his table. They would need to have everything ready tonight and then go directly to the prime minister with it. He was all agog to see what his three friends would find after sunset. He was convinced they were on the verge of discovering something that would make the Book of Kells seem like a garage-sale item in comparison.

He stood in amazement at the professor's knowledge of history and the American's resourcefulness. They had done extraordinary work in piecing together the puzzle so far. Later tonight, he would laugh with satisfaction as he watched the look of fascination on Mr.

Braden's face as Killian personally presented the man with not only the recovered booty of Ireland's greatest national treasure, but also with a new discovery that would utterly supplant that treasured book in Irish hearts.

Even though the general plan for the return of the book was proceeding as well as he could have hoped, it was the present moment that was shrouded in mystery. He couldn't get a bearing on what was happening. Normally, he could see right through things. But, at this moment, he wasn't sure how to pray for the expedition that was still underway at the Hill of Tara.

Then there was Sophie. His feelings for her had become so strong in recent weeks he felt like a love-struck adolescent from one of Shakespeare's sonnets. He was in love; there was no question about that.

Killian took another sip of coffee. It was no use praying. He felt no connection, and the heavens were still as brass as they'd been when he started his prayer in the morning. He thought about getting a refill, but the clerk at the counter was gone. The store was strangely empty.

Or was it?

He thought he heard something in the back. But maybe not.

A wave of uneasiness came over him so strong that he felt compelled to answer it. Maybe the girl had an emergency and had to leave without locking up. "Hello? Might I get some buns?" Killian asked aloud, although he was almost certain that nobody but himself had heard his words. There was certainly no reply.

Ah well, it was getting late anyway. They would probably close within the hour. He would go to Tara and join his friends, he decided. He was of no use here. His praying was ineffectual. Too much distraction in the air.

And then there was the briefcase and its precious contents. Perhaps it wasn't such a good idea to be alone with it. Although they did need it with them tonight when they took everything to the prime minister.

He rose from the table, clutched the briefcase tight in his hand, and carried it toward the door of the cafe, snug to his body. Still no sign of the lone employee. The lights were off in the back.

He exited the door. No other cars in the lot but his.

Nearly at his car, he saw the club at his periphery. Hurling toward his head.

Have to duck. Get a hand up. Block the . . .

But the synapses firing signals from his brain to his muscles weren't fast enough.

A loud crack to his cranium stunned him beyond pain.

His world was going grey as he fell toward the yellow line marking the parameter of a parking space on the black pavement. His eyes were almost unseeing, but he registered a face.

The scar.

His fingers slackened, then went limp, and the briefcase slipped from his hands.

He barely felt the asphalt as his shoulder hit with a thud. The last thing he heard before he lost consciousness was a thick voice. "Thank you Mr. Murchu, I shall see that the book meets its rightful end."

As he watched Murchu fade to unconsciousness, Kirby picked up the briefcase and then rifled through the man's pockets to find the key. When he finally opened it, he saw what he was looking for. He took the Book of Kells in one arm and reached for his handgun with the other.

He had the gun pointed to Murchu's head, when a car's headlights suddenly illuminated the parking lot. Kirby slipped into the shadows and made his way back to his vehicle. Another car came into the parking lot. Kirby decided to leave with the book and take it to Lorcan, who'd no doubt say, "Excellent" when he finally grasped it in his hands. No need to further attend to the bloody mess on the pavement; the man would probably die from the blow he'd delivered anyway.

CHAPTER TWENTY-SEVEN

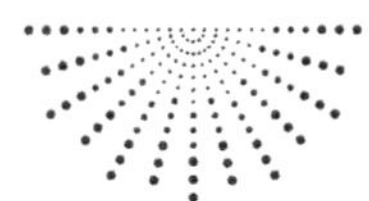

MARCH 17, 572 A.D

Patricius opened his eyes and stared at the thatched ceiling of his beehive hut. The Spirit, still ardent within him, had told him that today would be his last day on earth. His journey nearly finished, he called for his disciple. "Aban, come devout servant of God."

Aban, a slender man from years of fasting and prayers, was keeping vigil outside the hut. At his teacher's command, he entered with an uncertain smile. "Bishop, I am glad to see you. I thought perhaps—"

"Your thoughts are correct, my dear brother," Patricius tenderly interrupted, knowing the importance of the hour. "My time is short. I shall not be of this earth to make the evening vespers. The Spirit within me has shown that the prophecies and the visions I have faithfully recorded must now be preserved. They are to be entrusted to faithful men and then hidden and preserved for many generations in the future. For the last day people of our beloved land."

Patricius handed Aban a manuscript with a list of instructions. The bishop's eyesight had grown so weak in recent days he could barely write, and he could only read the largest of texts with difficulty. "I have written for you all that you must soon do, and I have earnestly beseeched my Lord that His hand would be with you, my dear brother, in all you undertake." His voice was strong, but his pale and wrinkled flesh was weak. He had come to the end of his days.

"This manuscript must eventually be buried in the earth for many generations," he continued, "and our eyes will be the last ones to see it for many days. We must never forget that with the Lord a day is as a thousand years and a thousand years is as a day. The years of many generations are like yesterday when it passes by. The grass withers, the flowers fade, but the Word of God shall stand forever."

"I want to be sad," Aban replied, "but I can only find joy in knowing that your course is finished, your work well pleasing to our Lord, and with a legacy left not only for the many thousands that have been baptized in your days, but also for a people yet to be created."

"You are most gracious. Know that you are much loved. I will lay hands on you before I depart. To pass on the gift of God within me. But first we must share in one last consolation: the priceless prophecy that I believe He has so graciously given for our latter day people. Would you be so kind as to read it aloud so we can share this together?"

"With great pleasure, Bishop."

Aban spread out the deer vellum script in his hands and began reading:

Here begins the last day oracle for the people of Eire. If you are reading these words, the time is now, the words of this prophecy will shortly come to pass, and all will be changed in an instant. The hope in these words must be shared with all of the people from the highest to lowest.

I, Patricius, am writing to you as the servant of the Lord. The servant of the same God and Lord who often warned me in advance of danger. As God is my everlasting witness, I have been rescued from death no less than a dozen times. And the many times I have been in great dangers are too many to number. One thing I can confidently say is that God knows all things before they happen and will share them with his friends.

I heard the Voice of the Irish calling me from many centuries in the future: "Describe for us the insights of God and give us wisdom and hope for the future!" And then I saw a strong angel with a giant scroll which he unfolded before me. I wrote down the words of the scroll and after that I had many visions of things to come so marvelous that my mind could hardly comprehend. I saw a time when travel and communication were greatly increased. A time of unimaginable advancement. But a time and people in desperate need of the holy word of God.

I saw, as it were, a famine in the earth for the words of the Lord. People starving for a morsel from heaven. And then I saw the people reading the prophecies of my manuscript. And they were fed, and they began to have an appetite for the Holy Scriptures passed down from the fathers, prophets, apostles, scribes and saints.

That you might know that the words of this prophecy are true, I tell you in advance that it will be discovered and brought to the people just before a great earthquake occurs in the land of Eire. It will shake the land from one end to the other. There will be no loss of life, however, because the people will take precaution. It will occur precisely at the sunset on the day the words of this prophecy are announced to all the people of the land. And the people will know to take precautions to save themselves. It will also coincide with the discovery of a great treasure that has been stored up for the people of the land to give them provision and a release of all debt and a storehouse for the future that the people might forge their way into the purpose of God for them in the last days.

When the earthquake occurs, all the people will know and fear. The righteous will experience joy, and the unrighteous terror. The terror of the Lord will grip the land, and all the people will mourn for their savior as a mother weeps for an only son who is slain. And it will come to pass that a nation will be born in a day.

Just as I was captured and placed into slavery just shy of my sixteenth birthday, the people of this time will be wicked and foolish. They will deserve slavery, and the yoke will be tightening around their necks. Pressures from within and constraints from without. There will be no human remedy for the problems this generation will be facing when my words are read. They will have gone through many centuries of chastening. The Most High says, "Oh you, whose land lay in the heart of the seas, I have gathered gold and silver into your treasuries, but you were not able to see it. Instead I brought foreigners upon you, the most ruthless of peoples, and they unsheathed their swords against you and took down the beauty of your splendor and carried off the luxuriance of your wealth."

But when the last day people of the land read my words, the Spirit himself will plead with their hearts: "Be reconciled to God! Come back to the Father that loves you." And they will hear the Spirit, and they will come with great rending of their hearts. And the earthquake will shatter all resistance as it is seen as a Voice from Heaven.

But the picture will be different in much of the world. Great darkness will cover the people and gross sin will cover much of the earth. False justice will grip many nations to their everlasting ruin in the Day of Doom.

And when the repentance is complete in Eire, a great rejoicing will come. There will be much joy in the cities and in the countryside. Dancing and laughing and people extending brotherly kindnesses. A new dawn of love will descend, and it will be the first fruits of a thousand years of light that will welcome the King to his throne in Jerusalem. And a great treaty of friendship will be forged between some of the people of Eire and the descendants of Abraham. But for the nations that know not the Lord, the robe will drip with blood and will be measured to the horses bridle.

There will come a time, as it will be in Israel, when it will no longer be necessary to say in the land of Eire, "Know the Lord?" I believe that a great multitude will come to know him here, from the little child to the oldest grandmother breathing her last breath. And it will come to pass that all this will be set in motion when the earth quakes. It will come at the setting sun on the Holy Day of the Church to honor all the Saints in Heaven—it will come in the evening following the very morning when the words of this prophecy are first read to all the people by the high king of the land. And it will come at the sunset. A sign that this word is true will be an incident from the gospel of John: the Nobleman whose son lay sick. The man went to Jesus, walking over 20 miles uphill from Capernaum to Cana to beg Jesus to heal his son who was close to death. I Patricius, my name means 'nobleman,' am that nobleman for the purpose of this prophecy. My beloved son? The nation of Eire is my son, and he lays sick far in the future. I have begged Jesus to come and heal him. And he has told me healing will come with the earthquake, at the setting of the sun. And then will be the time for the fulfillment of this prophecy. The scripture that will confirm my word and correspond with the setting of the sun and the quaking of the land in that day and hour will be this from the book of John: "So the nobleman knew that it was at that same hour, in which Jesus said unto him, 'Your son will live,' that he believed and his whole house." I tell you the time will come when the sun sets and the earth quakes on the Day of the Saints.

CHAPTER TWENTY-EIGHT

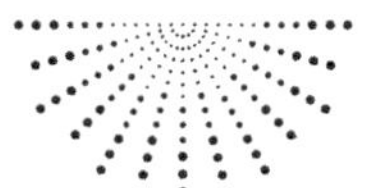

Saorla had the manuscript in hand, her heart pounding. Pulled in two directions. A terrible dread told her to run for her life, but the scholar in her head told her she was breathing in the rarified air of one standing in the presence of the greatest find in the history of archaeology, and how could she not stop for a moment of reverent awe. The scholar in her head became a little tyrant and won the battle . . . for the moment.

"Is it what we thought it would be?" Ian asked.

Saorla nodded in perplexed silence as she continued to read.

"Has to be from Patrick," she finally said with less emotion than she felt. The truth was that the writing had so staggered her that she was on the verge of fainting. Nothing in the history of the world could compare with what she'd just dissected. "The Latin is old," she finally managed to say. "The Scripture references aren't from the Vulgate or the common language version of Jerome, which would have been in use for many centuries after Patrick. Instead the text is Old Latin. The Latin Patrick would have used."

"But what does it say?"

"That everything is going to change." The dread was back, telling the tyrant scholar where to shove it. *Flee now!* it demanded.

"Huh?" Ian asked.

"Tomorrow. It all starts on the morrow—"

"What starts?"

"At sunset."

"Again, what starts?"

She knew she should bolt. Just begin running somewhere, anywhere, with the prophecy and hope to Heaven Ian and Sophie could catch up. Instead, she found herself replying, "The turning—"

Her words were interrupted by a rushing in the darkness to her right. A flash of metal in the weak spray of light from her lantern. "Stop right there!" a man from the shadows commanded.

There were at least four of them. Armed with assault rifles and pistols, they formed a semi-circle around her and the mound of dirt that Ian had displaced from the ground. The weapons were trained and ready to fire.

Saorla glanced at Ian. He was slowly moving his hand toward his waistband. *No!* She wanted to cry it out, but nothing came from her lips.

Please, Ian, don't try anything silly.

Why did the foolish Captain Hooligan have to give him a gun in the first place?

"Hands over your heads, please," a tall dark man stepped from the shadows pointing a revolver. "Allow me to introduce myself, my name is Lorcan Duibur—"

"I know who you are. What are you doing scaring us like this?" Saorla asked, even though she'd already put it all together.

She had never met Duibhur, but she'd viewed him on television newscasts over the years and then in the helicopter. She now stood face to face with the man who had been watching her, tailing her every move, trying to kill her. This could only end one way. Death was on the table.

Unless . . . prayer. She clung to a sliver of hope.

The dread and fear she held slowly receded as words formed on her lips in a whisper. "*I arise today with the power of Christ . . . to protect me against every merciless force that comes against my body and soul . . .*"

"Let's drop the pretense," Lorcan said. "You have already helped me immensely, and by the time the night is over your assistance will be complete."

The man reached from the shadows and wrenched the holy prophecy of Patrick from her hands. Saorla gasped.

"I have a fitting end in mind for it."

A deep wave of nausea swept through her stomach at the loss of the prophecy. And she couldn't escape the thought that Ian really did fancy himself a cowboy gunslinger from the American West, about to draw any second.

"Allow me the pleasure of introducing my friends," Lorcan said. A thick man with a hideous scar on his forehead stepped forward. "This is my assistant Mr. Hogan Kirby. Mr. Kirby, would you please search Mr. Shaw."

The thick man stepped into the glow of the lantern.

Ian pulled his arm back about to lash out a blow. Another man from the darkness behind Ian grabbed him in a bear hug. He was also a squat, thick man. She had seen him before, at the cliffs; he had been shooting at them, along with the man with the scar that Lorcan called Kirby.

Kirby placed the tip of the barrel of his weapon at Ian's head. Her heart raced out of her chest.

God, no, not Ian. I couldn't live without him, she screamed in the silence of her heart.

"It's not time for that . . ." Lorcan said to Kirby, pausing for effect with his index finger held in the air, then added, "yet."

Lorcan took a step closer to her. He waved the vellum prophecy in her face. "Be careful with that," she said, knowing she must sound ridiculous.

Lorcan stuffed the vellum inside his coat pocket, then pulled out a book he'd concealed under his armpit inside his coat. "Recognize this little codex?" he asked.

It was the Book of Kells.

He held it up like he was a priest celebrating Mass. "Isn't it nice to have both these works present for our ceremony? After tonight, no one shall ever see either of them again."

These priceless relics were going to be destroyed? The thought sickened her. She'd rather die than they perish, no question about it, but she didn't even have her life to bargain with.

"I also want you to meet another of my assistants, Mr. Torna Mag Vidhir," Lorcan said with a grin. He pointed to the man who'd stepped from the darkness behind Ian moments earlier and had grabbed him. "Kirby will keep his weapon trained on you, Mr. Shaw, so please don't try anything."

Saorla was glad to see that Ian had his hands raised over his head. But would anything they did or didn't do at this point really matter? *Anything except prayer*, she corrected.

Torna conducted a pat down, first under Ian's arm and then around his hips. "Look what we have here, boss," he said triumphantly, as he removed the Webley Revolver from Ian's waist, and then handed the gun to Lorcan. Lorcan stuffed it under his waistband.

"Excellent," Lorcan said, while he watched his men bind Ian's hands in medieval-style handcuffs, made of some kind of strong rope material.

"And now that we're safe, with all the weapons on one side, it's time for the grand finale of introductions." Lorcan announced this as if he were breathlessly emceeing a televised game show. "Meet your friend and confidant."

A woman stepped from the blackness into the glow cast by the lantern. Clothed in a black flowing dress and cape, the woman in the pall of the wan rays of light conjured images reminiscent of some sort of Wiccan rock star. The color drained from Saorla's face with the last drop of sanguinity from her soul.

Claire!

All this time she had been in on it. The strange meeting at Saorla's office when Claire ruminated suspicion and jealousy, causing her to distrust Ian. The probing questions. It all made sense. Claire was part of a cadre of darkness with this beast Lorcan, who couldn't even be called a human being.

Lorcan flashed perfect white teeth that illuminated his dark eyes. "I love this part the best—the look of surprise in the precise moment when ultimate treachery is revealed."

Saorla couldn't speak on her own initiative, but words were forming on her lips in spite of herself it seemed. "*I arise today with the comfort of God's nearness to keep me safe from all conspiracies of demons and the false deceits of woman . . . and the spells of witches . . .*"

"Prayer will not help you now," Claire said.

"How could you?" Saorla whispered.

"It was easy. Everyone wants to live for a purpose greater than themselves. I found mine." She slipped her hand into Lorcan's. "Academia is too slow a mode for changing the world."

"We don't need to justify ourselves," Lorcan said.

"You're right," Claire cooed at Lorcan. "But perhaps you'll allow me to indulge myself this once."

Claire turned to Saorla. "You see, you are our honored guests and a big part of the ceremony. I'm still new to this. But I've come to appreciate the organic, indigenous nature of the ancient Druids and the Queen of Prosperity. And maybe I'll get to see the world change. You may be interested to know we've found your treasure."

Saorla groaned. Claire must have taken the GPS coordinates from her desk she now realized. "You inimical witch, you—"

"Enough," Lorcan shouted.

Lorcan turned to Claire. "Don't stoop to the mortal need to explain your actions."

"I'd be happy to show you how weak and mortal you are if you'd just take off these handcuffs." Ian said it with a baffling calmness that belied the circumstances.

"Mr. Shaw, I've great admiration for you. But I'm not a street brawler. You must know that. My plans for you will become apparent soon enough."

Lorcan gave a nod and his brutes manhandled the captives, herding them where a couple of black SUVs waited. They were all three corralled into the back of one of the vehicles.

"Relax," Lorcan demanded from the front seat as Kirby drove. Torna and Claire rode in the other SUV.

The SUVs bounced over roadless open country of rough hills and thick grasses. Saorla lost all sense of direction as they careened onward. She glanced over at Sophie—they had tied and gagged her, then placed a blind-fold over her eyes. The thought that she was responsible for Sophie's being here sickened her.

"The night becomes fascinating at this point," Lorcan said. "Druids, human sacrifice, the reversal of ancient spiritual pathways. All of these are on the agenda for tonight's Samhain."

"You're nuts," Ian said. "You really ought to get some help."

"The biggest bonfire you've ever seen."

"You'll never get away with it," Ian said, still appearing confident. How he managed to do it, Saorla had no idea. She, on the other hand, was bouncing from terror to tacit resignation and back again. She suppressed the fear by reminding herself that the last few weeks had been a gift. She'd nearly died twice and had had a glimpse of the other side. But still she had so much more to live for. Now that she had Ian.

Especially now that she had him.

And she would always have the memory of Stuart.

But what about dear Sophie? And what had happened to Killian? Neither of them deserved any of this. It was her fault they'd become involved and were going to die tonight.

Then there was the prophecy. That alone was worth dying to save. And she had to save it somehow. She would do anything to prevent its destruction. Gladly throw herself into the flames to save it.

Lorcan laughed. "I'm a big fan of *Foxe's Book of Martyrs,* but perhaps not for the reason most people might think. I love reading about bonfires."

"Where are you taking us?" Ian demanded.

"Very good question. It's almost a shame I have to use you for this purpose."

The SUV came to a stop. It was deathly dark, but they hadn't traveled far from the Hill of Tara. Kirby exited and came around to open the back door.

Lorcan remained in the driver's seat. "The hill you see out there beyond this one is Slane. The professor will know of how the ancient inroads to Christianity were established there. We're going to bring a reversal of fortunes tonight."

Kirby and Torna dragged the three of them out of the SUV. Lorcan had arranged for rock music to blare into the atmosphere from speakers that had been set up on the mound ahead. "A loud party on the night of Samhain this far out in the country with a bright bonfire will not be unusual at all," Lorcan shouted into Saorla's ear.

The three captives were pulled and dragged up the hill. Zeroed out by the awful sardonic metronome of the music, Saorla couldn't hear her own screams. As they trudged her up the hill, words from the *Breastplate* formed again on her tongue. Deep conviction beyond anything she'd ever experienced rose in her soul. *"God's shield to guard me. God's angels to save me. From traps of demons. From temptations common to man. From all who wish me harm. Abroad and near. Alone and among the people."*

The three were tied to large wooden stakes. The scene redolent of the Hill at Golgotha over two thousand years ago absent the cross-beams and nails.

Lorcan was a hundred yards off in the distance now. A lighter that looked like a blow torch extended from his hand, while his face was agog.

The madman flicked the torch; the ground burst into flames.

Fire lapped and wound its way. Slow, but with deadly steadiness.

A minute passed. The fire snaking around the hilly ground was a quarter way to her now.

Moving faster than Lorcan had predicted. Ten minutes he'd said; at this rate, they only had about four.

Was it really coming down to this? The whirlwind her life had become, dissolving into a firestorm.

Lorcan had made his way over to them now. The volume of the music lowered, but he would probably arrange for it to reach a crescendo about the time the flames began to sear the flesh of his sacrifices.

The music softened even further. She suppressed the urge to scream. It wouldn't do any good. And she didn't want to give him the pleasure of causing her to suffer that last indignity.

She would go out noble, fighting in the spirit like Patrick, with the weapons of the spirit. She shouted a proclamation into the atmosphere. *"I summon today power to protect me from every evil. Against every merciless force that may assault my body and soul... Against the greed of idolatry. Against the spells of witches, wizards, smiths and druids."*

CHAPTER TWENTY-NINE

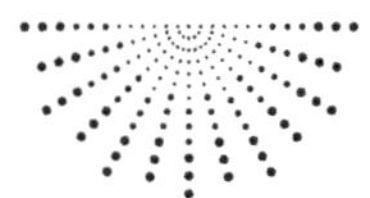

First in the queue for ignition, Ian watched the flames lick their way toward him. The line of fire had been making a tortuous route through the hills for several minutes now.

Thirty seconds to detonation, he surmised.

Energy coursed down his spine as he watched the flames grow closer and larger. Every hair on his body came erect; time slowed down. The most intense rush he had ever experienced filled his chest. He scolded himself for feeling this way, but it was no use.

The prospect of imminent disaster had always set his juices flowing.

His life began to play before him, drifting now to the spring of the year he graduated law school in Boulder. He'd met up with a buddy in the mountains for some backcountry skiing. The skiing itself was uneventful, but his solo car ride out of the Rockies had provided the premiere acute sensation of his life, at least up until the present moment and the incident at Mavs.

As he drove his rickety old Subaru around the winding curves of the steep mountain pass that day, a snow squall hit that was preceded by a long bout of freezing rain. Within a matter of seconds it was a near white-out blizzard. His Subaru hit a patch of ice exposed by the blowing snow. The brakes were useless and the car spun wildly out of control toward the edge of the road with nothing to separate him from a couple of thousand feet of exposure to the valley floor below. "God, save me!" he cried. And with that he took his hands from the wheel as if to say, *it's all yours now*. The vehicle did two complete three hundred and sixty spins. On the second rotation, he could swear that the front on of his vehicle hung out in space over the edge of the cliff. He wasn't sure how it managed to avoid plummeting over. In another second, the car continued straight down the road as if nothing had ever happened.

When Lorcan's music suddenly softened, Ian could hear the sound of Seer's voice. She was tied to the stake next to him, about ten feet away. He was about to call to her when he realized she was praying.

"Christ to shield me today. From poison and burning and fire ... So that I might attain the abundant reward . . . Christ with me . . . before me . . . behind me."

She had it exactly right, he decided. Prayer was their only weapon. It should have been his first option, too, he knew deep down. But he had been in such a rage over what they had likely done to Killian, and were about to do to Saorla and Sophie, that he'd only been able to think of revenge to this point.

Now, he decided to offer a prayer of his own. The music was back up again, suffocating the night air with an impressive din. He had tried to memorize Psalm 91 at the end of the summer, and some of it was still fresh. He plugged it into a desperate prayer for angelic help.

"God, I take my hands off the wheel. Please. Come. You said about the prayerful man, '*When he calls to me, I will answer him; I will be with him in trouble I will rescue him.*' God, I ask you to rescue us!"

The music intensified and was at an apex now. The fire just feet away. Probably twenty seconds to detonation.

Saorla's lips stilled moved. Still praying.

Good girl.

This was a noble way to go out. Papa would be proud of him if he knew how it had all come down. But Papa would never know what had happened.

Maybe on the other side he'd know.

The fires were three feet from detonation.

Lorcan stepped forward and stood down the hill about ten yards away and lowered the music to elevator-background level. Claire stood to his right. The two henchmen flanked the sorry couple on each side. Lorcan held up the manuscript of the Patrick prophecy and the Book of Kells, one in each hand. Lowering them now, he placed them in the old leather satchel, and made a mocked sign of the cross over it as he laughed. Ian realized he was going to toss it all into the bonfire when he sprung up.

"With these fires I reverse the Christian God's rule in the land. And summon forth Maeve to reign supreme as Goddess over all Ireland. Homeostasis restored."

Two feet to detonation.

Ian looked to Saorla. To say goodbye. He had to tell her he loved her more than life. She was looking at him too. "Seer, I—"

Ian saw a movement on the ground behind her. An animal creeping low? Perhaps a large dog?

Ian shook his head and rattled it against the wood stake at his back. The movement at the ground was faster now, and he could see a face. A human face.

One that he knew. It was mostly concealed in the darkness, but Ian could see it nonetheless. It couldn't be, but it was.

Captain Finn lay crouched to the ground with a rifle in hand. How in the world had he gotten here from Greyabbey? Had he followed them?

Twelve inches to the fiery apocalypse. Five seconds maybe.

"Tonight starts the reign of—"

Finn leapt from the cover of the hill and fired a shot. A bullet struck Kirby in the center of the hammer-head scar, and he collapsed in his tracks.

Torna rattled off a spree of rounds in Finn's direction. Ian couldn't tell if anyone had been hit.

Torna kept firing. But then he too dropped in his tracks.

With the Webley revolver now in hand that he'd taken from Ian earlier, Lorcan stepped forward and aimed at Saorla. "No," Ian wailed.

Finn fired off another shot. Ian could see now that the captain had been gravely wounded. But his last round had hit Lorcan in the arm, causing the foreign minister to drop his gun.

Four inches to detonation.

Lorcan dropped himself to the ground, recovered his gun, and fired. Blood spurted from the captain's chest.

Two inches to detonation.

Lorcan pointed the revolver again, this time at Ian, poised to pull the trigger.

The excitement snaked through Ian's spine as he waited to feel the hot metal piercing his heart. Better the hot metal to the heart than the hot flames torturing his skin.

Lorcan pulled the trigger. Ian felt nothing and heard nothing.

Lorcan slapped the gun and chambered another round. The gun had jammed. Ian cried tears of thankfulness for not having had the time to take Finn's advice about cleaning the weapon to prevent it from jamming.

Sirens rang off in the distance, piercing the night air and getting closer.

Lorcan, obviously befuddled now at the misfire, pointed the gun at Saorla and pulled the trigger again. Something clicked but it refused to fire, hopelessly jammed.

Louder and louder the sirens grew. And Ian could see the reflection of the Mars lights off the hills. Blue and red hue lit up the rolling grasses.

Lorcan threw the gun down and fled toward the forest to the west. He stumbled, fell to the ground, got up, and continued running again.

Ian's hands had been cut free of the constraints. How?

Finn laid, immobile and unresponsive, at Ian's feet with knife in hand. Somehow he'd cut Ian's ropes and hand constraints.

No time to loose. He had to free Saorla and the others.

Free of the ropes now, Ian grabbed the knife from Finn's listless hand.

A ball of flame knocked him from his feet and the mound around him exploded. Fire leapt to the battle.

Dazed, Ian struggled to get upright and clear his head.

A loud crack of thunder jolted him to his senses. And the skies opened up full throttle with a fierce deluge. Saorla would have called it a great lashing.

Lashing? "Saorla? Are you all right?" Ian screamed.

By now the rain was so loud he couldn't hear anything. The lapping inferno fought for a moment against the sheets of rain. But the flames were short-lived, having been reduced to a tiny smoldering by the great strokes of water from the sky.

Ian quickly surveyed the scene. Lorcan was getting away, escaping toward the forest. Where was Professor Curran? She was getting away too, heading the opposite direction.

Ian couldn't let Lorcan escape. He probably had a helicopter waiting nearby and had already set plans in motion to have the treasure removed from the cave. Who knew where the man would end up after that? To allow him to evade capture only to turn up somewhere else in the world where he would be free to wreak his own special brand of havoc would be intolerable. And where was the satchel with the prophecy and the Book of Kells? In the darkness and confusion, he'd lost track of it. Lorcan likely still had it.

Ian sprinted down the hill and toward the forest. If he was going to catch him, he'd have to have an effort worthy of the NFL scouting combine.

Have to end this now.

Ian was closing the gap, but Lorcan had a big lead.

Bounding down the hill and stretching his legs, Ian kept his balance despite the impossible speed he was traveling. All the while he kept Lorcan in his sights. But the forest edge was coming fast. He had to get as close as possible while they were still both in the clear.

Fifty yards, forty yards, thirty-five. And then Lorcan disappeared into the dense tangle of trees. Ian kept flying in the direction of the disappearing act that Lorcan had become, an act that would have made the ancient druids proud. In another couple seconds, Ian entered the darkness of the forest too.

The brush clawed at his arms, as he careened forward following the path of least resistance. Branches and leaves slapped his face; he kept pushing through. And then he slammed into a body.

Head collided with ribs. Body collided with the ground, Ian atop of Lorcan, who cursed a string of obscenities.

Ian wrestled against strong determined limbs, but couldn't tell arms from legs. Finally, he grabbed an arm, and tussling fiercely to subdue it, he felt the unmistakable coldness of a gun barrel.

Lorcan had a gun. Another gun. Why hadn't he used it up on the hill? It was all a chaotic blur. Perhaps it was the confusion of the moment. The panic that ensued from the sirens. There was no question Lorcan would use the gun now.

Have to get the gun before he kills me.

He flipped himself over and grabbed Lorcan's arm with both hands. Arms flayed wildly.

"I'll kill you here," Lorcan howled.

"Why do you hate God?" Ian grunted out through clenched teeth, as the two combatants rolled and grappled through the undercover of the forest.

Ian's arms were noodling from the struggle. The man was every bit his equal in strength and stamina, if not more.

Ian heaved and pulled, trying to keep the barrel of the gun point away from him. But the man pulled back. Interlocked, they fell over a ledge and tumbled down a steep hill like two monkeys with their tails tied together.

The gun discharged with a loud bang.

Blood spurted from the neck, and a body fell limp.

THE SMELL OF SAORLA'S SINGED HAIR STILL LINGERED IN THE AIR, BUT she couldn't feel any damage to her skin. The prayer for deliverance from burning had been answered so far.

The rain ended as suddenly as it had started, and when it did, she felt the embers hot beneath her despite the incumbent moisture. And in another second, fire started to spark up again. The flames, though low near her feet, were growing in strength. The heat set her squirming, and she struggled against her ropes, but nothing budged.

A number of Gardai were ascending the hill in full riot gear now, and she prayed they would lose their overabundance of caution and free her quick. It was getting so hot around her lower extremities she considered that her clothes might ignite any second.

Why weren't they hurrying?

At least the awful music had ceased. The rain had shorted out the electronics, and the relative quiet of the rural night was restored.

Without warning, a gunshot pierced the quiet, coming from the direction of the forest.

God, don't let it be Ian.

Why did he take the chance? He should have let Duihbur flee. Let the Gardai handle it.

But Ian's going after Duihbur was the only course that made sense, she suddenly realized. If he got away, he'd be free to do untold damage.

It was Lorcan, lying motionless.

Ian's hand grazed the metal of the gun. He picked it up, felt the weight of it, before casting it away out of the reach of Lorcan who was suddenly still now except for the rising and falling of his chest.

Ian fumbled for his cell phone, activated the small flashlight, beamed it toward Lorcan. He was barely conscious. Not dead yet, his breath came shallow.

Ian took off his coat and tried to plug the bleeding. "I'll get help for you."

"No," came the adamant reply. "To answer your question, I hate God because he killed my father."

"How could God kill your—"

"My father was a believing Christian like you. Gave me the name Luke. I was eleven when he went to see a famous preacher, from America. Came to Croke Park . . . My father was killed on the way to the meeting. A drunk driver . . ."

The life was draining out of him, and he didn't look like he could hold on much longer. Despite the rage Ian had felt earlier toward the man, he suddenly pitied him.

"Look, sir. With all due respect, God didn't kill your father. Satan is the one who kills and destroys. For a time, it may look like he wins. Things happen every day that aren't God's will. But He sees it from eternity. Even now, the fact that you hear me speak means he's giving you one last chance to receive his love."

There was a look on Lorcan's face that Ian couldn't read. Was it surrender or defiance?

Lorcan gasped heavily now. Ian's coat was wet with blood. Lorcan said something undecipherable, and then his chest stopped moving and his breath left.

CHAPTER THIRTY

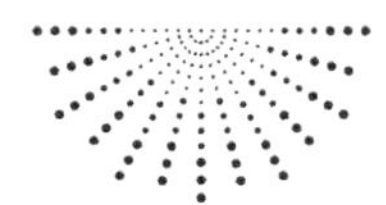

"You've all told me basically the same rotten story," Callahan said. "You've rehearsed it in case you were caught."

"Or it could mean we've been consistently telling you the truth," Ian shot back.

"That's a conclusion that is far from called for at this point. Remember, Mr. Shaw, you've as much as admitted that your actions were responsible for the death of at least one of the victims."

Ian shook his head at the man's stupidity. He'd told him the whole story, laid out in all its proper context. Why couldn't he see it?

The lawyer part of Ian had initially wanted to divulge as little as possible, but the part of him that was a man on a quest for the truth was anxious for resolution. Ian had opted for full disclosure and had been more forthcoming than any defense counsel in his right mind would prudently advise.

Following the failed human sacrifice, Detective Callahan had transported them from the barbaric scene straight to the main SDU headquarters in Dublin for questioning. For the past three hours, well into the wee hours of the morning now, he and his detectives had interrogated them in separate rooms from each other. Obviously not getting the results he'd hoped for, Callahan had finally brought them to a central conference room to address them all together. Ian was surprised to find that they had also snatched up Myrna in their dragnet. Seeing Myrna now in custody, Ian was finally able to grasp how Callahan had known that he and Saorla would be in the vicinity of Tara.

Ian had also learned that Killian had been transported to the nearest hospital for treatment. The initial report was that he'd suffered a bad concussion and was being treated to prevent further swelling to his brain. Beyond that, four men had died—the brave Captain Finn, as well as Lorcan Duihbur and his two henchmen, Hogan Kirby and Torna Mac Vidhir. As far as Ian knew, Professor Claire Curran was still on the run.

Jumbo came into the room now and handed Callahan the leather satchel, which Ian recognized as the one in which Lorcan had crammed both the Book of Kells and the Saint Patrick prophecy in anticipation of hurling them into the bonfire.

Callahan placed the satchel on the conference table and took out the book and the prophecy and sat them side by side next to the satchel. Ian marveled at the fact that both writings had been so well preserved despite the deluge. The satchel had clearly served its intended purpose.

"Basically, we snatched you from the hill red-handed with the Book of Kells within your reach and four men dead," Callahan said, laying out his indictment.

"You should have been after the foreign affairs minister and his two goons," Ian said.

Callahan's face turned carrot orange, and a vein bulged from his neck. "Mr. Lorcan Duihbur, was *helping me* on this case! Two of the others were his assistants. The fourth man, who you say was helping you, has a shady past. We know he has ties to revolutionary activities and domestic terrorism."

"His IRA connections were in the past," Ian said. "And his heroics tonight will be remembered and admired forever."

"Let me get this straight," Callahan said with a chortle, "you believe that Saint Patrick himself communicated a message for you to find so you could pass it on to the present-day millennials."

"Yes and no," Saorla corrected. "The message isn't just for millennials—it's for the young and the old, for all ages and for all of Ireland from the north to the south, from Portrush to Skibbereen."

"Yes, got it, a message for Ireland for which you needed to break the law and steal the Book of Kells to find."

"Look, you'll know soon enough if our story is a hoax," Saorla replied.

"Right. The earthquake's coming tomorrow and so is the Easter bunny. Now listen, you people have exhausted my patience. Unless you want to spend the rest of your lives in a prison cell, I need to have some real cooperation and—."

"We would each like to exercise our right to make a phone call," Ian said.

"—some answers fast."

"One call, Detective."

"What if I say you don't get a call?"

"I'd say you were violating our rights."

"Look, they already have a barrister in you, Mr. Shaw. Who could you possibly want to call anyway at this ungodly hour?"

Sophie cleared her throat. "I would like call to . . . the Taoiseach, Mr. David Braden."

Callahan laughed so hard Ian thought the detective would pop one of the buttons on his shirt that strung tight over his impressive belly. "The young Pole wants to call the Taoiseach, Jumbo. Can you fathom that?" He managed to spit the question out between guffaws. "If the lady wants to call the Taoiseach at four in the morning, who am I to deny the request."

Callahan yanked his cell from his coat and handed it to Sophie; all the while, he continued to laugh. She took the phone without bothering to explain how she might know the number.

Ian felt his head tilting. But nothing about Sophie surprised him anymore.

She dialed a number and waited. In a few seconds, she was

speaking to someone. Callahan and Jumbo flashed toothy grins at each other.

Sophie explained where she was and that she needed immediate assistance. Ian wanted to tell the detective that the smirk on the man's face would soon be disappearing, probably permanently, but he held back.

"And who would you like to call, Professor, the Dali Lama?" Callahan asked.

"Or maybe Indiana Jones?" Jumbo chimed in. Both detectives laughed uproariously.

"No, I would like to call a reporter," Saorla shot back.

Callahan sobered. "Go right ahead. I think that's just what we need, a little publicity, get the reporters in and let them know I've collared the thieves who stole the Book of Kells and who have moved on to felony murder, with four men dead."

It wasn't normal police protocol for the States, Ian knew. Sharing a cell phone with suspects and throwing out a cavalcade of one-liners weren't text-book interrogation procedures. And he doubted if Callahan was operating by the book here in Ireland. But there was no doubt he was in charge, a king amused by the jesters that had come to his court.

"All right, now that we've all had a good laugh," Callahan said, "I suggest we get down to business. If you tell me what really happened, I'll see what I can do with the judge." Callahan winked at Jumbo.

The room suddenly fell silent.

"We can even take a break if you want. Come back when you're ready to tell me the truth, and we can put it all on videotape. Make it nice and neat for everyone—the court, the justice system, the public, and the victims' families."

"I would still like to make my call," Saorla insisted.

Callahan handed her the phone. "You got it, Professor."

Saorla took it and began punching numbers. It seemed to ring for a long time. "Hello," she finally said. "I would like to speak to Mr. Seamus Murray . . . Mr. Murray I apologize for the rude interruption so early in the morning . . . This is Professor Saorla O'Rourke, Irish

History professor at Trinity College . . . You're very gracious. The reason for my call is that I have a story for you so astounding that it will warrant D-Day-size headlines . . . For starters, we have the Book of Kells with us here, and four men are confirmed dead . . . I'm at the SDU station on Harcourt Street . . . Yes, you can come now. The Gardai will be expecting you."

After Saorla ended the call, the light-hearted atmosphere that had spawned the inane ridicule by the two detectives dampened.

"Who's Seamus Murray?" Ian asked Saorla.

"A columnist at the Irish Times and a former reporter. He also has a morning news show on local television. Basically, everybody knows him."

"Obviously he knows you," Ian said, a tinge of jealously gripping him.

Saorla threw her long dark tresses over her shoulders. The rain water earlier in the evening had added a special shine to her hair that had somehow managed to enhance even its normal luxuriance. She was locked onto Ian's eyes now. "He's called me in the past when he needed information for stories involving Irish history and lore. Sometimes even linguistics questions. You, of all people should know I get that from time to time. Someone looking for an expert."

Ian nodded apprehensively. "Of course."

"All right," Callahan said, "I don't mean to interrupt the expert, but why don't we start with her. Then you can each take a turn telling me one more time about the events that led to the *Halloween Massacre,* as it will be called for years to come, I'm sure."

The four detainees, starting with Saorla, took a whack at giving their perspective on the events that had transpired over the last few weeks.

It was after four-thirty in the morning when a young detective interrupted with a knock at the conference room door. "Sir, I have some news you are going to want to hear in private," he announced breathlessly to Callahan.

"Nonsense, lad, I'm shaking everything up. Conducting a completely open investigation. Whatever you have to share, let's bring it out in the light for our suspects . . . uh, excuse me, our guests." Callahan chuckled and cupped his large strong hands together before fanning them out in a gesture that said the entire group was welcome to the news.

"All right, as long as you are keen," the young detective said, while looking unsure about Callahan's approach. "First off, we've arrested Professor Claire Curran trying to enter her apartment about a half hour ago. Your request to station men at her residence worked."

"Indeed," Callahan said scratching his chin. "Ms. O'Rourke has implicated Ms. Curran, and I'm not yet certain how she fits in. Most likely Professor Curran was an accomplice, helping the suspects in this room. Is that all?"

"No," the young detective said, still looking flummoxed.

"Come on, let's have it out," Callahan urged.

"All right. Prime Minister Braden has just arrived with a retinue. And also waiting in the lobby is Seamus Murray from the Irish Times."

"That's bloody blarney," Callahan bellowed.

"No, it's true, sir. I swear it on my mother's grave."

Callahan seemed to lose all the color in his face on learning that the prime minister was at the station. "Send them both in immediately," he mumbled.

"Sir, there are other men with Mr. Braden."

"Send them all in," Callahan said, his voice cracking.

The young detective went to the door and opened it. Seven men entered. Ian recognized the first one as the prime minister and a man that looked to be his body guard. He also immediately recognized another man with dark hair slicked back into a ducktail, as Joseph Egan, the Director of Public Prosecutions, whom Ian had battled in court a couple of weeks ago at Saorla's judicial hearing. Ian had no idea who the other four men were.

He glanced at Saorla, who seemed to have read his mind. She whispered to him that the gentleman with the curly hair, slightly greying at the temples, was Seamus Murray. She also identified the Attorney General and the Minister of Justice. The last of the seven men who had entered the room was in a military uniform and looked like he could be the country's top-ranking general.

Among the men assembled were the principal legal officers of the nation and one of the most influential members of its press, Ian realized, and collectively they could spin the wheels of justice in whatever direction they saw fit.

The prime minister explained to detective Callahan that despite his reluctance to interfere with the investigation, he'd ordered a shadow investigation with a particular emphasis on his minister of foreign affairs and the employees at the National Museum. The upshot was that Director Egan was in possession of evidence that revealed the full depth of the former curator's nefarious activity. Lorcan Duihbur, it seems, was running an international smuggling ring that had a corner on black market antiquities sales.

Taoiseach Braden then turned the meeting over to Director Egan, who explained in greater detail the outcome of his investigation. He concluded his presentation by revealing that a search conducted just hours ago of Lorcan's high-rise uncovered enough incriminating material to implicate Lorcan and his men ten times over. They'd also recovered a silver chalice, and from Egan's description of it, Ian concluded that it had to be the one that had been stolen from Papa when he was run off the road. Egan also explained that they had enough to implicate Lorcan in the death of Professor Greenwald in Wexford, and the excessive drugging of Ian's grandfather by a former nurse named Eva Morgan, a.k.a. Nurse Maureen. An arrest warrant for the nurse had already been sworn.

Callahan frowned. "But the fact remains that the people I'm holding in this room are guilty of both stealing the Book of Kells and of a conspiracy to keep that fact hidden from the Gardai. Is it now government policy to overlook crime?"

"Now that you mention it," the Taoiseach said, "you should know that I intend to issue full pardons later in the morning."

"And make them national heroes?" Callahan fumed.

"They are heroes," the Attorney General, Gordon Maher, now piped up.

"Preposterous," Callahan muttered.

"You won't think it far-fetched when you know all the facts," Maher said. "Some things seem to have eluded your normally careful investigatory skills. But other matters you had no way of knowing."

"For example?" Callahan asked, suddenly looking genuinely confused.

"What you don't know is that the Book of Kells was in the process of being turned over to the government," the Taoiseach said. "It was never intended to be taken off campus in the first place. But given what it has led to so far . . . the discovery of the treasure. I think the public and the justice system will be more than willing to make an accommodation."

"*Treasure*? You mean, you really found a treasure?"

The Taoiseach smiled. "Enough to pay off our national debt fifty times over if it were sold. But we're not going to sell it. We'll put all the artifacts in a brand new museum. Revenue from the tourist traffic in one year alone will set us in motion to wipe out all of our financial troubles."

Callahan looked dizzy. It was a good thing he was sitting down. "What about all this esoteric babble about a prophecy from Saint Patrick? And a prediction of an earthquake at sundown on All Saints Day? Don't you think that's cuckoo? Or am I the only sane one left in this room?"

Silence fell across table.

Callahan had his head down fidgeting with an app on his phone. Then he popped his head up. "Sundown comes at 4:53 p.m. That's exactly twelve hours from now. If the government expects me to stand around and wait for some dooms-day scenario to come to pass, I can tell you I'll put in my resignation right now."

"I intend to take a wait and see approach with the prophecy," Taoiseach Braden said. "I'll go ahead and read the prophecy. That's what it calls for. Then I'll announce the pardons and the safe return of the Book of Kells. The public will be thrilled with that. And they'll be even more thrilled when they hear about the discoveries in the cave that could end the days of economic austerity. We will also tell them all about the prophecy, every detail, and let the people draw their own conclusions. Detective, you can't lose sight of everything confirmed to be true so far."

Callahan's face grew pale, and he slumped himself deeper in his chair. "Pardons you say. Full . . . This morning?"

Director Egan made his way over to Callahan and put his arm on his shoulder. "Don't take it so hard, Sean. It's all going to turn out fine."

Callahan regained a measure of equilibrium. He looked at Ian. "If there are to be pardons. You are all free to go."

"Wait a minute, not so fast." Seamus Murray, the journalist, suddenly interjected himself into the meeting. "I don't suppose any of you would like to go on the record, starting at the beginning and explaining everything to me?"

"Seamus, it's your lucky day," the Taoiseach said. "You have a three-hour head start on the rest of the news world to run with the exclusive of the century before I call a press conference."

CHAPTER THIRTY-ONE

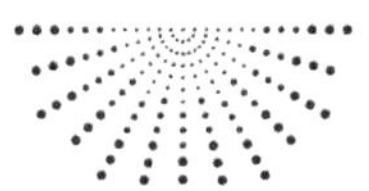

Ian spent the morning walking the streets of Dublin, alone, after watching Prime Minister Braden's press conference. Saorla, exhausted from another sleepless night, had returned to her Georgian manor safe in the knowledge that she could rest without being stalked by forces seeking to do her mortal harm.

The press would be another matter altogether.

It would be impossible to exaggerate the news coverage and the consequent hysteria that was gripping the city with ever-increasing intensity. Sporting events canceled. Schools let their students out early. Employers immediately closed up shop for the day where possible. Television sets in the restaurants and pubs were tuned to a constant cycle of repeating news clips, showing the Taoiseach's press conference and pictures of the recovered Book of Kells, along with items found in the *blackest cave*. The events had even taken over the American cable outlets, which were more skeptical than the Irish press about the going-ons, introducing their stories with such preludes as "What Have the Leprechauns Done to Ireland?" and "A Blarney Fit for the Irish."

The locals seemed to be digesting bits and pieces of the story but were having a hard time putting together a coherent whole. Mr.

Braden had read the prophecy on air to the nation, and it was published in its entirety on all of the online editions of Ireland's dailies. Although most people were adamant that they did not want to be inside a building when the sun set, it seemed that this was about as deep as the information had sunk so far. Ian had overheard conversations where it was asked, more than once, where ground zero would be.

Actually that was a fairly astute question, he decided. Where exactly would the epicenter of the quake be?

As Ian walked, he flitted away the stress of the past several weeks. But then new challenges came to mind. What was to become of a basically unemployable, disbarred attorney? What was he to do about his feelings for Saorla? His initial objections about not wanting to involve a woman in his adrenaline-overloaded life seemed laughable, schizophrenically hollow even, given the heroics Saorla had proven herself capable of.

Was there a chance they could stake out a life together now that this was all over?

As he strolled down Grafton Street, the mania in the air only increased. A long-haired guitar player, looking all the part of a 1960's Jim Morrison, sat on the pavement and played, "The End." Others were circling around the square, holding a variety of signs: *Ground Zero?* And *Calamity is Near* and *Judgment Over Government Chicanery*.

By eleven o'clock in the morning, Ian had had enough. He walked the ten blocks to Saorla's place, woke her from a sound sleep, and half an hour later, they pulled out of the driveway in her Land Rover with Ian at the wheel.

CHAPTER THIRTY-TWO

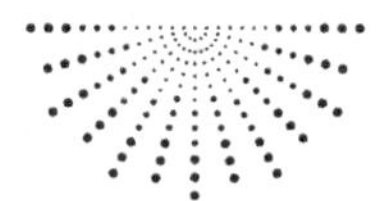

Three hours down the road, they were in the hills of Antrim and then on his grandmother's front porch. Ian was surprised beyond measure to find Papa George in bed, awake and alert. Ian hadn't wanted to call, fearing the worst—that he had passed in the night just before news of the discoveries shocked the nation.

For the next hour, Ian told his grandfather everything. The old man was so fiercely overcome with emotion that Ian considered several times that he might have to cut his story short. But each time George rallied and urged Ian to continue.

The look on the old man's face was all it took to let Ian know that it had all been worth it. The sleepless nights, the depredations of the cave and forest, the gunshot wound to the arm—they were all nothing in comparison to the joy he saw in his grandfather's eyes upon hearing about the discovery of Patrick's prophecy.

Before her release from the SDU station that morning, Saorla had been allowed to take photographs of Patrick's codex message to the nation, which began by noting the date it was written: March 17, the year of our Lord 562. Saorla had spent a good part of the ride to Antrim going over the translation she had worked onto her tablet from Latin to English.

Tears fell easily down George's cheeks as Saorla read. Ian wrestled to suppress the fluid building in his own eyes. The old man had really lived to see this day. And not just see it, but comprehend and appreciate it.

Saorla finished with the last bit about Patrick likening himself to the nobleman in John's gospel who had asked the Lord to heal his gravely-ill son. When Saorla reached the part about Jesus telling the man that his son would live, George threw his hands in the air. "Ireland will live too," he declared, "I am convinced of it."

Saorla had the passage up on her cell phone now. "The verse Patrick refers to is John 4:53, where it says: "The father knew that was the hour when Jesus had said to him, 'Your son will live.' And he himself believed and all his household."

When Ian heard Saorla say that the verse was 4:53, an idea clicked in his head. It was something Callahan had said about it being 4:53 in the morning and that sunset was precisely twelve hours away. "Wait a minute. Do you think?"

He had his cell out now and was googling the official time of sunset in Ireland. Ian felt his eyelids flutter and his eyeballs bulge. It was indeed 4:53 p.m. for November 1.

"Seer, this is John 4:53. Guess what time sunset is?"

"Uncanny," Saorla said, as her voice cracked with emotion. "The earthquake's timing is reinforced by the chapter and verse of the Biblical analogy Patrick makes to the nobleman. Especially amazing given that chapter divisions in the Bible weren't added until the thirteenth century and the verse numbers weren't added until the sixteenth."

George nodded from his bed. "It's after 4:30. Been up four hours now and I haven't felt this strong since the accident." He tried to push himself with his hands over toward the edge of the bed.

"Be careful," Aryana said, as she moved to George's bedside.

"Can you help me to the wheelchair?" the old man pleaded with Ian. "I want to see the sunset if it's the last thing I do."

Aryana shot both hands in the air, palms out. "I don't think that's a good idea, dear."

"I've lived this long, haven't I? This old Simeon needs to get out of bed and see what the Lord is doing."

Aryana just shook her head. The wrinkle lines magnified on her face. But she seemed almost resigned to the fact that George was going to give it a try.

Ian helped him from the bed to a wheelchair that had sat in the corner of the room for weeks, ever since George had come home from the hospital.

After steadying the rickety old codger into the chair, Ian pushed him across the living room floor toward the back porch. His atrophied legs stuck out from under his medical gown like two bleached-out femurs attached to a century old, desert island skeleton.

"Open the door," George said.

"There is a November chill in the air," Aryana protested.

"Cold didn't kill Simeon; it won't kill me."

"But stubbornness has killed plenty of foolish folks."

Ian and George ignored Aryana's protestations for the moment. Ian pushed the sliding patio door open and plunged the wheel chair and its occupant outside onto the uneven stone of the patio.

"Looks like about ten minutes to D-Day," George said. "Why don't you and Saorla head up the hill and watch from the top?"

Ian hesitated.

"Go on now," George urged.

The hill presented no obstacle for two healthy adults in the prime of life. It would probably only take all of three minutes to get to the crest. Though they still had plenty of time to make it to the summit before the quake hit, Ian wanted to get a move on it just to be safe. From the top, they'd be in a good position to see the point where the upper edge of the sun dipped below the horizon. A perfect spot.

"Come on, Seer." Ian took her hand and started a trot in the direction of the hill.

Soon enough they would know whether the words from the ancient scroll could be trusted. "The suspense is making me nervous," Ian said as they made their way up the incline of the long lush grass.

Several sheep clustered tight and gnawed at the green. A snapshot that could have been taken on any of a thousand hills of Erin.

"I thought you like suspense and like to be nervous."

"I do, but this is different."

"You got that right because we know there's going to be a quake," Saorla said confidently. "Where's the suspense in that?"

True, Ian had to admit. "Still, I feel like I'll be holding my breath till it comes to pass. I've never seen an earthquake predicted beforehand."

"Especially not a millennium-and-a-half beforehand," Saorla added.

They trudged their way up, and in a few minutes they crested the top and saw the valley spread before them. It was a mostly clear afternoon, but a puff of clouds in the vicinity of the horizon shrouded the sun in an amorphous haze. The sheep Ian had seen on the way up were no longer feasting on the grasses but were on the move now, bleating as they headed down.

What Ian hadn't told Saorla was that he felt a great suspense building over what would happen next in his life. There were so many unanswered questions. Would she consider a future with him? And did he even have a right to ask her about it?

Ian still held her hand. He turned his gaze from the horizon to face her. "I'm wondering what comes next," he said.

She smiled. "The ground shakes."

"I think if I leave for California . . . my world shakes apart."

She reached her hand tenderly around his back and pulled him close to her. Their lips met as she kissed him softly. Her hand caressed the hard stubble on his face. Their lips barely parted and she whispered, "Whatever shaking comes, we can take it on together."

In an instant, Ian knew that this would be true. He nodded his head in affirmation. His nostrils swelled with emotion and he fought to keep the tears out of his eyes. Tears of joy at the treasure he'd found in her. A priceless gem he'd stumbled upon in the land of his fathers.

"It was the glorious quest that brought us together," she said quietly, "and nothing's going to separate us now."

"And a new quest begins," he said, pushing his lips toward hers.

"Do you have any idea how much I . . . I love you . . ." His words were garbled by the intensity of her moist, eager lips on his.

A loud rumbling boom came with a violent shaking. It tilted him off his feet, and he fell sideways to the grass. Saorla tumbled on top of him, her head landing on his chest. Ian feigned a struggle to untangle himself, as the terrible shaking continued.

"*This has to be* ground zero," he said, already beginning to laugh like a kid going high on a coaster ride.

The rumbling endured for a full minute.

And even though predicted, it had come so suddenly and unexpectedly given their distraction with each other that they were immediately hit with wave upon wave of laughter. Laughter that started in their stomachs and filled their chests and erupted from their mouths. The giggling was uncontrollable now, catching them in a Maverick's-like spin cycle that consisted not of life-threatening surf but of sets of euphoria that undulated over them as the seconds moved by.

Over what exactly were they laughing, Ian wasn't able to precisely define. Perhaps over realizing that the words from the past were pearls of truth, that the stresses of these last weeks had been for them swallowed in the knowledge of what they'd uncovered, and that all of Ireland was privy to the oracles of hope. Perhaps it was over realizing that they'd been caught off guard despite knowing for the last eighteen hours that this moment was coming. And finally, it could have been over realizing that God had knit them together through the words of a faithful saint whose obedience had bridged the centuries to undeniably and irretrievably touch the present. Yes, it was each of these, Ian decided, and something more—a shift in the atmosphere.

The turning, Saorla had called it at the Hill of Tara.

When the shaking stopped and he finally came to himself, Ian rose to his feet and pulled Saorla up to him. She was still laughing when he looked in the direction of the farmhouse. What Ian saw next took his breath away. The sight of a ghost caused a knife-edge of fearful awe to poke through his spine. But it wasn't a ghost.

George and Aryana, hand-in-hand, side-by-side, *walking*. George was *walking* under his own power.

The impossibility of it froze Ian and Saorla in their tracks.

For his part, Ian let out a loud guttural, "Ho!," which was a three-way mix that consisted of equal measures of utter shock, unbounded joy, and sheer terror. Saorla emitted a gleeful scream that would have made a U2 devotee proud before she aped Ian's "Ho."

Tears flooded Ian's eyes as he bounded his way down the hill with his hand locked in Saorla's. The wonderful reality had settled. He knew it was the genesis. The genesis of the turning.

When he got closer, he saw that his grandparents were crying too. On their faces and deep in their eyes, he saw a recognition that matched his own. He sensed the same recognition in Saorla, as she squeezed his hand tight. Kindling in the dusk and dark—was the turning.

A white-tailed eagle flitted and danced on the air above. At the murky black horizon, the sky was streaked through with gold and crimson-stained clouds that floated like bubbles and formed a canopy over the now darkened but verdant hills that resounded with the lore of the long centuries. And a mild breeze bore the briny air of the Irish sea well inland.

In that moment he knew, and he knew it as profoundly as he had ever known anything, that the turning would spark a fire. And the fire would expel the darkness.

THE END.

ACKNOWLEDGMENTS

Special thanks to Erin Healy and Jenny Dunlap who offered advice early on. Much appreciation to Rowena Kuo and Meaghan Burnett and their team of editors at Brimstone. Thank you also to Elaina Lee who does amazing work.

A huge thank you to my sisters, Lynn Sandberg and Lee Hruby, for taking a trip to Ireland with me for "research," where we navigated the winding roads of the lush Irish hillsides, sometimes at great peril, but also having the time of our lives. The hope is that the landscape we viewed comes across as vivid as any character in the story.

Once again, writing a novel is a journey in faith, so I want to mention all those that read my tale while it was still a work in progress and offered their steadfast encouragement—Carole Troy, Joy Lang, Donna Friesz, both Patrick McNamaras, Randy Mead, Gunnar Dunlap, and especially Sarah Wagner.

And to Lydia, Liberty, Daniel, Patrick and Dawn, you five are best and are loved and appreciated deeply. Finally, thanks to my wife Laura who has always been there to offer her unfailing encouragement. There can be no doubt that without you I would never have written a single word of this book.

ABOUT THE AUTHOR

As a student at Saint Patrick's Grade School, Michael Penosky developed a love for Saint Patrick and all things Irish. That love led to a dozen trips to the Emerald Isle and the writing of ***The Patrician Prophecy Series***. He holds a Juris Doctorate from Northern Illinois University, and for the past decade, he's been a senior attorney for the Supreme Court of Illinois. When Michael is not writing, he can be found dusting the cobwebs from his basketball jump shot to avoid getting schooled by his teenage boys. He currently lives with his wife Laura, their five children, and his faithful Labrador Retriever, Colter.

Made in the USA
Monee, IL
27 March 2023